Mona Lisa

Robyn Sheridan

WALDORF PUBLISHING

Published by Waldorf Publishing
2140 Hall Johnson Road
#102-345
Grapevine, Texas 76051
www.WaldorfPublishing.com

Mona Lisa

ISBN: 978-1-945172-73-1
Library of Congress Control Number: 2016957010

Chapter 1

I guess most people would consider me a glass half-empty kind of girl. I'm sure it started the day I was born. My dad, Chick as he is known to everyone including his kids, said when he first saw me my lips were together in such a way he immediately thought of Leonardo's creation. He knew right then I had to be named Mona Lisa. Mona Lisa Annette Cicciarelli—Annette, because everyone needs a middle name and it also served as an homage to Chick's favorite Mouseketeer. Mona Lisa didn't really lend itself to a nickname, especially since my mother said Mona sounded like an old lady with leather skin from Boca Raton. Therefore, I began life saddled with the name Mona Lisa, which propelled me on my path toward pessimism and is why I wasn't surprised when I was left at the altar.

I sat in the bride's room of St. Luke's church with my head on the vanity, trying to ignore my husband-to-be's mother and the sobbing of my mother and sisters.

"You know, Mona Lisa, Joey is just sick over this, but it really is for the best," his mother said.

My father burst in and bellowed, "Where is he? I'm gonna kill that son of a bitch with my bare hands."

"Chick," my mother admonished. "We're in church."

"I don't care if we're in the friggin' Vatican. Where is that coward son of yours, Alice?"

"Chick, you're being unfair. My Joey feels so bad. You just don't know."

Why didn't I pay attention to the signs? Joey was such a mama's boy. He was thirty-five and still lived at home with his widowed mother, Alice. She was a piece of work. Small in stature, but a giant who was fiercely protective of her Joey, as she affectionately called him.

Alice was there when he proposed to me. Sign. We went to the same Italian restaurant as on our first date and it was just another night out as far as I was concerned. We had dated for five years, and we talked about marriage but never made any plans. As we ate, I felt someone staring at me. I looked over at the door and there was Alice.

Joey glanced over and said, "Ma, what are you doing here?"

"I couldn't wait," she answered with a huge smile plastered on her face.

Joey smiled apologetically and reached into his pocket. As he pulled out a black velvet box, he got down on one knee and asked, "Mona Lisa, I was wondering if you would do me the honor of being my wife?"

Before I could answer, Alice ran over to us and announced, "Of course she will!"

Joey thankfully waited to hear an answer from me.

"Yes. Yes, I'll marry you," I answered quietly before I cupped my hands on his face and kissed him. He placed a small, but elegant round diamond in an antique setting on my finger and I was so entranced I never noticed that Alice had slid into the booth across from me. Joey kissed me again and then sat next to his mom—another sign. That was the beginning of the end. Our relationship from that point on went from Mona Lisa and Joey to Mona Lisa, Joey, and Ma.

The ring was barely out of the box, but it didn't stop Alice.

"Joe senior gave me that ring thirty-eight years ago. God rest his soul. I always prayed that Joey would give it to his wife. And now that he has, I'd love for the two of you to get married on my birthday."

Joey smiled and said, "Great idea, Ma."

Big sign.

The increasing chaos at the church brought me back to reality; I had had enough. "I want to go home," I said to no one in particular. And then it hit me; home was the apartment I shared with Joey. We signed a lease and moved our furniture in last week. And though I technically still lived with my parents, all of my belongings were in the new apartment.

"Come home with Chick and me," my mom suggested.

"I don't have anything there, but I don't want to live in the apartment with Joey's things there."

Alice pulled a key from her purse and handed it to me. "He already moved them out. He didn't want to hurt you any more than he has."

My temples throbbed. "He knew he wasn't going to go through with the wedding and didn't have the common decency to tell me. That asshole let me come here and get dressed up and think that this was going to be the happiest day of my life. And all the while he knew he wasn't going to marry me." I moved closer to Alice and her eyes widened, so I got even closer. "And you! Look at you; you're not even dressed! You knew and did the dirty work for him. What is wrong with you people?" I shouted.

My middle sister, Rosie, grabbed my shoulder. "Mo, let's get out of here. Charlie and I will take you to our house. You can change and calm down."

I looked at my sister in disbelief. "Calm down? It's not like I missed a nail appointment or something. I've been stood up. Left at the altar. Jilted." I didn't want to relax. I wanted to get drunk, find Joey and beat the shit out of him.

Chapter 2

In the end, I decided to go to the apartment and my sisters and I looked like a wedding party that showed up on the wrong day. My sister, Nina, handed me the key, but the door was unlocked, and as we entered, we heard the rustling of papers and boxes coming from the bedroom.

"Great," I whispered to my older sister, Sophia. "I'm being robbed on top of everything else."

Joey appeared in the doorway and my sisters lined up next to me, forming a human barricade. Joey looked like a frightened child about to be attacked by the classroom bully.

"Nice of you to show up, chickenshit," Marilyn taunted.

"Aren't you the big man? Sending your mommy to be your messenger," Rosie added.

"Mona Lisa, I'm so sorry. I wanted to tell you myself, but I couldn't." Then he started to cry. Not quiet tears. He sobbed and wailed like a baby.

"Geez, Joe. Get it together," I said.

He was pitiful. I almost felt sorry for him until I saw what he had in his hand–a picture of Alice. Could this day get any worse?

"You came for a picture of your mother? Are you for real? Get out of here, Joe, and if I find anything that belongs to you or your mother, you can be sure that I'll take care of it," I replied sarcastically.

"You heard her," Sophia said as she gestured toward the door. "And don't come back here again."

He wiped his eyes with his sleeve and he walked toward the door. He looked back at me but said nothing.

My baby sister, Nina, walked to the door and slammed it shut. "Asshole."

I couldn't help but laugh. Nina never had a bad thing to say about anyone. If nothing else, I could always count on my sisters. After we changed, and assembled on the new sectional sofa Joe and I bought, tears welled in my eyes. I let them roll down my cheeks.

"Oh, Mona Lisa, don't cry. You'll get through this," Marilyn assured me as she wrapped her arms around me. I rested my head on her shoulder.

"Is there something wrong with me?" I asked quietly.

My sisters surrounded me for a group hug. "Are you kidding me?" Rosie asked. "You're a Cicciarelli."

We all laughed.

"That's encouraging," I replied.

The Cicciarelli's were quite a bunch and our leader, Chick, was eccentric, to say the least. His real name was Carmine, but as a kid, he would go crazy when people mispronounced his last name. He was constantly saying 'It's pronounced Chick A Relli' so his friends started calling him Chick. The nickname stuck. Carmine faded into the sunset and Chick's penchant for unique names grew. While my name was the most unusual, my sisters were also named according to Chick's whims. Sophia was named after the Italian Bombshell and Marilyn was named after the infamous Ms. Monroe. Rosie's full name was Rosemary after the singer and star of White Christmas, Rosemary Clooney. The baby, Nina, was born on Columbus Day—I guess Pinta and Santa Maria would have been too obvious.

I wiped the tears from my eyes and said, "Seriously, though, you three are happily married and Nina has Nick. I've only had one other boyfriend in thirty-two years. What's the matter with me?"

"I'm having an affair," Rosie blurted out.

The room went silent and all eyes turned to Ro. There went my spotlight.

"Don't worry; I'm not sleeping with him."

We all gave her the "sure, you're not" look.

"Really," she replied. "I'm not happy and I think I want a divorce."

We all gasped.

Again she answered the unasked, "I know, Chick forbids divorce, but he isn't in charge of my life."

Chick's motto was, "Divorce is not an option. Murder is, but not divorce." We had been hearing that since we were old enough to date. "Make wise choices girls. You will be together 'til death."

Maybe I was lucky to be left at the altar after all.

My sisters assaulted Ro with questions and I slipped away and climbed into bed. I thought for sure I'd never sleep, but was awakened the next morning by the ringing of the phone. I never even said hello, but I'm not sure my mother cared.

"Mona Lisa," she acknowledged, "since you won't be going on your honeymoon, we'll expect you for family dinner at noon."

Chapter 3

The last thing I wanted to do was have Sunday dinner with my family and the thought of it brought me to the brink of a nervous breakdown. Lying in bed was all I wanted to do, but my mother called out the troops, and I was pretty much dragged out of bed by my sister Marilyn and her husband, Mike.

"Let's go, Mary Sunshine," Marilyn sing-songed as she threw the covers back.

Mike had the decency to turn away from me.

"Jeez, you people have no hearts. Don't you realize what a shitty day I had yesterday? I should at least be given time off for extenuating circumstances!" I protested.

"Sorry, Mona Lisa," Marilyn said. "I'm under strict orders from Ma and Chick to bring you to dinner even if we have to carry you."

"I'm not going!"

Marilyn crawled into bed with me and I started to cry.

"I'll be in the living room," Mike said before leaving us alone.

"Sweetie, I know you're hurting, but you shouldn't be by yourself. Being with family is what you need. We love you and we want to help you get through this."

"Are Rosie and Charlie coming? I don't think I can handle any more drama today."

"Don't worry," Marilyn assured me. "I talked to Ro after we left last night and she's not going to do anything rash. She's all talk."

"I really don't want to go," I whined.

"I know, but if you don't get your ass out of that bed, Mike is gonna come back in here and throw you over his shoulder, so you decide."

Since I didn't have a choice, I dressed and drove the ten minutes to my parents' house. They lived in an old ranch house with a huge kitchen and dining room on an acre of land. Our neighbors were like family, and if they caught you doing something wrong, they had no qualms about reprimanding you. We looked out for each other and now that some of them were in their last years, my mom and Chick made sure to be there for them.

I took a deep breath before I turned the knob to enter my parents' kitchen. I thought I could sneak in quietly and avoid a big fuss, but that wasn't to be. The door flew open, and two of my nephews almost knocked me down as they ran outside to play. The men were sitting while the women worked around them, but they all looked at me in unison and let out a collective sigh.

I was hugged and kissed, and finally, I stepped back, and said, "I'm fine. Let's not talk about it."

My grandmother pulled me aside and said, "I never liked him anyway. He's a *shmendrick*! I don't think Alice ever cut the umbilical cord. You deserve better, Mona Lisa."

I smiled though I didn't know what a *shmendrick* was, but I assumed it was an appropriate choice, so I said,

"Thanks, Noni. How are you?"

"Eh, a little constipated, but other than that, I'm old."

Italians were notoriously free with discussions about their bowels. It was one of those things you got accustomed to.

"You're not old, Noni. Mrs. Shemansky was telling me that she thinks Marshall Bernbaum is sweet on you," I teased.

"That Mabel Shemansky is nothing but a *yenta*. At least, she's letting you color her hair now. Miss Clairol she is not."

I laughed at my grandmother's sudden use of Yiddish phrases as that gave her away more than Mabel Shemansky.

"She does look better," I agreed. "Blue is not a natural hair color."

I walked over to my mom who was cutting pepperoni for the antipasto.

"Need any help?"

"No thanks, honey. You doing alright?" she asked quietly.

I just shrugged my shoulders.

"I'm here if you need anything," she said before kissing me on the cheek.

I helped my sisters get the kids settled at the kitchen table, before joining the adults in the dining room. We all took our places and waited for Chick to say Grace.

After the usual, "Bless us O Lord…" he added, "We

have a little something else to be grateful for. Mona Lisa, I arranged for Evelyn Colletti's grandson to take you on a date!"

Chapter 4

I gasped as my grandmother let out an "*Oy Gevalt!*"

"Ma, enough with the Yiddish already!" my mother snapped. "And Chick, I think it's a little soon for you to be finding dates for Mona Lisa."

"What too soon? She's not getting any younger," he protested.

"She was j-i-l-t-e-d yesterday," my mother countered.

I stood, "Hello? I'm in the room and I know how to spell. I do not want to date anyone right now."

I turned to leave the table when my mother grabbed my arm and pulled me down.

"Sit."

"If wanting my daughters to be happy and married before I die is a crime, then I'm guilty," Chick said throwing his hands in the air.

I lightly banged my head on the table, when my mother chided me, "Mona Lisa, don't be so dramatic. Believe you me, you're not the first girl to be left at the altar and you won't be the last."

"What do I have to do to get a little sympathy here? Lose a limb?" I whined.

"You're *meshuggeneh*, Chick!" Noni added.

"Between the Yiddish and the drama, I have a terrible case of *agita*. I don't even feel like eating," my mother complained. "Pass the garlic bread, Mike and can we please have some normal conversation?"

13

My brother-in-law winked at me and smiled before announcing, "I heard that a certain person we know is having an affair!"

My sisters and I stopped breathing. I looked at Marilyn as if to say, "Did you tell Mike about Ro?"

"I heard that old man Battaglia was seen in Hoboken with a young blonde who is not Mrs. Battaglia."

We all let out our breath.

"I hardly think that is appropriate dinner conversation, Michael," Chick admonished. "Besides, that's old news."

I sat back as the conversation turned to kids and work and off of me. I was supposed to be on the beach in Cancun right now with a margarita in my hand, and yet here I was—enduring another Sunday meal with the family.

I managed to make it through dinner by daydreaming and trying not to partake in the conversation, which never proved difficult with this group. When the meal was over, the women rose to clear the table while the men sat waiting for coffee and dessert. I grabbed a few dishes when the doorbell rang.

"He's here!" Chick announced. "Punctual, too."

I nearly dropped the plates.

"Who's here, Chick?" I asked.

"I told you, Evelyn Colletti's grandson, Dante."

"Dante Colletti?" Charlie asked. "Did he just get off the boat?"

"Chick, you're crazy if you think that I am going on a date with him!" I announced as I ran into the kitchen.

The doorbell rang again as Chick called to me, "Of course, you're not going on a date today. I invited him over to get a look at you!"

I sat on the floor in the corner and put my hands over my ears and hummed loudly.

My sisters and mother just stared until my mother finally said, "Mona Lisa, stop that!"

"Your husband is crazy, do you know that? It hasn't even been twenty-four hours since I was at the church waiting to get married and he's having strange men come over to get a look at me. What am I—a show dog?"

"He means well, honey."

"Ma, it's way too soon," my sister, Marilyn, countered. "She needs some time."

"Thank you for being the voice of reason," I said before I let out a sigh.

It was quiet for a moment when Chick called out, "Mona Lisa you have a visitor."

"I don't believe this," I shouted. "I am not going out there. Soph, go get my purse from the living room and I'll leave through the back."

She bumped into Chick, who caught my eye and said, "Mona Lisa, please come to the dining room—now!"

It was times like these when I realized how much of an adult I was not. I stood and followed my father into the dining room where I found Dante Colletti listening to Noni explain to him that she was feeling bloated because my mother insisted on serving escarole salad when she knew darn well that it gave my grandmother gas.

Dante seemed mildly amused and turned toward me as I entered the room. He stood and offered me his hand as Chick made the introductions.

"Dante, this is my beautiful and available daughter, Mona Lisa. Mona Lisa meet Dante Colletti. Hey, Angie," he called to my mother. "Bring out the dessert and the coffee."

I motioned for Dante to sit and said to my father, "I have to go now Chick. I have a lot of things to take care of. Dante, sorry you came all this way for nothing."

"Mona Lisa, you have a guest and you're being rude. I will not tolerate this kind of behavior in my home."

I was determined to put a stop to this once and for all. "I don't mean to be rude, but I did not invite him here and given the day I had yesterday, I have every right to be a little testy."

As I grabbed my purse from the living room, Chick told Dante, "She's a little emotional today. Give her a few days and I'm sure she'll come around. How about an espresso?"

I stood motionless for a minute, debating if I should go back in and try to make Chick understand what I was going through when he came up behind me.

"I gave Dante your number. He'll call you next week."

Chapter 5

I spent the first three days of my "honeymoon" as most other brides spend theirs … in bed. I, however, was alone except for the cartons of ice cream I bought to keep me company. I didn't answer the phone and spent my time eating, napping and watching Lifetime Original Movies. It somehow made me feel better to see women who had it worse than me.

On day four, I decided to shower as I could no longer stand the smell of myself and when I came out there was the daily message from my mom, begging me to call and let her know I was alright.

Then there was a message from my sister, Sophia. "Mona Lisa, please call me. Mom and Chick are going batshit crazy because they haven't heard from you and they're making the rest of us nuts because they love to share the misery. So, here's the deal. Call me in the next two hours or the entire Cicciarelli clan will be there tonight for an intervention. I love you, kiddo." She paused and added, "I'm really not kidding about the intervention part."

Sophia was the sister I felt closest to. She was the oldest and I was the middle. There were enough years between us so there was no competition. She was my biggest cheerleader and most trusted confidante. If I were to call anyone, it would be her.

I dialed and she didn't even say hello. "It's about time you called me. I tried to give you some space, but Mom and

Chick are seriously freaking out. She blames him for trying to get you a date, and he's mad at her for not making you stay and have dessert with Dante. Those two are quite a pair."

"I'm fine. Thanks for asking."

"I'm so sorry, honey," she replied. "How are you—really?"

"I showered today so that's progress and I don't want to eat any more ice cream."

"Why don't I come get you for lunch?"

"Then would you help me get rid of these wedding gifts? I can't keep them and I can't stand looking at them anymore."

"Sure thing. Why don't I get Marilyn to bring over her SUV and we can take care of it all today."

"Thanks, Soph. I don't know what I'd do without you," I admitted.

"I love you, Mo and I'm just glad I can do something to help. We'll be there in an hour."

"Be sure to call off the dogs. Tell them you spoke to me and I'll talk to them later, okay?" I asked.

I actually felt a little better and started to rearrange some furniture. I was ready to make this place my own and wipe away all traces of Joey and his mother. When my sisters arrived, we gathered up all of the wedding presents and loaded them in Marilyn's truck.

We climbed in and Sophia asked, "You ready, Mona Lisa?"

"Ready as I'll ever be."

Ten minutes later we arrived at Alice's house and quietly, we unpacked the car and deposited the boxes on her porch. We crept silently back and forth, and when we placed the last load on the steps, I taped a note on top giving Joey and Alice the responsibility of returning the gifts to their senders. Marilyn uncapped a thick black marker and wrote "Coward, Asshole and Mama's Boy" in huge letters for anyone who passed by to see.

Once back in the car, we broke into a fit of laughter so intense, we had to pull over after we turned the corner.

"That was fantastic," I said. "Totally liberating. I am free of Joey and Alice forever."

Then my laughter turned to tears.

"Oh, Mona Lisa," Sophia said as she offered me a tissue. "It's going to get better."

"What if I'm alone forever?" I wailed.

"I know it seems dismal now, but it will get better."

"Remember when Paulie and I broke up?" Marilyn asked. "It took me a month to recover."

"But you were in high school," I cried, "and now you're married to Mike and have two kids. I have nothing."

Sophia climbed in the back seat with me and held me as I got it all out of my system. When I was able to quiet my sobs, I looked at my sisters and asked, "What now?"

"Let's go eat!" Marilyn suggested because every Italian knows that no matter the ailment, food always provided a cure.

Chapter 6

The next big hurdle I had to get over was returning to work. As I stood outside the salon door, I wished there was a way to avoid that inevitable moment when I walk in and all eyes turn to me with that look of pity. There was no way around it, so I took a deep breath and pushed open the door and found all of my co-workers standing under a banner that read, "We Never Liked Him Anyway." I couldn't help but laugh as one by one they hugged me and told me specifically what they disliked about Joey.

When they each had a turn, my boss, Vinnie, handed me a curling iron microphone and asked me to speak.

"Your outpouring of sympathy is overwhelming. It's nice to know that when the chips are down, I can count on you guys to continue to bust my balls. Let's get to work."

After a standing ovation, I went to my station and looked at my schedule. I had completely forgotten about Alice's standing Monday morning appointment and was relieved to see that she was crossed off my list.

I turned to my friend, Mary Kathleen, and said, "Thank goodness Alice had the decency to cancel her appointment."

"She didn't cancel, hon. She's seeing Caroline instead. Thoughtful, huh?"

"She's psychotic. God forbid Vinnie turn away a paying customer. I guess that's why he took that banner down so quickly."

Just then the salon door opened and in walked Alice looking badly sunburned.

"*Hola*, everyone," she sang. "Guess who just got back from Meh hee co?"

I was speechless. That loser took his mother on our honeymoon. Would this nightmare ever end?

Caroline quickly pulled Alice to the side and spoke to her in a whisper.

Alice, who didn't know the meaning of the word tact, answered loudly enough for everyone to hear. "My Joey paid for the trip and we couldn't let that money go to waste. Mona Lisa should certainly understand that."

Again, Caroline spoke to Alice in a hushed tone.

She responded by announcing, "I don't see why we can't be friends, Mona Lisa. In the words of Rodney King, 'Can't we all just get along?'" she laughed.

I stood and Vinnie rushed to my side. He ushered me into the break room and sat next to me on the sofa.

"Let it go, Mona Lisa," he suggested. "I'll tell Alice to find another salon. Please don't let her get to you."

"I can't escape them," I cried. "Joey and Ma. Joey and Ma. They're like a bad rash that won't go away."

"Time, honey. Give it some time and hopefully one day you'll be able to laugh about this."

"I don't know, Vinnie. Right now, it seems impossible."

Mary Kathleen interrupted, "Mona Lisa, your grandmother is here, and she's raking Alice over the coals. It's awesome."

I returned to find Noni sitting in my chair and Alice wiping away tears as Caroline went at her with a hairbrush.

Noni smiled and said, "I thought you might be having a tough time today so I wanted to check up on you. Who knew that *Nudnik* would be here? I swear some people have no common sense."

"Thanks, Noni. It's been a shitty day. I don't know if things will ever get better."

"Mona Lisa, one plus of being such an old lady is that I know you will get past this. You're too good for that boy and his lunatic of a mother. Your true love is out there, sweetheart, and when you find him, you'll be glad you didn't settle for Joey," Noni said in a comforting tone.

"I hope you're right," I replied.

"Will you be okay if I leave now? Marshall and I are going to Atlantic City to play the slots and hit the buffet."

"I'll be fine. I love you, Noni."

"I love you, too, Mona Lisa, and remember, this too shall pass."

"Like a kidney stone, eh, Noni?"

Chapter 7

The rest of the week passed by mostly without incident. The pitying looks and the squeezing of the hands as
they said, "Mona Lisa, God has something better in store
for you" finally came to an end. It was comforting to have
the routine of work, and though several of my friends had
invited me to go out, I was still in a funk. I was lonely but
not ready to date as the thought of investing any of myself
in another relationship exhausted me beyond comprehen-
sion. When the phone rang, I never bothered to check the
caller ID as my mother called the same time each day to
check on me.

"Hi, Ma," I answered.

"Mona Lisa, it's Dante Colletti. We met at your parents' house. Remember?"

I laughed, "It's a little hard to forget. Not many women
are set up on a date the day after they're left at the altar."

He coughed nervously and added, "I guess not. I'm
sorry to bother you, but I told your dad I would call. He
cares about you a lot."

I relaxed a bit and said, "I know he does, but his timing
leaves a lot to be desired."

"I understand. Families can be tough. Between my
mother and grandmother, the guilt for not being married is
monumental. My grandmother threatens that if I'm not
married by the time she dies, she'll come back and haunt
me."

"Oh, I understand. Chick loves to announce how his life will only be complete when all of his girls are married."

"Italians are very dramatic, aren't they? I know you're probably tired of being asked, but how are you doing?"

I smiled. "I'm okay. Taking it day by day. I'm just waiting to find my new normal."

"I'm sure it will happen soon. I know you probably aren't ready to date yet, but would you like to go out for a drink sometime? Strictly platonic, of course."

While part of me was intrigued, my heart was still heavy. "Thanks for the offer, but I'm not there yet."

"I understand. If you change your mind, we will make a lot of old people very happy."

"Tempting as that sounds, I think I'll pass. Thanks for calling, Dante."

"My pleasure, Mona Lisa. Feel free to give me a call if you want some company."

I hung up the phone and it immediately rang. I had ignored the call waiting while I was talking to Dante and knew this time it was my mother.

"Mona Lisa," she yelled. "Are you alright? I was a nervous wreck when you didn't answer the phone. It rang and rang and rang."

"Calm down, Ma. I was talking to Dante Colletti."

"Oh, Mona Lisa. I'm so happy for you." She then called out to my father, "Chick, Mona Lisa was talking to Dante Colletti."

He cheered in the background.

"Shit." *Why can't I keep my mouth shut?*

"No need to talk like trash, Mona Lisa. What would Dante think?" she asked.

"I don't give a rat's ass what Dante thinks, Ma."

"Language, please. You'll care after you go on a few dates with him."

"I'm not going out with him or anyone else right now."

"Chick, she refuses to go out with Dante," she called out.

"Listen, I have to go, Ma. Talk to you tomorrow."

I hung up to the sounds of my parents arguing in disbelief and waited for the phone to ring again, which it did. I let the answering machine pick up.

"Mona Lisa, it's Chick. I know you can hear me. I understand you're not ready to date right now, but remember you're not getting any younger. Take another week and get it out of your system. I'll tell Dante to call you then."

Chapter 8

Sensing my continued depression, Sophia arranged for a Cicciarelli girls night at her house. Every once in awhile, we got together for a sleepover, which was basically an excuse for us to eat, drink, and gossip and I was in need of all three.

I got there early to have a little one-on-one time with Sophia. Her home was so warm and inviting—a total reflection of my sister.

"So, how have the past few weeks been?" she asked as we sat with the first of our many glasses of wine.

"I don't know. I hoped it would be easier by now. I thought I was done with having to talk about it, but yesterday an old client came in and the first thing she did was ask to see the pictures from the wedding. She had no way of knowing, but it got to me."

"Eventually everything will settle down. Are you doing anything for fun?"

"I go out with the girls sometimes, but I don't have the energy to go on a date right now. This town is so small sometimes. Nobody ever leaves and all the guys I know are friends of Joey's."

"There's always Dante," she kidded.

"Thanks, Soph. You sound like Ma and Chick. Maybe I'll just marry him and move next door to them. Then everyone would be happy."

We laughed as the front door opened and the rest of the

girls arrived, carrying pizzas and cannolis.

We filled our plates and glasses and made ourselves comfortable in Sophia's family room. We talked about work, the kids, and thankfully none of the conversation focused on me. I relaxed hoping that maybe I was starting to move forward.

"I know the last time we were together I dropped a bomb on you guys about Charlie and me, but things aren't getting any better," Rosie admitted.

Marilyn asked, "What's going on that's so bad?"

"It's not that we fight or anything like that. It's just that I think there might be something better out there."

"Are you still seeing the other guy?" Nina asked quietly.

"No. I never actually went out with him. We only talked online," Ro confessed.

Something inside me snapped. "You met him online? Are you crazy? Don't you know how unsafe that is?" I asked.

"Gee, Ma. I didn't know," she replied sarcastically. "It's not like I gave him my real name or anything. Plus he wasn't honest with me so I broke it off."

"He wasn't honest with you?" I countered. "Please tell me you're not going to use the Internet to find a guy again."

"I should hope not," Marilyn chimed in. "We're going to have to put filters on your computer like I do with the kids. You really need to be more careful, Ro."

"I knew you guys would judge me," Rosie complained. "I'm really unhappy and he was sweet to me. It made me forget about my life for a while."

"We're not judging. We're concerned about your safety. I know marriage isn't easy, but an affair isn't the answer," Sophia proclaimed. "Dom and I have gone through some really tough times, but I couldn't imagine going through life without anyone to share it with."

All eyes turned to me, but instead of tears, I felt a little anger well up inside of me.

"There are plenty of single women who are happy, you know," I challenged.

Nina, ever the peacemaker, added, "Of course there are, Mona Lisa. You don't need a man to complete your life."

I sighed and thought, *I don't need a man to complete me. Lather, rinse, repeat.*

Chapter 9

Though it had been a few weeks, I wasn't sure I was ready to start dating. However, everyone else in my life couldn't understand what I was waiting for. A guy who worked with my brother-in-law, Mike, was divorced and he thought we would hit it off. I was very resistant at first and not in the mood to meet someone new, but Marilyn called and used her powers of persuasion to change my mind.

"Alright, I will go, but no double dates! It's awkward enough to meet him on a blind date—I don't want you and Mike there to witness it for posterity."

"Fair enough, Mona Lisa. Mike says he's super sweet."

"He used the words super sweet?" I asked.

"No. Guys don't talk like that, but I could tell that's what he meant."

"Give him my number and we'll see what happens." I hung up and began assembling a series of photographs I had framed. I smiled because the apartment was finally starting to feel like my home. It had a nice casual feel and I enjoyed decorating it. I found my hammer and began to put a nail in the wall when the phone rang. I answered without checking the caller ID.

"Hello."

"This is Ben Wallington. I work with Mike. Is this Mona Lisa?" he asked nervously.

"Hi, Ben. This is Mona Lisa. How are you?"

"Good, thanks. Mona Lisa, huh? That's one heck of a

moniker. Is it an Italian thing?" he quipped.

Are you kidding me? That's the first thing you ask? And who uses the word moniker? "No. It's just my dad's whacked-out baby naming skills," I answered dryly.

Silence.

Finally, he spoke. "I was wondering if you'd like to go out for coffee tomorrow night."

Ooh, big spender. "Sure. Where do you want to go?"

"How about Coffee Time on Amboy Avenue?"

We firmed up the details, and I was already dreading our date. I was less than impressed with him after our phone call. Who makes fun of someone's name before they even meet them?

* * * *

When I entered the coffee house, I spotted a nice look-ing blonde gentleman in khakis and a polo shirt who was on the phone and a couple with a baby in a stroller. I as-sumed that Ben hadn't arrived and was surprised when the blonde man approached me.

"Mona Lisa?" he asked cautiously.

"I guess that makes you Ben," I said offering my hand. "Let's order some coffee."

After we had our drinks, we settled at a table, and he opened the conversation by saying, "I hear you were left at the altar." He didn't wait for me to reply. "What a jerk, huh? I was talking to my ex-wife and I was telling her about what happened to you. She said to give you her sym-pathy."

"Do you always talk to your ex-wife about your dates?" I asked.

"Oh, sure. We're very close. We talk three or four times every day. You know when we got married, it was the best day of my life. We planned every detail together and it was pretty spectacular if I do say so myself. We took dance lessons for weeks and put on quite a show for our first dance as husband and wife." He reached into his pocket and pulled a photo from his wallet. "This was us on the big day."

Kill me now! "What do you do for a living?" I asked, fervently hoping to change the subject.

"I work with Mike, remember?"

"Oh, yeah. Sorry. I work at Vincenzo's hair salon."

"What a coincidence," he replied. "Melanie gets her hair done there."

"Who's Melanie?" I asked while praying a small fire would spontaneously ignite and set me free.

"My wife," he answered casually.

I raised an eyebrow and he corrected himself.

"My ex-wife. She gets her hair done by Vinnie himself. She says he's a master at highlights. It doesn't hurt that she has great hair."

"Lucky girl," I muttered.

"She's the best. She takes such great care of herself. She's into Pilates and yoga. What about you? Have you ever tried either of those?" he asked with genuine interest.

"I've tried yoga, but it makes me dizzy. I don't think

humans were meant to bend like that."

"Melanie says it takes practice. You should go with her sometime. I think you two would really hit it off. She gets along with everyone."

I was speechless, which was fine because he kept on talking. I looked around, certain there was a camera and this whole scene would end up on a reality television show. However, I wasn't that lucky. Ben went on about how they used to work out together all the time and what great shape Melanie was in. When I couldn't stand it anymore, I excused myself and went to the bathroom. I quickly pulled out my cell phone and called Mary Kathleen.

"M.K., I am on the worst blind date ever. Call me in ninety seconds and make up a reason for me to leave." When she started to ask questions, I got impatient and yelled, "Just do it!"

I returned to the table and Ben was on the phone again, so I walked over to him and said, "I have to go. Thanks for the coffee."

He stood, but I waved and walked out of the door. As I headed to my car, the rescue call came.

"Thanks, girl, but I managed to escape on my own."

"What happened?" she asked. "Was it really that bad?"

"Oh, yeah. I can't wait to share my story at Sunday dinner. Afterward, I'm going to take a poll and see if I should settle for spinster aunt or try for a nun. I'll keep you posted."

Chapter 10

After my coffee with Ben, I called my sister Sophia, and she managed to make me laugh about it. She could put a positive spin on a root canal and that's what I loved most about her. Despite her good humor, my date left me somewhat shell-shocked. At this point, I'd rather be alone than endure another encounter like I had with Ben.

As I drove to my parents' house, I asked myself which was worse—dating or the family dinner. I could always choose not to date, but my weekly obligation to Chick and company was unavoidable. If being left at the altar wasn't a good enough reason to skip the Sunday meal, I'm not sure anything would give me a pass.

I pulled my car into their driveway, and my shoulders relaxed as I was actually looking forward to seeing everyone. I was feeling down and there was nothing like family to make you forget your troubles. Mostly because they didn't really want to hear about your problems—they wanted to tell you about theirs.

When I opened the back door, all heads turned toward me and conversation came to an abrupt halt. The looks on my sister's faces resembled fear. I was used to the looks of pity, but this was a new one.

"What?" I asked.

Then I saw my father come into the kitchen with his arm around Dante Colletti.

"Mona Lisa, look who's here for dinner?" he boasted.

I took a deep breath and opened my mouth, but nothing came out.

"Hey, where are your manners? Dante gave up his Sunday afternoon to be with you. The least you can do is be polite," he ordered.

"I don't recall asking him to do that, so I don't think I owe him anything," I answered.

"Mona Lisa, he is a guest in our house," my mother admonished. "Chick, why don't you and the boys go sit in the dining room and we'll be right in with dinner."

"I'm leaving," I announced.

My mother cornered me in the kitchen and gave me a "what for" look as she liked to call it.

"Mona Lisa, you're acting like a spoiled child. Your father loves you and thought you might like some company. That poor boy did nothing to you and doesn't deserve to be treated so rudely. Grow up and act like a civilized adult."

She grabbed a bowl of meatballs from the counter and placed them in my hands fully expecting me to take them into the dining room. And of course, I did. The chair next to Dante was open, but I purposely avoided him and sat next to Noni. I was not going to make this easy.

Noni leaned over and whispered, "You better be careful or Chick will put you in timeout."

"I love you, Noni."

"You too, kiddo. This should be interesting, if nothing else."

My mother was the last one to the table, and when she saw where I was sitting, she stopped and stared at me. I put my head down but glanced up to find everyone watching so I stood and took the chair next to Dante.

He whispered, "Sorry."

"Me too, because this is going to be the most uncomfortable meal you've ever had," I said under my breath.

"I can leave."

"Why don't you?" I countered.

"Because that would be rude."

"And coming here after I told you I wasn't ready to date isn't?"

Chick interrupted, "Hey, you two, I know you're excited to get to know one another, but let's say Grace first."

I rolled my eyes and grabbed Dante's hand so hard he winced. When I let go, I excused myself and went to the bathroom. I tried to stay in there long enough to convey the message that I was not happy, but when my stomach started growling, I realized I had only succeeded in starving myself.

I slipped into my seat and Dante passed me the pasta. My dad was in the middle of a story about me being left at the church after Catechism.

"...Then we sat at the table and realized Mona Lisa was missing. I thought Ange had picked her up and she thought I did. I grabbed the car keys and drove like a bat outta hell to the church, and there was Mona Lisa sitting on the steps bawling while Sister Pauline yelled at her to quiet

35

down. Poor Mona Lisa thought we left her to live with the nuns."

Everyone laughed.

"Sister Mona Lisa has a nice ring to it!" Dante quipped.

"Gee, Chick. The way things are going these days, there might still be hope," I retorted.

"Mona Lisa," my mother answered, "you're a little old to be getting the calling, don't you think?" Then without waiting for an answer she moved on. "So, Dante, tell me a little bit about yourself? What do you do for a living?"

"I'm a pilot for Eastwest Airlines. I fly domestically mostly to Florida, Boston and Chicago. I moved back to Jersey a few years ago because I fly out of Newark now."

"How exciting," my mother gushed.

She went on to ask him if he had ever flown any celebrities and he wowed them with his stories. Dinner seemed interminable, but when it was finally over and all the dishes were put away, I said my goodbyes.

"Thank you for dinner, Ma. I'll talk to you in a few days."

I ignored her response as I walked toward the front door. I stupidly stopped to zip up my jacket when I felt a hand grab my arm. I turned and was face to face with Dante.

"I really am sorry, Mona Lisa," he said before lightly kissing me on the lips.

I lost myself in his kiss for a moment, but it didn't last

long. The uneasy feeling returned that I didn't belong anywhere anymore. The nagging question was whether I needed a vacation or a fresh start somewhere new.

Chapter 11

I was in a funk and wasn't sure what to do about it. I hadn't had a date since Ben, and Dante assured me I wouldn't hear from him again. I was relieved, but depressed. I fought back tears as I put the permanent solution in Donna Donatucci's hair and I pretended to listen to her drone on about what a bitch her daughter-in-law was. I wanted to scream, *Who cares, lady? Maybe if your son paid more attention to his wife, she'd be nicer to you.*

Somehow, I held it together until I could excuse myself and go to the restroom.

When I came out, Vinnie was waiting for me.

"Mona Lisa, what's going on? You look horrible."

"I don't know, Vinnie. I'm a mess today."

"Come here," he said as he held out his arms to hug me.

I sobbed for a few minutes, then gave my nose a good blow and said, "Thanks, Vinnie. I swear I think I'm more miserable now than the day of the wedding."

"I know, sweetheart. I wish there was something I could do to make everything better, but according to my wife I know nothing about women. She says I use up all my sympathy on these old broads that come in here and am useless when it comes to her."

I laughed, "I'll be okay one of these days. I think that I may need to get away from here for a while. It's so hard to move on when I feel like I'm living in a cocoon."

"Do you want some time off? Tell me what you need."

"Thanks, but I don't even know myself. I'm wondering if I should move somewhere and start over."

"Where do you want to go?" he asked.

"Who knows? Some place that is not Edison, New Jersey."

"I have a cousin who owns a salon in Atlanta. I could see about getting you a job," he offered.

"Georgia?"

"Well, yeah. The last time I checked, Atlanta was in Georgia. She has a place in some *hoity-toity* suburban area. You might like it."

Suddenly my head was spinning. Atlanta. Atlanta? I had never been farther south than Cape May and even that was a little slow for me. Would it be like living in Hee-Hawville? I wasn't sure I could handle that. Surely, it was more progressive than that.

When I got home, I looked online and found the salon and looked at some pictures of Atlanta. Then I called Sophia.

"What would you say if I told you I was thinking about moving to Atlanta?"

"I would ask if you've been smoking crack?"

"I'm thinking about moving there and I haven't had so much as a wine cooler," I confessed.

"Why would you even be thinking about leaving?" she asked.

"Because I can't take it anymore. This town is so

small, and everyone knows everyone else's business, and I'm never going to find a guy if I stay here."

"Whoa, slow down." Her voice quivered as she realized I wasn't kidding. "There are plenty of people who don't know about you and Joey. Besides, you've only been on one date since the wedding."

"And that was a stellar moment in my life."

"It wasn't ideal, but you wouldn't want to marry the first guy you dated after the break-up anyway."

"Marry him? All he cared about was his ex-wife. The bagger at Shop Rite is more attentive than that guy."

"Come on, Mona Lisa, aren't you being a little over-sensitive?"

"Gee, thanks, Ma. Soph, I thought you of all people would understand."

She was silent a moment. "I do understand, but you're my best friend and … I don't want you to move away."

"I need to do something. I'm broken inside, Soph."

"I'm sorry, honey. I didn't realize it was this bad. Let's get the girls together and come up with a plan. But if you think I reacted badly, wait until you tell Ma and Chick."

Chapter 12

I didn't even want to think about my parents' reaction to a possible move, but the one person I needed to discuss it with was Noni. I showed up at her house with donuts and coffee, hoping to get some reassurance in exchange.

I knocked and when Noni peered out of the door, she jumped when she saw me. She was still in her nightclothes, but she let me in and said, "Listen, you're a big girl so you might as well know Marshall is here. I don't think you need to say anything to your mother, though. I swear I think she's turning into a nun in her old age."

I laughed. "I'm glad one of us is getting some action, Noni."

Marshall came out of the bedroom adjusting his belt with a big smile on his face and said, "Mona Lisa! What a wonderful way to start my day," before he kissed my cheek. "And good morning to you, my little s*hiksa*," he said to Noni.

"He's a keeper, Noni."

"I might as well tell you that Marshall moved in with me, and again, your mother doesn't need to know. He got tired of *schlepping* his stuff back and forth plus he was here all the time anyway."

"Well, Noni, I'm sure you both have given this plenty of thought, but you're Catholic and he's Jewish. What religion are you going to raise the kids in?" I kidded.

"Listen, smart-ass, I figure with Marshall I've got all

my religious bases covered. It's like heaven insurance. I should be safe no matter what. So now that you have the goods on me, what's up?" she asked.

We sat at the kitchen table and I blurted out, "I'm thinking of moving to Atlanta."

Her mouth fell open. "Wow, I didn't see that coming. Why Atlanta? And does Chick know?"

"Vinnie has a cousin who owns a shop there and can give me a job. And no he doesn't. Sophia is the only person I've told so far."

"He's not going to be happy, but I think you should go for it. It's time to spread your wings, Mona Lisa."

"That's what I think, but I'm scared."

"Open your mind and your heart, kiddo. After Papa died, I thought my life was over and then I met Marshall. We have our differences, but he makes me laugh. I can't imagine missing out on this."

"You're right. I need to make a change and maybe Atlanta will be what I need."

"Why don't you go visit and see what you think?" she suggested.

"The girls are all getting together tonight. I'll see if I can talk one of them into going on a little road trip with me."

"You're very lucky to have your sisters. They will always be there for you."

"Even if I move nine hundred miles away?" I asked.

"Yes. My sister Yolanda lived in Italy and we were

best friends until the day she died. We saw each other once a year and when we were together, it was like we had never been apart."

"I couldn't imagine only seeing my family once a year."

"Believe it or not, some families don't have dinner together every Sunday and they survive just fine. Not that I'm complaining, but right now I think a little time away will be the best thing for you."

"Noni, have I told you how much I love you?"

"Yes, but it does an old lady good to hear it again."

"I love you, Noni. Will you tell my parents about Atlanta?" I kidded.

"I love you too and hell, no."

Chapter 13

I was the last to arrive at Sophia's house and the conversation and wine were flowing freely. I joined in and we had a good laugh recalling the dinner with Dante.

Marilyn chuckled, "He should have said, 'Mona Lisa, I'm ordering you to marry Dante. I invited Father Flanagan to dinner, too and he'll perform the ceremony after dessert.'"

"Subtlety is not Chick's strong point," I added. "He won't rest until I'm married."

"You can have Charlie," Rosie offered.

"Nice," I replied. "Does Charlie know that you're auctioning him off to the highest bidder?"

"Mona Lisa, please. You couldn't possibly understand," Ro replied.

"Maybe that's true," I responded. "But I feel kind of bad for him."

"Gee, thanks," she replied sarcastically. "I thought you were my sister."

"I am. Lighten up. I didn't realize he was so bad," I offered.

"He's not bad. He's … nothing."

Marilyn had little patience for Ro's immaturity and challenged, "What do you mean, he's nothing?"

"Don't get snippy with me," Ro barked. "Why are you all ganging up on me?"

Nina rushed to Ro's side and gave her a hug.

"Ganging up on you? What's the matter? You got your thin skin on?" Marilyn asked.

I bit my lip to keep from smiling because, as much as it irritated her, Marilyn was turning into our mother.

"I'm sorry we all don't have the perfect husband like you do," Ro mocked.

"All right, everybody, let's take it down a notch," Sophia ordered. "What's really going on, Ro?"

"I don't want to talk about it anymore," Ro said.

"No need to be a martyr, Ro," Marilyn said dryly.

I rolled my eyes and got up to get another drink. When I went to the kitchen, Nina followed me.

"How are you doing, Mona Lisa?" she asked quietly.

"I'm fine, hon. How's that handsome Nick doing? Does he know how lucky he is?" I asked.

"He does. I'm pretty lucky, too. He's a great guy," she replied then quickly added, "I'm sorry."

"Why are you sorry? You deserve to be happy, Nina."

"So do you."

"I will be happy one day. In fact, I wanted to talk to everyone tonight about my plan. I'm thinking about moving."

"You can't!" she wailed.

Marilyn, Sophia, and Ro ran in.

Marilyn asked, "What's the matter?"

"Nothing," I answered.

Nina blurted out, "She's moving."

They all began yelling at once.

I put my hand up in protest and said, "Let's go back into the living room and I'll explain."

When we were assembled, I said, "I might move to Atlanta."

"Chick won't allow it," Marilyn said dismissing me with a wave of her hand. "Should we get back to Ro and her marital troubles?"

"No," I snapped. "Chick has no say in this. I'm over eighteen. I can do what I want."

Nina gasped.

"It's true," echoed Ro. "Why are we so afraid of him? We're grown women and if we want to move or get a divorce, we can."

I winced as I didn't want Ro to join my bandwagon, although, a divorce would trump a move to Atlanta any day. It might take some heat off of me, but a divorce would kill my parents.

As if she read my thoughts, Nina said, "A divorce? That's way worse."

"Thanks, Judge Judy," Ro replied. "Why am I always the bad one?"

"Can we get back to me, people?" I interjected. "I've been thinking about leaving for a while. I can't seem to move forward with my life and I thought maybe a change of scenery would do me good."

"Why not take a vacation, Mona Lisa? Why make such a drastic move?" Marilyn asked.

"I could do that, but when I came back, the same old

bullshit would be here waiting for me. Alice, Joey and the whole wedding mess. I want to go where nobody knows about any of that."

"Why Atlanta?" Nina asked, her eyes brimming with tears.

"Vinnie has a cousin who owns a shop down there, so I'd have a job. I looked it up online and it looks nice. Different."

Nina dabbed her eyes and asked, "When are you leaving?"

"It's not for sure. I want to take a road trip to check it out and I was hoping one of you would come along with me."

At once they all replied, "I will."

Secretly, I was hoping it would be me and Soph or Nina. Now I had to choose.

"You all want to go?" I asked.

Again, a collective, "Yes."

"Alright, then. It's a Cicciarelli girls' road trip."

Calendars and computers came out as we planned dates and routes. Marilyn was in charge of sights along the way and Soph was handling the accommodations. We were like the elves in Santa's workshop when Ro's phone rang.

Ro answered, "Hi, Ma. Yeah, we're all together." Panic rose in me as I lunged unsuccessfully toward Ro to grab the phone as she blurted out, "We're planning Mona Lisa's move to Atlanta."

No, Mona Lisa, there really isn't a Santa Claus.

Chapter 14

I heard the scream through the phone as Ro handed it to me. I shook my head. No way was I talking to her.

I walked away and heard Ro say, "Ma, she won't, um can't come to the phone now. She'll call you later and explain everything."

She quickly hung up and we looked at her in disbelief.

"Do you hate me, Ro?" I yelled. "Is that it? I didn't give you enough sympathy when you were complaining about Charlie? Why don't I call Chick right now and tell him about your little cyber affair? Let's see how much sympathy you get from Ma and Chick."

Sophia stepped in between us and ordered, "Stop right now."

"Yeah, Mona Lisa," Ro added sounding like a five-year-old.

Soph raised her eyebrows and said, "Both of you. Neither one of you say another word and we'll figure out how to fix this."

Marilyn said, "Let's tell them you're going on vacation to Atlanta."

"Oh, right. They'll believe that after she said the word moving. Let's face it, I'm screwed."

"Maybe it's not meant to be," Nina responded.

"I'm tired of that excuse. If only I hadn't believed that everything happens for a reason, I would have broken up with Joey years ago. Everyone said we were meant to be

48

and now look at me. I'm alone and miserable. I'm going to Atlanta."

The door burst open and Chick flew in and announced, "Girls, I want to talk to Mona Lisa alone."

"They can stay," I countered as they all scattered like ants crawling back into the woodwork. "Thanks, cowards."

"Just so you know, your mother is hysterical. I never saw her this upset."

"Maybe you shouldn't have left her alone," I remarked.

"Listen, 'Miss I'm Too Good for the Family', I will not allow you to move away from home."

"Chick, the last time I checked, I didn't live at your house."

"Aren't you a wiseass these days? What happened to you, Mona Lisa? You used to be such a good girl."

"I'm still good, Chick. But, I'm not a girl anymore, and if I choose to move to Atlanta, you can't stop me." I wasn't sure where this bravado was coming from, but it sure felt good, so I continued. "I have to do what's best for me and right now it may include moving away."

"Oh, so that's how you justify selfishness? You have to take care of yourself? Family is number one and we don't abandon our family." With that declaration, he turned and walked out of the door.

I jumped at the sound of the door slamming.

Nina looked to see if it was safe before coming back into the room. "I heard everything," she admitted. "You really are screwed."

Chapter 15

It had been two days since my showdown with Chick, and I hadn't heard from either of my parents. My pride kept me from calling them, but I was surprised that Chick had not summoned me for a meeting or come by. As I dressed for Sunday dinner with the family, or as it was becoming lately, The Mona Lisa Hour, I seriously considered staying home. However, the situation was pretty bad and missing dinner would only make it worse.

I was running late and rushed to my parents' door. And as was becoming routine, I entered the house and conversation ceased.

"I'm starting to get a complex," I joked. "I seem to be able to bring all activity to a halt just by walking in the room. Maybe I should try bending spoons with my mind."

Not so much as a smile. This was a tough crowd.

"I didn't think you'd show," Chick challenged, "seeing as how you want to disassociate yourself from the family. Really, Mona Lisa, you don't have to lower yourself and spend time with us."

All heads immediately went down as if bowing to Chick. I searched the crowd for a friendly face, but no one met my gaze. Where was Noni?

I approached my mother who busied herself with preparing the salad.

She rebuffed my kiss, so I quietly said, "Hi, Ma."

"Hello, Mona Lisa," she said tersely and turned her

back to me. "Sophia, please get me the vegetable platter from the china cabinet."

"I'll get it," I offered.

"No, thank you. Your sister can do it."

Despite my efforts, tears brimmed in my eyes. When Ma was upset, she refused to talk to the offending party and I was no exception. I went to sit in the living room where my niece Gina was coloring.

Gina looked up at me and said, "You're in big trouble, Aunt Mo."

"Don't I know it, kiddo. What have you heard?"

"Chick told Grandma that you either got with the program or you were out of the family."

"Geez. What did Grandma say?" I asked.

"She said he was being a cop toaster," Gina cackled.

Sophia had snuck into the room and said, "I think you mean *capatosta*. It means hardheaded, like when you refuse to go to bed when I tell you to even though you know you'll be cranky in the morning. So, listen my little *capatosta,* go find your brother and wash up for dinner."

As Gina scampered off, I asked Sophia, "Are they still aiming to kill in there or have they dropped their weapons?"

"Mona Lisa, you know how they are. Instead of telling you that they're sad and will miss you, they get mad. It's how they deal."

"It sucks," I admitted.

"I know it does, but they'll get over it. Give them time

and work on Ma first. She'll crack a lot faster than Chick. He can be a real cop toaster," she added.

We went in the kitchen and my heart lifted when I saw Noni and Marshall.

"Hey there, you two." I leaned in to kiss Noni's cheek and whispered, "Help me. They know about Atlanta."

Noni smiled and replied quietly, "I heard."

My mother called us to dinner. As we prepared for Grace, I said a silent prayer for my sanity, which obviously was ignored as Chick provided his addendum to the blessing of the food.

"God, please help those who think they are better off without their family to see the error of their self-centered ways. Amen."

I took a deep breath and then counted to ten. The rage was still bubbling within me, so I took a large gulp of wine. It seemed to help. So I took another and stood to refill my glass. I had a few bites of pasta but was enjoying the liquid part of my meal more, so I had a third glass.

My mother took notice and said, "Watch yourself, Mona Lisa. Drunkenness is unbecoming."

"So is living your life apparently," I retorted.

"You will not ruin another family meal, young lady," Chick admonished. "I have had enough of your antics. First the wedding fiasco, then Dante and now this so-called move to Atlanta. You have a responsibility to this family and I will not allow you to treat us this way."

I started to cry. Uncontrollable, heaving, wracking

sobs while everyone stared with open mouths. I felt my stomach start to heave and ran to the restroom. My mother followed and held my head while I paid the price for too much wine combined with Italian, Catholic guilt.

When I was finished, my mom asked, "Have you been feeling like this since the wedding?"

"Yes, and I seem to be feeling worse instead of better."

We sat in silence for a few minutes and finally I said, "I don't want to leave you and Chick. I need a change. I don't even know if I'll like it there."

"I think you should go, Mona Lisa."

"Really, Ma? What about Chick?"

"I'll handle Chick. Give me some time and before you know it he'll be offering to take you to Atlanta himself."

Chapter 16

My mother was true to her word. After my Sunday dinner breakdown, Chick came around—as much as he could. He referred to my trip to Atlanta as "The Mona Lisa Search for Happiness Tour", but he never spoke to me about it directly. Ma assured me that Chick was on board, so I focused my energy on our trip south.

The night before we left, the girls and I stayed at Marilyn's and awoke to a beautiful late winter day of clear blue skies and sunshine. We had a *bon voyage* family dinner and said our goodbyes as Ma quietly cried. Chick hugged me but said nothing, which was why I was shocked when he showed up the next morning as we loaded the car.

"Marilyn, let me do this. Those bags will fall out the first time you open the back door," he said as he removed all of the suitcases and put them in the right way.

When he was finished, I approached him and said, "Thanks, Chick."

"You're welcome, Mona Lisa. I have a few things I want you to take with you."

He walked to his car and returned with two shoeboxes.

"This one has lasagna."

I must have made a face.

He shrugged and said, "Your mother. There are forks and napkins and each piece is individually wrapped."

"Okay, then. What's in box number two?"

He looked around to make sure no one could hear. He

leaned in and whispered, "There's one thousand dollars in cash and a gun."

"A gun?" I asked in disbelief. "I'm not taking a gun. What the hell? We're not going to a Third World country, Chick. Last time I checked, Georgia was in the United States."

"Mona Lisa, I'm serious. Who knows what kind of people you'll run into on this trip. I insist you take the money and the gun." He shoved both boxes in my hands and got in his car and left.

I was dumbfounded when Sophia came up and asked, "What's in the boxes?"

"Apparently dinner, cash, and a gun. Isn't that what everyone packs when they cross the Mason-Dixon line?"

"You're kidding, right?"

"Wish I was. Let me ask Marilyn if she has a place to keep these while we're away. Although, there's a thousand bucks in here. We could have one hell of a dinner on Chick's dime and tell him we got robbed by a couple of tobacco farmers who forced us to drive off the road with their tractors."

"Mona Lisa, you really do need to get out of here."

I found Marilyn, who gave the gun box to Dom who promised to put it in their safe. Then we piled in the car and drove out.

As we drove along, I was enthralled by the majestic mountains and amazed at the world outside of New Jersey. We ate lunch in Pennsylvania and did some shopping at the outlets before stopping for the night in a quaint little town in Virginia. We ate at a hole in the wall restaurant where the servers called us all ma'am and we could detect a hint of a southern accent.

"Do you hear how funny they talk?" Ro asked.

"They probably think we have an accent," Sophia replied.

"Right. Like we have an accent," Ro laughed.

"We do, you moron," I countered.

She looked at me in disbelief and I laughed. If I stayed in Atlanta, I would miss my sisters tremendously and the thought terrified me. I pushed it out of my head until I was alone with Sophia and Nina in the hotel.

I sat on the bed and pulled my knees to my chest. Soph sat next to me.

"You okay, Mona Lisa?" she asked.

"I'm scared. We haven't even gotten there and I'm already anxious. What if I hate it? What if I don't make any friends? What if I love it there and never come home?"

She smiled and asked, "Is that all that's got you worried?"

"I sound like a lunatic. How will I make it without you?" I asked, my eyes tearing up.

"Mona Lisa, you and I have a special bond. We always have and we always will. Nothing will change that."

I hugged her and said, "Thanks."

My cell phone rang and the caller ID revealed that it was my parents.

"Hi, Ma," I answered.

"It's Chick. I wanted to remind you to keep the gun in the hotel safe. You have a safe, don't you?"

"Yes, Chick, we do."

"Okay, here's your mother."

"Our trip was fine. Thanks for asking," I said as my mother took the phone.

"Hi, honey. How was the drive?"

"It was great, Ma. We'll get there tomorrow sometime mid-afternoon. I'm getting a little nervous," I admitted.

"Mona Lisa, try to enjoy yourself and the time with your sisters. If you don't like it, you don't have to go back."

"I love you, Ma."

"I love you, too. Don't forget to put on some makeup. You might meet a southern gentleman and you wouldn't want to scare him away with an unmade face."

"Of course I wouldn't. Goodnight, Ma."

Chapter 17

As we drove on I-85 into the state of Georgia, I immediately loved the lush, green foliage everywhere. Stopping
for gas, I noticed the accents were heavier, but people
looked you in the eye and said hello. There was genuine
warmth in their smile and it was very welcoming. My
nerves abated as we settled into our hotel room in downtown Atlanta. I unpacked, and then called Vinnie's cousin,
Bobbie Lee.

The phone rang, and a sweet, southern voice answered,
"Bobbie Lee Salon. How may I *hep* you?"

"Can I speak to Bobbie Lee, please?"

"You got her. Who do I have the pleasure of speakin'
to?"

"Hi, Bobbie Lee. This is Mona Lisa Cicciarelli. I work
for Vinnie."

"Well, hey, Mona Lisa. I love, love, love that name,
girl. So Italian. You don't hear names like yours around
here."

"I was thinking the same thing about your name."

"Honey, I was named after the General himself. My
parents are very fond of their southern heritage. My full
name is Roberta Ellen Lee Adcock. Quite a mouthful, isn't
it? Are you in Atlanta?" she asked.

"Yes. I'm here with my sisters and we're staying at the
Omni. It's a beautiful city."

"There's a lot to see and do. Ya'll will love the great

restaurants down there."

"We're getting ready to do some exploring. When would be a good time for us to get together?"

"Are you free for lunch tomorrow?"

"Sure," I replied as I felt anxiety settle in my stomach.

"Come by at noon. I'll show you around the shop and we'll go grab a bite. How does that sound?"

"Great. Thanks so much, Bobbie Lee."

She gave me directions and said, "All right, darlin'. I'll see you tomorrow and have fun visiting our fair city."

I smiled as I hung up the phone. I picked it back up and called Marilyn and Ro.

"Let's meet in the lobby and see what this town has to offer."

Sophia, Nina and I met them at the concierge desk.

"We're visiting for the first time and want to get a feel for the city. What would you recommend?" I asked the concierge.

He was an older gentleman, with kind, blue eyes, and a slow, sophisticated drawl.

"No visit to Atlanta is complete without lunch at the Varsity. It's an institution around these parts, but not for those with a delicate stomach. Then there's the Aquarium, the Coca-Cola Museum, and the Fox Theater. For some fine southern dining, there are numerous restaurants to fit any budget."

I grabbed some brochures and we set off.

* * * * *

After a day of playing tourist, we capped off our adventure with dinner at an upscale seafood restaurant.

"Here's to new experiences," I toasted.

"At the risk of sounding like Noni, *oy vey*, but that hot dog at the Varsity gave me *agita*," Marilyn announced.

"The concierge warned you," Ro replied.

"Atlanta seems great so far," Nina chimed in.

"It's not how I pictured it. I thought it would be more *Gone with the Wind*," I admitted.

"Everyone sitting on their porches drinking mint Juleps and talking about the Civil War?" Marilyn cracked.

I nodded. "It will be interesting to check out the area where Bobbie Lee's shop is."

"What do you know about it?" Sophia asked.

"It's a pretty affluent part of town. Vinnie says it's all nice neighborhoods with pools and tennis courts. A lot of famous athletes live in the area."

"Sounds nice," Marilyn said.

"Yes, but it doesn't sound like the place for singles," I admitted.

"You don't have to live there. Couldn't you commute from downtown? It would be fun to live in a city, don't you think?" Nina asked.

"I guess so. There's so much to think about. I hope Bobbie Lee can give me some recommendations. Nothing like asking a total stranger to tell you what to do with your life."

"You don't have to take her advice, Mona Lisa. Nothing is set in stone," Sophia replied. "Right now let's be grateful for a wonderful trip so far."

"Here's to sisters on vacation," Ro toasted. "And the best part is … we get to miss Sunday dinner."

Chapter 18

As I drove to the salon the next day, I wished that I had
asked Sophia or Nina to come with me. I thought about it
the night before, but knew it would cause hurt feelings.
More importantly, this was something I needed to do on my
own. It would be my decision to make, even though the
thought of it terrified me.

I had a death grip on the steering wheel as my naviga-
tion system called out directions. I had never driven on a
circular highway system before and I was more than a little
freaked out; roads crossed over each other and there was a
ton of traffic at eleven o'clock in the morning. This could
be a definite strike against Atlanta. I was used to the Park-
way and Turnpike where it only went in two directions.
Sure, people made fun of us by asking 'What exit?' but it
was a piece of cake compared to this nightmare.

When I pulled into the parking lot, I sat for a moment
to compose myself and allow my heartbeat to slow down. I
eventually mustered up my courage and entered the salon
where I was greeted by a woman whose smile was instantly
recognizable because she was the female version of Vinnie.

"Bobbie Lee?"

"That's me. Mona Lisa?"

"Yes. Wow. I can't believe how much you and your
cousin look alike."

"Crazy, isn't it? Our mamas have some strong genes.
Let me show you around. We run our place pretty much

like Vinnie runs his. We opened our salons at the same time, so we compared notes frequently."

We walked past the reception area into the work-station.

"Hey, ya'll. I want you to meet Mona Lisa. She's visiting from New Jersey," Bobbie Lee announced.

I was greeted by a chorus of hellos before Bobbie Lee led me into her office.

"This is my hideout. Some days I need a quiet place to escape to, so pardon my mess. I'll grab my bag and let's get some lunch. There's a great place just down the road."

When we settled in her car, she asked, "How was your ride to the salon? Atlanta traffic takes some getting used to."

"That section where the roads cross over each other scared the hell out of me."

"That's Spaghetti Junction. Honey, I've lived here all my life and I still don't know which way to go on the perimeter."

We pulled into a parking lot behind an old house that had been converted into a restaurant.

"My friend, Anna Jo, grew up in this house and about two years ago, she and her husband opened this café. They only serve lunch, so Anna Jo is home when her kids come home from school in the afternoon."

We walked in and were seated at a corner table where we could look out at the gazebo. Our waitress smiled as she approached our table before leaning over to give Bobbie

Lee a light hug.

"Hey, girl," she addressed Bobbie Lee. "I haven't seen you in ages."

"It's been crazy over at the salon. Most days I barely get to eat, but today my friend is visiting from New Jersey, so I made sure to get out for lunch. Mona Lisa, this is Brandy."

"It's nice to meet you."

"You, too. What can I get ya'll to drink? The tea is fresh and sweet. I made it myself."

"Do you have Diet Pepsi?" I asked concerned about the calories and sugar.

Bobbie Lee raised her eyebrows. "Honey, you're in the south now, and the only cola that exists in these parts is Coca-Cola. As far as tea goes, we only drink it sweet. We like to feel the sugar rot our teeth with each sip," she said giving me a wink. "Just try it."

"Why not? I might as well get the whole experience."

We ordered our lunch and I managed to choke down some tea.

"Mona Lisa, Vinnie told me about the wedding. Bless your heart. You sure have been through a lot lately."

"That, my new friend, is an understatement. Actually, I'm doing better since I got here. It really helps to be physically removed from the situation."

"I'm glad. Vinnie told me about your work, so I know you're qualified. You have a job if you want one. The question is are you ready to make the move?" she asked.

"Right now I am. Ask me in an hour and the answer might be different," I admitted.

"Why don't you spend some time at the salon and talk to the girls. They can tell you more about what the nightlife is like because I can't remember the last time my husband and I went out. We've got three kids and we eat in my car more than we do at any restaurant. I always say I could live for three days on the fries I find in my car."

I laughed and said, "You sound just like my sister."

"Well, maybe you need a southern sister to get your butt back on track."

I raised my glass of tea and said, "I think that's exactly what I need."

Chapter 19

After lunch, Bobbie Lee and I returned to the salon, and I sat in the break room with Brightleigh, a darling blonde and Atlanta native.

"Mona Lisa, it's great to meet you. You must get a lot of comments about your name, huh?" Brightleigh asked in such a sweet voice, I could swear honey was about to pour out of her mouth.

"I do," I admitted. "I've never heard your name before. Is it a family name?"

"My mama's maiden name was Bright, so they named me Brightleigh. It's a southern thing. My brothers are Bostwick and Mize, which are my grandmothers' maiden names. It's a tradition I'd like to put a stop to."

I laughed. "I know what you mean. My dad picked quirky names for all of my sisters too, but mine is by far the most dubious. Are your parents from Atlanta too?"

"Sure are. Mama met Daddy in high school and they both went to the University of Georgia. Go Bulldogs. They've been together ever since."

"So, what's the dating scene like?" I asked.

"I reckon like any place. There are a lot of fun clubs. It's not New York City, but there's still bunches to do. I live in a great apartment complex. Lots of singles and parties. I might be biased, but Atlanta men are good lookin'."

"Do you mind me asking if you're dating anyone?"

"Not at all. I'm single and happily so. I guess you are

too, or you wouldn't be moving."

"I am. I wasn't happy about it at first, but I'm feeling better every day," I confessed.

"Well, girl, there's plenty of guys to go around. Did you meet Amy? She works here, too. She's also my room-mate and a hoot. She's from Brooklyn and she can tell you what it was like when she came here."

There was so much to consider and I was feeling overwhelmed.

"We live about thirty minutes from the salon. It's a great town for work, but it's all families in this area and not good for meeting men—single men, that is. There are plen-ty of married guys who have tried to get me to go out with them, but I'm not into that at all."

"Me either. I've dealt with enough bullshit recently and don't need anymore."

Brightleigh laughed. "Ya'll crack me up with your cussing. My mama would wash my mouth out with soap if she heard me say that."

"Seriously?" I asked. "I think cursing is a prerequisite for getting into kindergarten in New Jersey."

Brightleigh's eyes widened.

"I'm kidding," I explained. "I use humor as a coping mechanism."

"Mama always says you gotta use the talents God done give you."

I wasn't sure what she meant by that, so I asked, "Is Amy busy? I'd love to meet her. I also need some advice on apartments. Thirty minutes seems like a long commute."

"That's nothing for Atlanta. How far do you live from your job in Jersey?"

"Ten minutes. I guess I'm spoiled," I admitted.

"Maybe a little," Brightleigh said before giving me a wink. "I'd have to talk to Amy, but we have an extra bedroom. Our last roommate got married and we haven't worked hard at getting a new one."

The muscles in my neck relaxed. "Thanks. Everyone has been so friendly and helpful."

"It's our way. Let me see if Amy can pop in for a few minutes."

I sat back in my chair and closed my eyes while I tried to take it all in.

Amy stuck her head in the doorway and said, "I'm in the middle of a color, but I just wanted to say I love Georgia. When I first moved down, it was a definite culture shock, but eventually, you get used to it. And now that I can get some good Italian food, it's even better. They still could use a decent bakery, but they would never be able to make a cannoli like Little Italy."

"Thanks, Amy."

"Anytime. Call me if you want to talk more. Bobbie Lee can give you my number."

For some reason, I was smiling and I thought, *I can do this ... I think.*

Chapter 20

I unlocked the hotel room door and was relieved to be alone. I wasn't ready to talk to my sisters, but I did want to talk with Noni, so I fluffed my pillow, sat back on the bed and dialed.

"Hi, Noni. Do you miss me yet?" I asked.

"I might be old, kiddo, but I have a life. You've only been gone for a few days. Ask me in a month," she said.

I laughed. "You sure are a tough, old broad. How are you?"

"Still kicking, baby. Marshall and I are enjoying every moment we have. What about you? Are you back?"

"No. I just visited the salon and met the boss and some of the girls that work there. I have a job if I want it and maybe a place to live."

When I didn't say anything else, she said, "And why are you not bursting with excitement? What gives?"

"It's scary. That's all."

"Mona Lisa, I think you need a good kick in the ass."

I chuckled. "That's why I love you, Noni. No nonsense."

"I'm serious," she continued. "You act like you're the first person to ever make a big change in your life. Guess what?" she asked not waiting for me to answer. "People do it all the time and they live to tell about it too."

"I know you're right. I need to make a decision and stick with it."

70

"Time to put up or shut up as I like to say," Noni replied.

"You are full of wisdom, old lady."

"And don't you forget it. Mona Lisa, no one likes change, but what kind of life would you have without it?"

I thought about it before answering, "Pretty dull, I guess."

"Do you want to lead a boring, monotonous existence or do you want to live your life? They are two very different things, Mona Lisa."

"Once again, you're the voice of sanity. You're my rock, Noni."

"Mona Lisa, you don't need a rock. You're stronger than you think."

Tears pooled in my eyes. "Thanks, Noni. I can't wait to see you."

"When are you coming home?" she asked.

"I think we'll probably get on the road tomorrow."

Noni yawned, "Excuse me. I love Marshall, but he is tiring me out. This morning we got up early and went to the racetrack."

"How exciting. Nothing like betting on the ponies to keep your blood pumping."

"Tomorrow we're going into the city to see a show. Marshall doesn't like to stay still for very long. He claims the Grim Reaper can't catch him if he keeps moving."

"Isn't tomorrow Sunday? Ma isn't making you go to Mass and dinner?" I asked.

"Your mother may think she is in charge of me, but I do what I want when I want. And as far as dinner goes, it must be your lucky week because Chick said he wanted to wait until the night you girls got back, so you get two dinners."

I shook my head and sighed. "Lucky indeed."

Chapter 21

My sisters and I enjoyed another great evening in Atlanta, but despite my good mood, I had trouble sleeping. I
slipped out of bed and quietly dressed, before sneaking out
of our room. I needed some air and hoped it would help me
clear my head so that I could get some rest before the long
ride home. I walked around the block marveling at the
cleanliness of the city. I felt very safe as I strolled letting
my mind wander.

I was much more at ease and when I returned to the
hotel, I passed the bar and saw Ro sitting alone with a
drink.

I walked up and quietly asked, "Couldn't sleep either?"

"Nope," she replied. "Want to join me?"

"Sure," I answered. "We can let the others do the driving tomorrow. I ordered a glass of pinot noir and after it
arrived, I asked Ro, "So, why can't you sleep?"

"I don't want to go home, Mona Lisa," she answered
simply.

"That's a tough one. Does Charlie have any idea how
you feel?"

"I've tried to tell him that I'm not happy and it's as if
he either doesn't believe me or thinks it's a phase I'm
going through. I've felt like this for over six months. It's
not a phase."

"Have you thought of going to counseling?" I asked.

"Yes, but first I want to be alone for awhile. I think I

need to figure out what's going on with me before I try to fix Charlie and me. I wish I could do that without the whole town knowing. Hell, I wish I could do it without having to let Ma and Chick know."

"Believe me, I feel your pain. And I hate to say this, but I think they will take a divorce very badly."

"Badly? I think Chick will have a meltdown of nuclear proportions. And Ma will never talk to me again. Maybe they'll disown me and I'll never have to endure another family dinner again."

"Speaking of which, they're planning on having two dinners this week to make up for the one we missed."

"Are you kidding?" she asked.

"Wish I was."

"Maybe I'll have a nervous breakdown on the ride home."

"I tried that. Remember the day after my wedding? I can see Chick dragging you out of your padded cell for some homemade manicotti. According to Chick, there is nothing that can't be fixed by a good bowl of pasta."

"He really is a lunatic," Ro laughed.

"Yes, but he's our lunatic and he'd do anything for us. He may make us crazy in the process, but he means well."

"I know he does. It's hard enough to deal with my marriage problems without worrying what it will do to him and Ma."

"I know. That's one of the reasons I'm having trouble deciding on the move," I admitted. "That, and I'm scared out of my mind."

"We're quite a pair, aren't we, Mona Lisa? Maybe I'll move down here with you and we can both be excommunicated from the family."

"If only it were that easy. What are you going to do?" I asked.

"I had an idea. If you come back here, maybe I can live in your apartment."

"Wow, you really have been putting some thought into this. I guess that would work out. I hadn't even considered what I'd do with my place in Jersey. I have a lot of time left on my lease."

"Maybe the universe is telling you this is the right thing to do, Mona Lisa."

"I'm not sure I trust the universe these days, but my other advisor thinks I need to do this."

"Who's that?" Ro asked.

"Noni. She told me to stop whining and do it."

"I think she's right. It's good advice for the both of us."

"I wish the decision were clear-cut. Maybe I'll meet my soulmate before we head home."

Ro drained the last of her martini from the glass, then said, "Ha! And maybe Chick will cancel the family dinner."

Chapter 22

We drove home in one day stopping only to fuel up the car, get some food and use the bathroom. There was much less enthusiasm on this trip than on the way down and all I wanted was to get home and sleep in my own bed.

That wish was short-lived as my phone rang at eight the next morning.

"Mona Lisa, it's your mother."

"I know, Ma. No one else calls this early."

"I've been up since five-thirty. Anyone who sleeps longer than eight hours is lazy if you ask me."

"I got to sleep at one in the morning," I replied.

"If you can't manage to get yourself to bed at a decent hour, you have no right to complain."

I opened my mouth to argue that I wasn't complaining, but realized that would serve no purpose, so I asked, "What's up Ma?"

"I wanted to tell you we will be expecting you for dinner tonight at six."

"Got it, Ma. Chick isn't planning any surprise visitors for me, is he?"

"No, Mona Lisa. I'm afraid the world doesn't always revolve around you."

"I know that, Ma. I'm tired and I don't want to have to make small talk with Chick's latest choice of boyfriends for me."

"He loves you, Mona Lisa, and wants you to be happy.

You'll miss us when we're gone."

And there it was, the ultimate guilt trip—you'll be sorry when we're dead.

"I know he does and I love you both, too. I'll see you at six."

I tried to go back to sleep, but it wasn't going to happen, so I showered and dressed and went to the salon to talk with Vinnie.

After I said hello to the girls, I joined Vinnie in his office.

"How about some coffee?" he asked.

"Sure. What did I miss while I was gone?"

He poured two cups and handed me one.

"A resident of the assisted living escaped and went around flashing people. He put on quite a show in our front window. You chose the wrong week to go on vacation. What about you? How's my cousin?"

"She didn't flash me, so that was good." Vinnie laughed. "She's the southern version of you. She was so sweet and helpful. I really like her."

"She's a good egg, that one. So are you moving or not?"

"I haven't made up my mind yet."

"Are you waiting for Prince Charming to show up and whisk you off into the sunset? I hate to tell you this, but your fairy Godmother isn't going to wave her wand and help you out either."

"Thanks, Vinnie. You're a real pal. I hope you never

answer my call at the suicide prevention hotline."

"They took my privileges away years ago. Seriously, Mona Lisa, I love you like a sister and I want you to do something with your life."

"I want that, too."

"Keep me posted on your decision, okay?"

"You got it. I'll see you tomorrow. And Vinnie? Thanks."

I walked out of his office and looked for Mary Kathleen, who patted her chair as an invitation to me.

"Hi, girl," she greeted me with a hug. "How was your trip?" she asked as I plopped myself in her chair.

"It was good. It's a nice town and the salon is beautiful. I haven't made a decision yet, though."

"There's no rush, is there?"

"No, but the longer I wait, the easier it will be to stay. You know me, I have to be hit over the head before I make a change."

I heard the jangle of the bell on the door and saw Alice walk in looking like a giddy schoolgirl.

"Excuse me," she said as she clapped her hands to get everyone's attention. I turned my chair to face her and immediately felt a gnawing in my gut.

"I wanted you all to be the first to know that my Joey has met someone and last night they got engaged. Wedding bells will be ringing soon."

I struggled to catch my breath when Mary Kathleen asked, "How's that head feeling? Was that a hard enough hit?"

Chapter 23

In my mind, I lunged at Alice and scratched her eyes out. In reality, Vinnie stepped in and said, "You are the most insensitive, vile woman I have ever met. Do you even care about anyone besides yourself and your lame-ass son? I mean, really Alice, do you not have one ounce of common sense in that messed up head of yours?"

Alice looked aghast. "What did I do? I thought you would all be happy for my Joey and me."

The room was silent as we all stared at her in disbelief.

I stood and said, "Thanks for helping me make my decision, Alice."

I walked into Vinnie's office and pulled out my cell. I dialed and felt a sense of calm come over me as Bobbie Lee answered the phone.

"Hi. It's Mona Lisa. I'm ready to do it. I'm coming to Atlanta."

Vinnie put a hand on my shoulder and gave a squeeze as he nodded his approval.

* * * *

I decided to make an official announcement after dinner. I kissed my mother who was showing my niece, Gina, how to grate Parmesan cheese.

"Am I the last one here?" I asked.

"Yes, but we can't eat until we have our cheese," Gina said.

Everyone seemed okay, so I assumed the details of the

scene at the shop hadn't hit the gossip mill, but that was not the case. When I saw Noni, she immediately pulled me aside.

"I heard what that crazy Alice did to you today. I'm sure there's a Yiddish word to describe how incredibly awful and tactless she is, but I'm too pissed to ask Marshall. I'm so sorry, Mona Lisa."

"You know what, Noni, I think it's good. It helped me finalize my decision. I'm moving in two weeks."

"*Mazel tov*, Mona Lisa."

"Noni, you kill me with the Yiddish. You're getting pretty good at it."

"You know what?" she asked. "I love it. I can usually manage one Yiddish phrase in each conversation. At first, I did it because it bugged your mother so much, but now it's like a special bond between Marshall and me."

"You never cease to amaze me, Noni. You and Marshall better be my first visitors."

"Let's eat," my mother announced so I quickly hugged Noni and we sat down at the table.

Chick's grace ended with "And thank you for getting our girls safely back to us, and now that they've gotten that nonsense out of their systems, please help Mona Lisa to find a husband."

I took a deep breath and said, "I guess this is as good a time as any to tell you I liked Atlanta and am moving there in two weeks."

No one said a word, but all heads turned toward Chick

who appeared shocked, then sad.

"It's going to be great," I continued. "I'm sure everyone heard Joey and his mother are marrying someone else, so it's a good time for me to do this."

My brother-in-law, Dom, raised his glass and said, "Here's to you, Mona Lisa. *Salut.*"

Everyone raised their glass except Chick who started eating. My mother nudged him, but he ignored her and kept on attacking his ziti like it had physically harmed him in some way.

"Tell us about your trip," Marshall asked.

"It was great. The ride down was easy and we ate, shopped and laughed. Who could ask for more?" I said.

My sisters each took turns telling stories about our visit as I stole glances at Chick who would not look up at me. I turned to Noni who just waved her hand as if to say, let him be.

Mike asked, "Do you definitely have a job down there?"

This must have gotten Chick's attention as his head came up out of his plate.

"I do. Vinnie's cousin is going to hire me. In two weeks I will be an official employee of the Bobbie Lee Salon. She seems wonderful and so sweet. We hit it off and I think I'll be happy there. They cut a lot of the Atlanta Braves' players' hair, so I may even work on a genuine celebrity."

"You better not turn into a Braves fan, Mona Lisa. We

might not let you back into Mets' territory if you start rooting for them," Dom kidded.

"No worries. I'm a northern girl through and through."

"Where are you going to live?" my mother asked. "Did you get an apartment?"

Before I could answer, Chick asked, "And what about your place here? You can't walk out on your lease?"

Ro cleared her throat and said, "I'm going to live there. Charlie and I separated this morning."

There was a collective gasp as we all turned to look at Chick, who said, "Mona Lisa, you created this mess. Now fix it."

"Me?" I asked in disbelief. "I had nothing to do with her decision, Chick. She's wanted to do this for a long time."

There was another collective gasp.

"Shit. Sorry, Ro. All I meant was that if Ro made this decision, she must have given it a lot of thought."

"Like your decision to run away because you were left at the altar," Chick countered.

My mother stood and said, "Enough, Chick. Stop talking before you say something stupid."

He opened his mouth to answer, but Ma pursed her lips and said, "I mean it, Chick. Our girls are grown women and you have to stop trying to control every aspect of their lives."

My heart soared with pride and awe as I wondered where this version of my mother had been all my life.

"No more talking until we are done with dinner," she ordered.

Chick stood and threw his napkin on his plate.

My mother responded, "And dinner's not over until I say so."

Chick sat back down and I had to stifle a laugh. This was priceless. I winked at Noni.

She shrugged her shoulders as if to say, "Who knew?"

The dinner continued in silence with the only noise coming from the kids' table.

It was very awkward and I was relieved when my mother stood and announced, "Now, we will do the dishes and then we will talk with Mona Lisa and Ro." She looked at the others, and added, "In private."

As we cleared the table, I managed to whisper to Sophia, "Oh, my gosh. That was amazing."

"I know. What happened to Ma? It's like she was taken over by aliens."

"Seriously. I've never seen her stand up to Chick like that."

I looked up to find Chick staring at me, so I smiled and went back to work.

When we had finished putting all of the dishes away, Chick came into the kitchen.

He said, "Mona Lisa and Rosemary, come into the living room so we can talk. The rest of you find something to do until we have dessert."

Ro and I followed Chick, and I couldn't help feeling like I was being led to the electric chair. I sat next to Ro and she grabbed my hand. It was cold and damp—not a comforting gesture. My mother joined us but deferred to Chick as he began his lecture.

"Girls, I know you think you're old enough to make important decisions, but you are both making huge mistakes, and I can't let it happen. Mona Lisa, you're running away from your problems instead of facing them. So what if Joey is marrying someone else? You need to show them they can't hurt you, but leaving town is what a coward does. And Rosemary, you and Charlie promised to stay together until death so unless one of you is dying, I see no reason to discuss this any further. Let's have dessert."

Now it was Ro's turn to speak up. "Chick, we are not babies," she stated matter of factly.

He started to protest, but my mother put a hand on his arm and he retreated.

"Mona Lisa and I have two separate issues going on and you can't tell us what to do. She is unhappy living in New Jersey and is going to move. Charlie and I have some problems and I am going to live in her apartment until we come to a resolution. We may get back together or we may not, and unfortunately, you have no say in the matter. It's between me and Charlie and it's going to stay that way."

I wanted to add something, but she had said it all and had done it so very well. Chick shook his head and walked out of the room.

The three of us sat in silence for a few moments.

Then I said, "Ma, we had to do that. I know he loves us, but it feels like he's smothering us. We don't want to be disrespectful, but sometimes he leaves us no choice."

"I understand about your wanting to leave, Mona Lisa. I don't want you to go. It hurts my heart to think of you living so far away, but I want you to be happy, so I will support you. Divorce is another thing, Ro. You and Charlie took a vow, and I hope you are not taking that lightly. Marriages are disposable these days, and Chick and I both hate that. It's as if nothing is sacred anymore. Please promise me you will do all that you can to save your marriage."

Ro's eyes teared up. "I promise, Ma. I don't want a divorce, but right now Charlie and I need some time apart from each other."

"Being apart doesn't always help you come back together. Keep that in mind Ro, and try to remember why you fell in love with him in the first place. It's easy to forget and take your love for granted. That's all I'm going to say on both of these matters. Your father will come around. After being married for forty-six years, I know him very well, and his love for you will overrule his need to fix everything and everyone."

She stood and kissed us each on the top of our heads and a feeling of melancholy washed over me.

"As crazy as these dinners get, I'm going to miss them," I admitted.

"I know you will, Mona Lisa, but it's going to be good for you to get away," Ro said.

"What about you, Ro? Is there hope for you and Charlie?"

"After hearing what Ma had to say, I'm definitely going to work hard to find some. She's made me think."

I smiled.

She added, "And if you repeat that to Ma or Chick, I'll kill you."

Chapter 24

The days flew by as I saw each of my customers one last time. It wasn't as sad as I had anticipated, but on my last day, I felt as if my heart were literally going to break. I sat in my chair and watched the others while they worked, knowing that come Monday this would all continue as if I had never been there. I tried to hold back my tears when I felt Mary Kathleen's hand on my shoulder.

"You're really going to leave me, aren't you?" she asked.

"It sounds terrible when you say it like that. You can come with me, you know. We could be like Lucy and Ethel—the southern version."

She laughed and said, "I wish I could. You know my mom still needs me or I'd be right there with you."

"I'm going to miss you so much, M.K. Promise me you'll keep in touch."

"Mona Lisa, you're my best friend and a few miles won't change that. I'll get one of my brothers to stay with my mom and I'll come visit soon. I love you, girl."

I couldn't control the tears anymore as I hugged Mary Kathleen. When I released her from my grasp, the bell on the door rang and I looked over to see Alice slowly walking toward me.

"Can we talk, Mona Lisa?" Alice asked sheepishly.

Mary Kathleen shook her head and mouthed, "No," behind Alice's back.

I hesitated.

Alice asked, "Please?"

Reluctantly I said, "Sure, Alice. Let's go to Vinnie's office."

We sat on the sofa and I waited for Alice to speak as she fidgeted in her seat.

When I couldn't tolerate it any longer, I asked, "What did you want to talk to me about, Alice?"

"You know how much I love Joey and I want what's best for him. You were never right for him. And his new fianceé, she's great and she loves me so much and …."

"Gee, Alice, you came all this way to tell me how wonderful Joey and his girlfriend are?"

"Yes, well no. Mona Lisa, I want to say I'm sorry if Joey and I hurt you. We didn't mean it."

The tears flowed again and I composed myself as I said, "It's okay, Alice. Joey and I weren't meant to be."

"I know, Mona Lisa. You'd love Jenny, though. She and I are the best of friends. We'd like you to come to the wedding. They're getting married on the same day I married Joe senior."

I stood up and said, "Thanks for coming by, Alice and tell Joey congratulations."

"I guess I did it again," Alice said as she put her purse over her arm. "Good luck, Mona Lisa. I mean it."

"Goodbye, Alice."

* * * *

My car was packed with all of my worldly possessions, and since Ro had already moved into my apartment, I agreed to spend my last night at my parents' house. The entire family gathered for my final family dinner and I wanted more than anything to keep it unemotional, and for the most part, it was. That is, until it was time for everyone to go.

My sisters gathered me into a huddle and began to sing *We Are Family*. Then I lost it. I sobbed uncontrollably which created a sea of tears among the five of us.

We were allowed to get it out of our systems for about fifteen seconds when Chick broke in and said, "Enough, girls. Remember, she chose to leave us."

"Geez, Chick. You sure know how to make a girl feel good," I whined.

"The truth hurts, doesn't it?" he asked not expecting an answer.

I wiped my eyes with my sleeve and hugged Marilyn first.

"Mona Lisa, you're going to be fine. I love you."

"I'll take good care of the apartment," Ro whispered through tears. "You've always got a place to stay when you visit."

I could barely look at Nina who hated to show emotion and was biting her lip to keep her composure. I grabbed her and said, "Don't let the others push you around while I'm gone."

She managed a small laugh and said, "I hate you for leaving me, you know."

"I know. I'll be back soon and I'll call you every day. You'll be sick of me."

I turned to Sophia and felt a fresh wave of sadness come over me as we embraced. I tried to speak, but nothing would come out.

"It's okay, Mona Lisa. This is your time," she assured me.

And then there was Noni, who held me tightly as I tried unsuccessfully to choke back my tears.

When she released me, she grabbed my shoulders and said, "You're a strong girl, Mona Lisa. Make each day count. Try new things and enjoy the journey. Now go take Atlanta by the balls."

Chapter 25

I had a hard time sleeping that night, so I crept down-stairs for something to eat. I found some cookies and poured myself a glass of milk and sat one last time at the family kitchen table. I heard footsteps and looked up to see my mother.

"Did I wake you up?" I asked.

"No, honey. When you get to be my age, sleep is a rarity. Are you okay?"

"Sure," I replied. "I hate change, you know? I'm ready to be there and get this waiting period over. I think this is the hardest part."

"You're going to have a great time, Mona Lisa. I can feel it."

"Old Italian intuition."

"Yes, if you must know, Italians have a gift for that sort of thing."

I laughed. "Intuition and guilt. Do you think Chick is ever going to be normal around me again?"

"Give him time, Mona Lisa. He worries about you be-ing so far away, but sometimes he has a *facacta* way of showing it."

"Wow, Noni's rubbing off on you."

"Listen, you. Enough with that. My goal in life is to live long enough to see your kids bust your chops like you do to me."

"That's a great goal, Ma."

"Hey, why didn't I get invited to this party?" Chick asked.

"I wasn't sure you would want to come," I answered honestly.

"I'm going back to bed. I'll see you in the morning," my mother said giving Chick and I some alone time.

Chick sat across from me and took a cookie from my plate. "Mona Lisa, I'm the father of five girls. When you were little, my job was to protect you, and as you grew, I wanted to protect you even more. That feeling never goes away. I'll never stop worrying about my girls."

"I know, Chick, but you and Ma did a great job with us. None of us are in jail. We don't smoke. We don't do drugs. You did good."

"Yes, we did, but I can't stop feeling protective. You'll understand when you're a parent." Then he looked up and added, "God willing."

"Better start that Novena to St. Jude, Chick, so I can find a husband."

"Start?" he kidded.

I hugged him and said, "I'll be fine Chick."

"I know you will, Mona Lisa. Make sure to call your mother every day. You know how she is."

"Will do, Chick. I love you."

"You too, kiddo."

* * * *

The next morning, I dressed and took a cup of coffee for the road. Ma and Chick walked me out to my car, and there were my sisters holding signs that read, "Haven't you left, yet?" and "Don't let the door hit you in the ass on the way out," and "Please, just go already."

I didn't want to have another hugging and crying session, so I gave them the finger, blew them a kiss and started my engine.

Chapter 26

I decided to make the drive in one day. I drank a lot of coffee and ate large quantities of Twizzlers to stay awake, plus I chatted with each of my sisters. I also listened to the *Change Your Attitude, Change your Life* CD, but had a hard time concentrating and ended up talking to myself. I was starting to lose it when I saw the *Welcome to Georgia* sign. That totally re-energized me, and when my GPS let me know that I was only ninety minutes away from my new home, I let out a shout.

I called Brightleigh to let her know that I was close.

"Is that you, roomie?" she asked.

"Sure is and I'm about an hour-and-a-half away."

"Mona Lisa, I'm so excited for you to get here. Are you haulin' a trailer?"

"Oh, no. I only brought my clothes and a few things I can't live without. I left everything else—mostly stuff I picked out with my ex, so I didn't want to bring it with me. I have an air mattress and a pillow and will be set until I buy new furniture."

"That's great. You really are starting with a clean slate."

"You got that right. I'm ready to leave all the bullshit of my former life behind and find out who Mona Lisa Cicciarelli is," I declared.

"Amen, girl."

* * * *

It was dark when I pulled into the apartment complex and navigated my way to our unit. I got out of the car and stretched, feeling so relieved and proud I had made it on my own. I slowly walked toward the entrance and felt my stomach tighten. I knocked and the door flew open.

"What are you knocking for? You live here now," Brightleigh said as she motioned for me to enter.

Amy sat on the sofa with a beer in hand which she raised as she said, "Welcome home."

"Thanks, guys. It's good to be here."

"Want a beer?" Amy asked.

"I'd love one," I replied. "Let me use the restroom first."

I heard Amy and Brightleigh talking animatedly. When I returned, the dining room table was set complete with sandwiches, flowers, and beer.

"Oh, my gosh. You guys didn't have to do this."

"Martha Stewart did it all," Amy admitted as she gestured toward Brightleigh.

"I wanted to welcome you properly and besides, my mama made all the food."

I instantly relaxed and said, "Thank you. It looks great."

We sat in the dining room and put a good dent in the spread. We each talked a little about ourselves, but I wasn't forthcoming with any personal information. That didn't deter Amy, though.

She asked, "I hear you ditched Jersey after a bad relationship. What happened?"

"Amy," Brightleigh admonished. "Where are your manners?"

"I think I left them in Brooklyn, Emily Post. Do you care, Mona Lisa?" Amy asked.

"No. In fact, I love how direct you are. It's like being home."

Amy gave Brightleigh a smug *I told you so* look.

I placed a hand on Brightleigh's arm and said, "It's fine. It feels like another life ago. Basically, I was engaged to Joey whose umbilical cord was still attached to his mother, Alice. She called the shots and apparently thought it would be best to leave me at the altar on our wedding day. I'm more embarrassed because I was left by those two, not because I was left. Don't get me wrong. It sucked, but the two of them only made it worse. Alice found a more suitable wife for her and Joey and I didn't want to be around to see them bring children into the world."

"I'm so sorry," Brightleigh said.

Amy laughed and said, "I think it's funny. You've got one hell of a story."

"Yes, I do. And it's even funnier when you go through it in a small town and with a large family. More gossip and advice than I could handle, so here I am. Tell me about you guys," I asked.

Amy nodded for Brightleigh to go first.

"I was born and raised here. My parents and grandparents are from Atlanta, and they want nothing more than for me to find a husband and start making grandbabies. Right now all I want to do is have fun, but they keep pestering me to get married."

"They sound like the southern Cicciarelli's. What about you, Amy?" I asked.

"I was born and raised in Brooklyn. My mom was really young when she had me and I never knew my dad. We lived with my Bubee and she raised me."

"Bubee is her grandmother," Brightleigh informed me.

"I know. My own grandmother likes to dabble in Yiddish," I admitted.

"Is she Jewish?" Amy asked.

"No. Noni's boyfriend is Jewish, so Yiddish is her new hobby. Plus it irritates my mother for some reason, so it makes her do it even more. We're Catholic, which I like to think of as Jewish with extra guilt."

Amy laughed, but Brightleigh seemed confused. Just then, my phone rang and the caller ID read Cicciarelli. It also told me that I had missed two of their calls already. I was so focused and determined during the last stage of my trip, I never heard the phone ring.

"It's my parents," I said. "This will only take a few minutes."

"Hello."

"Mona Lisa, where are you?" Chick demanded.

"I'm here. In my apartment."

"When were you going to tell us? We called three times. Your mother was going crazy thinking you had an accident."

"Geez, Chick, I'm sorry."

"The damage is done. Call your mother tomorrow," he ordered.

"Doesn't she want to talk to me now?"

"No, she's too upset."

I hung up and went back to the table, determined not to let them ruin my first night with the girls. "Now that I've had my daily dose of guilt, I believe I'll wash it away with another beer."

Chapter 27

I awoke to the sun shining on my face and smiled at
the dawn of a spring day in Atlanta. Then I started sneezing. And I couldn't seem to stop. I wandered into the kitch-
en to make a cup of coffee hoping that would help stop the
sneezing fit. It slowed as I sipped my coffee, so I was relieved.

Amy joined me at the table and said, "Welcome to
spring in Atlanta."

"What do you mean? The sneezing? I don't have allergies."

"You do now. The pollen count is two thousand today.
High is like five hundred."

"Are you kidding me?" I asked in disbelief.

"Wish I were. I'll give you my allergist's card."

"Great," I answered.

I put on my shoes and went outside to empty out my
car and was instantly assaulted by pollen. Everything was
covered in thick yellow dust. I had never seen anything like
it before. My car was covered and the sneezing began
again. I managed to empty out my car in between sneezes,
however once inside it wouldn't stop. I decided to shower
in the hopes that it would wash away whatever it was that
was attacking my nose.

I felt a little better after the shower, but now I suffered
with watery eyes and a runny nose. I grabbed some tissues
and began to hang my clothes in the closet when I saw a

card fall to the ground. The handwriting was unmistakably Noni's so I sat down and opened the letter.

Dear Mona Lisa:

There were some things I wanted to tell you but didn't want to say in person. You know I pride myself on being a tough old broad and I didn't want to blow my image, so I thought I'd tell you in a letter. I guess you know I think you're pretty special. From the time you were little, there was a bond between the two of us that has only grown stronger. Of all the people in the family, you are the one that gets me, Mona Lisa. And in spite of that, you still love me, so you've always had a special place in my heart, kiddo.

Promise me you'll try hard in Atlanta. Open your mind and heart and don't be afraid to let people get to know the real you. You are an amazing woman and I know you are going to find everything you are hoping for. So have fun, go crazy.

I miss you and love you.
Noni

I put the letter down and started to cry and sneeze. I needed more tissues and nearly collided with Brightleigh in the hallway.

"Oh, my gosh, Mona Lisa. What's wrong, sugar?"

"Nothing."

"Bless your heart, but something must be wrong 'cause you look all tore up. Sit on the couch and I'll get some tissues."

She came back with an entire box.

"Thanks, Brightleigh. I'll be okay. My grandmother slipped a note in my suitcase and it made me homesick. That combined with the yellow gook everywhere—let's say my morning got off to a bad start."

Amy walked in and asked, "What's wrong with you?"

I smiled at her no-nonsense approach.

"I'm fine. Having a moment," I admitted.

"She's homesick. Mona Lisa, you get it all out of your system. We don't mind," Brightleigh said as she patted my arm.

"Screw that," Amy contradicted. "Today's my day off and I don't want to sit around watching you feel sorry for yourself. Besides, you haven't even been here twenty-four hours. How can you be homesick? I'm a survival of the fittest type myself. You wanna survive? Go get dressed, take one of my allergy pills and let's go shopping. Only losers sleep on plastic beds filled with air."

Brightleigh was about to object when I replied, "Next time, I'll bend over so it makes it easier for you to kick my butt."

Chapter 28

I bought a new bed and dresser and completely updated my wardrobe. After all, we dressed differently in Atlanta and I wanted to do my best to fit in. Despite the misery of my allergies, I enjoyed the sunshine and warmer weather especially when I heard it was snowing in New Jersey.

It was my first day of work and I was more than ready. I had begun to have periods of melancholy when I was alone in the apartment. I explored the city a little on my own, but it was boring without anyone to share it with. I definitely needed the regular routine of work to keep my mind and body busy.

I was so excited I actually woke up at 6 A.M. and went for a run. I stepped outside and stretched when the sneezing began. Ten, eleven, twelve. I stopped counting when I was approached by a neighbor I had seen a few times before.

"Need this?" he asked holding a monogrammed handkerchief out to me.

He was gorgeous. Blonde hair, blue eyes, in a designer suit. And classy. He was the epitome of perfection and here I was trying to contain the river of mucous that was coming from my nose.

I took it and mumbled, "Thanks."

"You just moved in, didn't you?" he asked.

I nodded while I blew my nose and I tried not to think about how pathetic I must have looked.

"I'm Jamie," he said as he stuck his hand out to shake.

I pointed to the dirty handkerchief.

"Mona Lisa," I replied. "It's nice to meet you."

"That's a name you don't hear very often."

I smiled and said, "And let's thank God for that."

He laughed and said, "You're not from around here, are you?"

I noticed a subtle twang in his speech.

"No. I'm from New Jersey. How about you?"

"Ooh, a Yankee. Know the difference between a Yankee and a damn Yankee?" he asked. "A damn Yankee is one that doesn't go back home," he answered before letting out a guffaw.

"That's hilarious," I replied and uncomfortably shoved the used handkerchief into his hand.

I turned to go back into my apartment when he called after me, "Hey, I was kidding. Want to go out for a drink sometime?"

"Maybe," I answered not turning around.

I shut the apartment door and locked it.

"Asshole," I thought aloud.

"Who's an asshole?"

I jumped and turned to see Amy sitting on the sofa with a cup of coffee.

"Some guy who lives a few doors down. He's still fighting the Civil War."

"I bet that's Jamie. A blonde, pretty boy?" Amy asked. I nodded.

"He's harmless. Not very bright, though. He asked me out when I moved here and acted as if New York was a foreign country."

"Please tell me all the guys down here aren't like that," I begged.

"Nah. Most of the people I meet aren't even from Atlanta. This place has really evolved since I first moved down here. You'll get used to it or you'll move back home," she said matter of factly.

"No bullshit from you, huh?"

"No point, sister. You ready for your first day at the shop?" Amy asked.

"Yes. I'm about to go stir-crazy. I need to be busy."

"I'm sure Bobbie Lee will find plenty for you to do. I'd be happy to let you clean up my station today if it helps you out."

"Gee, thanks. You're all heart."

"Any time. And see an allergist. You'll never get a guy with that nose, Rudolph."

Chapter 29

My heart raced as I opened the door to the salon, but I quickly calmed down when Bobbie Lee welcomed me with a bear hug.

"Everyone," she announced, "this is our newest family member, Mona Lisa. Please take a moment today and introduce yourself."

I was greeted with a chorus of hellos and Bobbie Lee walked me over to my station.

"Here's your new home, girlie. For the next few weeks, you won't be too busy, so I'd love for you to help out wherever you see a need. And, we'll steer a lot of walk-ins your way until you develop a client base. As a bonus, you get to take care of my mama and grandmother today. They're coming in for their weekly wash and style."

Great, I thought.

My face must have betrayed me because Bobbie Lee laughed and said, "They're harmless. You're gonna love G-Mama. She's a hoot. Plus, they're easy. They always want the same old style. Maybe you can update their dos."

I took her word for it and when they arrived, my fears were once again abated.

Bobbie Lee made the introductions. "Ya'll, this is Mona Lisa. She's going to be doin' your hair today. Mona Lisa, meet Mama and G-Mama."

I shook both of their hands and asked, "Who would like to be first?"

"You go first," G-Mama ordered. "That way I can see if I want her to touch my head or not."

I laughed as Bobbie Lee and her mother groaned.

Bobbie Lee's mother followed me to my station and I asked, "What would you like me to call you?"

"Well, darlin' you can call me Bitsy. I'm the youngest of the clan and that's been my nickname for as long as I can remember. My real name is Gertrude, so I am very grateful to have a nickname. Sorry about my mama. I swear, some days I never know what's goin' to come out of her mouth."

"No worries. I like feisty women. My grandmother is a lot like that and I adore her."

"That's so sweet. I know you haven't been here long, but how do you like Atlanta?" Bitsy asked.

"I haven't seen too much, but I like the people. I could do without the pollen, though. I've never seen anything like it."

"Well, bless your heart. I'm so sorry you're having trouble with allergies. A good allergist can make a killin' in Atlanta."

"I have an appointment with one next week."

"Good for you. I'm sure you'll be feeling up to snuff soon. How's my nephew Vinnie doing these days?" she asked.

"He's great. I loved working for him and was sad to leave, but he was very supportive of my decision."

"I heard about the wedding mess. Good Lord. If some-one had done that to my little girl, I'd have knocked him into tomorrow."

I laughed, "That doesn't sound good."

"You got that right. Now, what can you do with this mop of hair? Bobbie Lee does the same old thing every week, but I don't have the heart to tell her I want something different. So why don't you have at it and surprise me."

I changed the color, added some highlights and gave her a shorter cut. She looked amazing—younger and radi-ant.

I turned the chair so she could see herself in the mirror.

"Oh, my stars, Mona Lisa. I look fabulous. Bobbie Lee, come out of your office," she commanded.

A moment later Bobbie Lee appeared with a huge grin.

"Mama, you are gorgeous. Daddy's gonna think he's got himself a new woman. He'll be chasin' you around the house tonight."

"Don't be crass, Bobbie Lee. I do look wonderful, though, don't I?"

"Yes, you do," I replied.

"Mama, you're next," Bitsy announced. "Mona Lisa's fixin' to transform you too."

"We'll see about that," she said.

I cleaned off the chair and motioned for G-Mama to sit.

Again, I asked, "What would you like me to call you?"

"For now, you can call me Mrs. Willbanks. If I like

how you do my hair, then I might let you call me Mary. Let's not get ahead of ourselves, though."

"What would you like me to do today?" I asked somewhat timidly.

"First, I'd like you to speak like you have some confidence in your abilities and then I want you to give me a nice hairdo. Think you can manage that?"

She sounded so sweet with that Southern drawl, but she wasn't about to cut me any slack.

"Yes, ma'am. I think I can."

I softened her color, trimmed the ends and styled her hair into a lovely, updated bob.

When I finished, I summoned up my courage and asked, "So, what's it going to be? Mrs. Willbanks or Mary?"

She slowly smiled and said, "I reckon you do good work for a Yankee."

"So it's Mary?"

"We'll see after my appointment with you next week. This might be beginner's luck."

"Okay, Mrs. Mary Willbanks. I'll see you next week," I said, giving her a wink.

"Don't let this go to your head, Yankee. I have an image to uphold."

"Your secret's safe with me."

After they left, Bobbie Lee said, "Well, darlin'. You won over the grouchiest old lady in town. You're going to fit in here just fine."

I smiled because I felt like she was right.

Chapter 30

At the end of my first week, I was exhausted but happy. So far I liked my job and my roommates and the best part was I stopped thinking about Joey. And when he did come to mind, I felt nothing. No sadness or anger and that was extremely liberating. I was finally free of him and his mother, and I was ready to join the dating world. If I thought I had some say in the matter, I was mistaken because as far as Amy was concerned, it was way past time for dating and a whole lot more.

"Listen, we're going out tonight, and you're going to let loose, girlfriend," she commanded as the three of us finished our morning coffee.

"Do you think I'm that uptight?" I asked.

She smirked and raised her eyebrows in response.

"What? I know how to have a good time," I said trying to convince us both.

It had been a long time since I had gone to a bar looking for a guy. Feelings of dread came over me.

"Let me be the judge. Between you and Scarlett O'Hara, it ought to be an interesting evening."

"Hey, now. Us southern girls know how to have fun," Brightleigh chimed in.

"Well bless your heart. You sure do, sugar," Amy said dryly.

"Amy, you're startin' to sound like a native, girl," Brightleigh replied.

"Never," Amy countered.

"Never say never," Brightleigh challenged. "Before I forget, Mother wanted me to invite you both for lunch tomorrow. Ya'll don't have to go to church, you can just come and eat."

"I'm out," Amy answered before I could even open my mouth. "I don't do church or family."

"Not all of us northerners feel that way. I'd love to come. I'll even go to church. That will flip my mother out. I'll tell her I'm thinking of converting."

"Oh, you can't treat your mama like that. You'll upset her."

"She's used to me busting her chops."

Brightleigh looked confused.

"That's Jersey speak for teasing somebody. It's how my family survives," I explained.

"Isn't that cute," Brightleigh said still looking unsure.

"I'm not sure that's how I'd describe it, but it works for us. I'm looking forward to meeting your family tomorrow, though."

"I'm glad you're coming too. I'm going to call home and tell Mama to expect you."

"I'm going back to bed so I can stay awake tonight," I said. "I haven't been out in ages and nothing turns a guy off faster than yawning."

* * * *

Before Amy would let us out of the car, she gave us strict instructions.

"Listen, you two. Don't be clingy. We're here to min-

112

gle and meet other people. If I wanted to spend a night with just the two of you, I wouldn't have wasted an hour shaving and plucking. Got it?"

I saluted. "Yes, captain."

We walked to the entrance and paid our fee. The club was hopping, but we managed to find a table and order a round of drinks. After I had a few sips of my vodka and cranberry, I began to relax and enjoy myself. It was great people-watching and there were several cute guys I had my eye on, but I wasn't as bold as Amy, who had no trouble going after what she wanted. Two guys were talking at the bar and she placed herself right in the middle of their conversation. Before I knew it, she grabbed the hand of one of the men and pointed the other in the direction of our table. He looked us both over and asked Brightleigh to dance.

Amy and Brightleigh were dancing up a storm, but I was starting to feel like Cinderella's stepsister. I was working on my second drink and planning my exit when a nice-looking man who seemed a little old for the bar scene approached. I immediately checked his left hand for the infamous wedding ring tan line and was pleasantly surprised at its absence.

"You look like you're in pain. Not much for the bar scene are you?" he asked.

"Am I that obvious?"

"Um, yeah, you are. Sorry but you look kind of pitiful."

"And you came over here to tell me that?" I asked.

He laughed. "I wanted to see if I could buy you another drink."

"I think I'm good for right now," I replied cautiously though my drink was almost empty. "Would you like to sit?" I asked.

"Sure, I'm Sterling."

"Hi. I'm Mona Lisa."

"Wow. That's a name you don't hear every day. You must be I-talian," he said in a thick drawl.

"One hundred percent. How about you?"

"Oh, I'm one hundred percent Atlantan. Third generation."

"Is that a nationality now? Atlantan?" I asked laughing.

Sterling's face went flat.

"It is in my world, honey. You must be from up north," he said somewhat as a challenge.

"I am. I'm from New Jersey, and if you want to tell me the damn Yankee joke, I heard it already."

He laughed. "That didn't cross my mind. I'm proud of my heritage, but I'm also a gentleman. How about I get you another drink and we start this conversation over again."

"I'd like that."

"Great. Before I head to the bar, I need to make a quick call. My mama likes to hear my voice right before she goes to bed each night."

My face fell, then I scanned the room to see if there was an exit close by as that was my cue to call it a night.

114

Chapter 31

I was looking forward to going to church the next morning because I needed to say some serious prayers for my social life. A little time on my knees in holy surroundings would do me good, but much to my surprise, Brightleigh's church didn't even have kneelers.

We sat with her mom and dad, Tandy and Beau, and her nana, Eugenia who gave me a wink and said, "Hey, there. You ready to be saved?"

I raised my eyebrows in question and apprehension.

"Mama, cut it out. You're about to frighten poor Mona Lisa to death. Don't you worry, honey. We welcome all kinds here," Tandy said in reassurance.

It didn't make me feel any better. I started to question the wisdom of my decision to attend services when the pastor, as Brightleigh called him, asked that all visitors approach the altar.

Brightleigh and her mother gave me gentle nudges to go, but I shook my head vehemently.

"No way. I can't do it."

I looked around and didn't see anyone else moving toward the front, so I put my head down to wait for the moment to pass, but my plan didn't work. I lifted my head and there was the pastor with a microphone in hand at the end of our pew.

"I believe our friends the Walkers brought a visitor today. Stand up and come talk with us for a minute."

I felt my face flush with searing heat as I made my way to the end of the row.

"Welcome. Why don't you tell us your name?"

"I'm Mona Lisa Cicciarelli."

The congregation shouted, "Hello, Mona Lisa."

I felt like I should confess I was an addict of some sort, but for once I kept my mouth shut.

"Tell us a little bit about yourself."

"I just moved to Atlanta and I'm happy to be here," I said making a conscious decision not to mention anything about being from the north.

I turned to make my way back to my seat when the pastor said, "We got us a shy one, brothers and sisters. Everyone, please make sure and say hello to Mona Lisa before you leave today."

I sat next to Brightleigh who was all smiles. I wanted to pinch her for putting me through that, but the joy on her face deflated my anger.

"Oh, Mona Lisa, I'm so happy you're here today."

"Me, too," I lied.

* * * *

The service finished and my hopes for a hasty exit were dashed as the parishioners made good on their orders to visit with me. I believe I shook more hands than a politician at the opening of a Wal-Mart. As Brightleigh and I drove to her parents' house, I realized it was a nice morning and wouldn't my mother be thrilled to know that more than ever I was happy to be a Catholic.

Chapter 32

Lunch at Brightleigh's was as lively as any Cicciarelli family dinner. Kids were running around the house. The men sat in the family room and the women prepared the meal.

"Mrs. Walker, what can I do to help?" I asked hoping for a job so that I didn't feel so awkward.

"Nothing, sugar. You're our guest. And please call me Tandy."

I looked over at Brightleigh who was doing something to green beans and was grateful when she said, "Mona Lisa, come over here and meet my sisters-in-law."

Each of the women was busy attacking their assigned vegetable when I sat at the kitchen table.

"Mona Lisa, this here is Ashley. She's married to my brother, Mize, and they have four boys— Miller, Mack, Mason and Monroe."

We smiled our hellos.

"And this is Kayla. She's married to Bostwick, and they have Emmalee and Jefferson."

"It's nice to meet you both. Wow. Six kids between you two. That's a lot."

They both looked at me as if to say, *No Kidding*.

"Mize kept wanting to try for a girl and now I'm living in a frat house," Ashley laughed. "I can't have anything nice. Those boys are like human cyclones. They destroy everything in their paths."

117

She was calm and kind as she described her boys.

"They're good boys. Just rambunctious is all," Kayla added.

"You guys are so relaxed. You must be great moms."

They both chuckled.

"Oh, honey, do I have you fooled," Ashley admitted. "Every day, I pray to make it to bedtime without killing one of them. Yesterday, Miller and Mason were fighting so bad I actually told them, 'If you two don't stop, I'm gonna chop your arms off and beat you with the bloody stumps'."

Kayla and Brightleigh gasped as I tried to hide a smile.

"I know. Not my finest parenting moment. Miller started to cry and Mason wanted to know what a stump was. I swear they make me say and do things I never thought I would."

"Don't be so hard on yourself," Kayla offered. "At the rate I'm going, I'll be in Betty Ford before Jefferson gets out of preschool. I live for bedtime so I can have my glass of wine."

"You sound like my sisters," I said, feeling a pang of loneliness for my family. "I really miss them."

"Bless your heart, Mona Lisa, we don't want to make you homesick," Kayla said sweetly.

"I'll be fine. Now that I'm away, I tend to romanticize the family get-togethers, but in reality, everyone is a little bit crazy."

"Well then, you ought to feel right at home," Nana butted in. She had been listening in on our conversation and

I gave her a big smile in reply.

Kayla and Ashley corralled their kids and got them situated in the kitchen, then the adults settled in the dining room and I got the seat of honor next to Nana. The table was covered with a southern feast of fried chicken, ham, coleslaw, biscuits and more vegetables than I knew existed. Suddenly I was starving.

Beau sat at the head of the table and said, "Mona Lisa, we are so pleased that you and Brightleigh have become friends and we are beyond thrilled to have you join us for Sunday dinner. Now, bow your heads for the blessing. Dear Lord, we thank you for this wonderful meal prepared for us by my lovely wife, Tandy and her mama, Eugenia. We thank you for our new friend, Mona Lisa. We give special thanks for our children and grandchildren and ask that you see it in your grace to send a husband for Brightleigh, so that we may have one less worry on our hearts. Amen."

I turned to Nana and said, "Yep, just like being at home." So much so, I could probably skip my weekly call during my family's Sunday dinner later that afternoon, but I missed everyone and was actually looking forward to my weekly dose of gossip and guilt.

Chapter 33

My cell phone rang just as I put my key in the door to the apartment. I looked and saw that it was my mother and plopped myself on the sofa as I answered.

"Hi, Ma."

"I thought you were going to call."

"I was. You beat me to it."

"Only because you didn't call me."

"Okay, well we're talking now, Ma. How are you? Is everybody there for dinner?"

"Not Rosie. She's trying to find herself, whatever the hell that means, and needs some time alone. If you ask me, it's a crock."

I laughed and said, "I miss you, Ma."

"I've got a cure for that. Come home."

"Not yet. I haven't found myself," I quipped.

"Nice. I don't miss your smart mouth."

"I bet you do."

"Maybe a little. What's going on with you, Miss Georgia Peach?" she asked.

"Nothing much. Brightleigh's family invited me for lunch today and it made me want to be at Sunday dinner with all of you. I want to hear everything that's happening up there."

"We had some sad news. Evelyn Colletti, Dante's grandmother, died this week. She was so young. Just eighty-six. She looked beautiful, though. Rosalie Genovese did her makeup and she made Evelyn look ten years younger. When I go, you girls better make sure that Rosalie does me."

"Ma, I hate it when you talk about such morbid things."

"Mona Lisa, we're all going to die, and when I do, I want to look as good as poor Evelyn, God rest her soul."

I could picture my mother making the sign of the cross as she spoke.

"How was Dante?" I asked knowing how I would feel if it were Noni that died.

"Oh, he was really broken up. His mother said he was taking it pretty hard."

Chick yelled into the phone, "Too bad you aren't here to console him."

I rolled my eyes, "Nice to know he never changes."

"Truer words were never spoken, honey. Chick, come say hi to Mona Lisa. I love you, here's Chick."

"Mona Lisa, how's the car? Have you checked your oil lately?"

"Yes, Chick and the car is fine. What's new with you?" I asked.

Chick was not one for talking on the phone. "Nothing. Here's your grandmother."

"Love you, too, Chick."

"Mona Lisa, how are you?" Noni asked.

"I'm great, Noni. I miss you, though," I admitted.

"Marshall and I want to come visit. What do they have

for casinos down there?"

I laughed. "I live in Atlanta, not Las Vegas."

"What do old people do for fun?"

"I'll look into it and get back to you. How's Marshall?"

"He's the best. A real *mensch*. I'm not sure what I did to deserve him, but I'm not going to question it."

"You're pretty special, too. Let me know when you want to come visit and I'll make sure we have a rockin' time."

"You got it, girl. I love you, Mona Lisa. Have some fun. Go crazy, okay?"

I laughed and then heard my mother say to Noni, "Ma, for God's sake. Why don't you just tell her to prostitute herself?"

"Noni, you are so bad," I playfully admonished.

"Yes, she is," my mother agreed after taking the phone back from Noni. "Mona Lisa, I raised you to be a lady and I expect you to act like one."

"Yes, Ma'am," I replied. "See, I already sound like a southerner."

"Between you and your grandmother, you are both trying to kill me."

"I love you, Ma. Can I talk to Sophia?"

"Yes, but not for long. The water for the *gnocchi* is starting to boil and you know how Chick has to have his food served steaming hot."

"I'll be quick. I promise."

Sophia got on the phone, "Hey, there. I was going to call you later. It's hard to talk with all these raving lunatics around here."

"I know. I wanted to hear your voice. Sundays are hard for me. As much as I dreaded those dinners, I miss them now."

"The grass is always greener, huh?"

"I guess so. How's Ro? Ma said she's not coming to dinner."

"She's a little wild," Sophia whispered. "I can't get into it. Too many big ears, if you get my drift."

"I guess she's enjoying the single life. And my apartment," I added.

"Yes, and isn't that supposed to be your job?"

"You and Noni seem to think so."

I heard my mother holler, "Dinner!"

"I gotta go. Ma will have my ass on a platter if dinner gets cold. Love you."

"Love you, too. I'll call you later."

Amy walked in as I hung up and smirked.

"Now that you're all depressed from calling home, go change out of those church clothes and put on something fun. We're going out."

I stood and said, "Yes, boss," and prepared to get a little crazy.

Chapter 34

Amy and I went out on the town a few times and I was managing to have a lot of fun. I hadn't gone on any dates but was enjoying myself and I loved getting to know the people at work. I liked my job a lot and my client list was growing. I seemed to be a hit with the older ladies and was gaining popularity on what the salon had termed, Old Biddy Monday. It seems that Monday was the day most of the older ladies liked to come in to get their weekly wash, curl, and style and because I was the newbie, I got the ones that no one wanted to deal with.

I walked over to the reception desk after I looked at my schedule and saw a name I didn't recognize—W. Smithson.

"Tell me about her," I asked Bobbie Lee pointing to the name on my schedule.

"She's a trip. Old money. Born and raised in Atlanta. About as uppity as they come. You'll do just fine with her."

The door opened and in walked an attractive, older blonde woman who looked like she just stepped out of a salon.

"That's her," Bobbie Lee whispered.

I walked over and extended my hand, "Ms. Smithson? I'm Mona Lisa Cicciarelli. I'll be doing your hair today."

She looked me up then down and said, "That's quite a name you've got there. You're not from around here, are you?"

"No, I'm not," I replied not wanting to give her any

impression of weakness.

We stared at each other and she finally spoke. "Well, then. Let's get started."

We discussed what she wanted me to do to her hair, but she offered little in the way of conversation.

"Have you been coming to this salon for awhile?" I asked.

"Long enough," she replied as she turned the page and buried her head in Southern Living magazine.

I stopped trying and only interrupted her reading if I needed to ask her something about her style. When I was finished, she looked in the mirror and smiled.

"Nice," was all she said as I reached for the can to give her one last blast of spray.

"It was great to meet you, Ms. Smithson," I said when I was finished.

"You can call me Wink," she said matter-of-factly.

"Wink? And you commented on my name?"

She laughed and said, "I was trying to see what you were made of. My real name is Winifred, but I've been called Wink since I was a girl. Winifred is a God awful name."

"Mona Lisa isn't so hot, either. I really enjoyed meeting you, Wink. I hope I see you again."

"Not so fast," she ordered. "Are you married?"

This was never a good question coming from a customer.

"No."

She reached into her bag and pulled out a cell phone and dialed.

"Come in. There's somebody I'd like you to meet."

Through the window, I saw a man on the phone, but only from the back. My stomach flipped over in dread as the door opened and I heard the jingle of the bells on the door. However, when a gorgeous blonde-haired, blue-eyed guy came over to us and kissed Wink on the cheek, I swooned.

"Mona Lisa, this is my grandson, Anderson. Anderson, this is Mona Lisa and she's a pistol. I think you two would like each other a great deal. I am going to change now and Anderson, if you have any sense at all, you will get her number. Ya'll talk a minute and I'll be right back."

"What is it with grandmothers and their lack of subtlety?" I asked.

Anderson laughed and said, "Wink doesn't know the meaning of the word. Nor does she know how to mind her own business."

"I'm sorry," I replied feeling very embarrassed.

"Don't be. Every once in a while, she gets it right and I think this might be one of those times. Would you like to have dinner with me sometime, Mona Lisa?"

"I would," I replied as I wrote my cell number on my business card.

He took it and flashed me the whitest, most perfect smile I had ever seen.

Wink came out of the restroom, joined us and said, "I

will see you next week Mona Lisa," before giving me an over-exaggerated wink.

I sat in my chair, enjoying my little bit of happiness as I watched Wink and Anderson leave the shop after she paid the receptionist. Amy sauntered over to the reception desk and looked my way, before coming over to me.

"Wink must have liked you. She left you one hell of a tip. Did she try to fix you up with her grandson?"

"Yes and I happily agreed."

"He's quite the catch," she said sarcastically. "Especially if you like gifts that leave a lasting impression. He gave a friend of mine herpes."

"Herpes, huh? I guess that means flowers are passé."

Chapter 35

It seemed as though the dating gods were against me
no matter where I lived, yet I persevered and accepted a
blind date that was set up by my coworker, Brittany. She
was newly engaged and was eager to try out her matchmaking skills on me. Her fiancé worked with a guy who she
knew would be perfect for me, but after I received his first
email, the voice inside my head told me to run. I tuned it
out, trying to be optimistic and went on the date anyway.
We exchanged photos and he was nice enough looking, but
something didn't seem quite right. When I arrived at the
restaurant and saw him sitting at a table waiting, it hit me.
The photo was about twenty years old. I froze a moment
and was about to turn around and leave when he saw me
and waved. I took a deep breath in and walked over to the
table.

"Hi. I'm Mona Lisa," I said offering my hand.

He leaned over to kiss me, but I pulled my head back
and pushed my hand out.

He took it and said, "I'm Ken."

I sat down and said, "So, Ken, how old is that picture
you sent me?"

"I don't know. A few years, but people are always telling me I never age so what difference does it make?"

"I thought you were my age, so I was thrown."

"I'm fifty-two. That's not that much older than you.
What are you, forty? Forty-five?"

I stared at him and exhaled loudly.

"I'm thirty-two, thanks."

"Whoa. Sorry. No need to get your panties in a bunch. Brittany said we'd get along because we're both from the north, but jeez, you're a bit uptight."

"I am not uptight. I'm annoyed because you pretended to be much younger."

"I didn't pretend anything and besides, age is just a number."

"Yeah, and your number is very similar to my father's," I replied dryly.

"And I've got a daughter your age, so what? If we've got chemistry, who gives a shit? Let's have a drink."

"I think I'm going to go."

"I ironed a shirt to come out here tonight. The least you can do is have a drink with me."

I sighed and said, "I'll have a beer. Whatever is on tap."

He went to the bar and returned with two beers. I drank half of it in one shot.

"Thirsty, huh?" he asked.

"You could say that."

We sat in silence for a while and finally I said, "Listen, Ken. This has been nice, but I don't see a future for us, so I'm going to head out. Thanks for the beer."

"Let me walk you to your car," he said.

"No. I'm fine."

"I insist," he said before telling the waiter, "I'll be

right back."

We walked to my car and as I turned to say goodbye he grabbed me, pulled me into him and proceeded to shove his tongue down my throat. I managed to get out of his grasp and wiped my mouth with my sleeve.

He laughed and said, "I'll call you, baby."

"Thanks, anyway Ken, but my mom only lets me play with boys my own age."

Chapter 36

I decided to take a break from dating and focus on training for the famous Peachtree Road Race—an Atlanta tradition—even though running a 5K on the Fourth of July in one of the hottest cities seemed idiotic to me. I didn't want to be one of those people who moved to a new town and questioned how and why they did everything, but this was another story. The month of June began with ten straight days over ninety degrees and it technically wasn't even summer yet. With only two weeks left to train, I woke up at 6 a.m. to get my run out of the way while it was still cool, but was drenched in sweat when I finished.

I quietly unlocked the door to my apartment and found Brightleigh sitting on the sofa staring intently at her laptop.

"Check and see what the temperature is today," I asked. "It already feels like it's ninety."

"Oh, Mona Lisa it isn't even that hot out yet. Wait until August."

Amy wandered into the kitchen and came out holding a glass of juice.

"August is great," she said dryly. "Like living on the surface of the sun."

"I don't know if I'll make it," I admitted. "I already feel like I'm going through menopause. It's so hot."

"Ya'll stop your complaining. The summer is hot, but that's why the good Lord made air conditioning."

Amy smirked and asked, "The Lord made the air conditioning? Gee, and I thought creating man was big, but air conditioning? That's something."

"Amy, hush. You are so bad. I'll take the heat any day over snow and ice."

"She's got a point," I admitted. "What are you working on this early in the morning, Bright?"

Her face immediately flushed red, so I perched myself on the sofa right next to her, sweat and all. She tried to hide the screen, but I caught a glimpse of a dating website.

"Ooh. It's come to that, has it? Online dating?" I teased.

"I'm just looking. Fix Me Up Atlanta has a great reputation. My cousin met her husband on it. They have all these criteria and very high standards. Plus the first month is free."

"And if you act right now, you get a free set of steak knives that can double as weapons if your date doesn't work out," Amy announced.

Brightleigh's face fell.

"I knew ya'll would make fun of it."

"We're busting your chops," Amy said. "You need to be careful. There are a lot of creeps out there."

"We love you, Brightleigh and want you to be safe," I added.

"I'm only looking around. I haven't actually signed up, but if I don't have to pay anything for thirty days, I may go ahead and do it."

"Let me see," I asked, my curiosity piqued.

I took the laptop and scrolled through some of the photos and glanced at the testimonials.

"It looks interesting," I admitted.

"I'm going to shower and leave you cyber daters alone. Don't come running to me if you find out your new boyfriend is a serial killer," Amy warned.

"Wow, thanks for that, Mary Sunshine. You can be the flower girl at the wedding," I retorted.

Amy grunted.

"I'm going to get my computer," I told Brightleigh. "Let's do this together."

We sat at the kitchen table and filled out the lengthy application. The questions were standard at first. Age, occupation, religion, but then they got tougher. What am I most afraid of in a relationship? What kind of marriage did my parents have? How did my previous relationships end? Would "Not well" be a good enough answer? I wondered.

"This is work," I said to Brightleigh.

"Seriously. It makes me sad that I have to resort to this to find a man," she admitted. "My mama would have a hissy fit if she knew I was using the Internet to get a date."

"Then don't tell her. Let's have fun with it and when the free trial is over, we'll quit."

"Maybe by then we'll have met Prince Charming and live happily ever after."

"I'm hoping we won't need those steak knives!" I said as I hit send and propelled myself into the world of online dating.

Chapter 37

I found myself checking my email every free minute I had to see if I had any responses to my profile submission. My inbox was not overflowing. Bob was forty, divorced and had five children all under the age of twelve. I think he needed a nanny more than a date, so I deleted him. Carson was thirty-six, never married and his picture looked like it was fairly recent, so I placed him in the maybe column. Lastly, there was Will. He was forty-two, divorced, from Ohio. Nice enough looking, so I emailed him.

Hi Will:

I'm Mona Lisa and I just moved to Atlanta from New Jersey. Tell me a little about yourself.

A response came within ten minutes, and I wasn't sure if that was a good sign or not.

Hi Mona Lisa:

Great name. I moved here after my divorce and I like it a lot. I'd love to take you to dinner and get to know you better. Are you available tomorrow night? I know a great Italian place in Midtown. Why don't I pick you up?

Will:

I'd love to have dinner, but I'd rather meet you at the restaurant.

A few more emails passed between us before we settled on a meeting time and exchanged cell phone numbers.

I was nervous but excited as I dressed for my date. I bought a new dress and it fit quite nicely due to my training for the upcoming race. I took one last look in the mirror when my phone rang. It was Will. My stomach sank as I thought he must be canceling.

"Hi, Will," I answered.

"I was making sure you were still coming."

"I was planning to. Why?" I asked.

"No reason. I also wanted to tell you that I have a little skin condition. It's nothing really and it's going away, but I wanted you to know."

I bit my lip then said, "Thanks for the heads up. I'll see you soon."

I picked up my purse and keys and walked out to my car before I lost my nerve. I turned on my Bluetooth and called Sophia en route to my date.

"Help me. I'm about to go on my first online date. He just called to tell me about his skin condition. Should I turn around and go home?"

She laughed. "You have some life. No. You cannot leave the poor guy stranded at the restaurant. I think you know how it feels to be left hanging."

"Ouch. You sure know how to get to the heart of the matter, don't you? I hope he doesn't spend the whole night talking about his ailments."

"Maybe he'll be like Noni and he'll tell you all about

his bowel troubles."

"Geez, Soph. Way to kill my appetite. That's one thing I don't miss. What's new with you?"

"Same old, same old. I live in my car taking the kids everywhere. Anthony's voice is starting to crack and he's giving me attitude. At least my Gina is still sweet."

"I miss you guys."

"When are you coming home to visit?" she asked.

"I'll check my calendar. I have a very busy social life, you know. I'm almost at the restaurant so let me go. I'll call you when it's over. Wish me luck."

I found the restaurant and handed my keys to the valet. I took a deep breath and walked in. I immediately recognized Will as he sat at the bar and scratched. I said a silent prayer that he wasn't contagious and walked over to him.

"Will?" I asked.

"Mona Lisa," he said smiling. "It's good to see you."

His scratching became more intense, so I was grateful he didn't try to kiss me. The hostess showed us to our table and suddenly I needed a drink.

"I'm glad you came. My last date never showed."

"I would never do that." I was eager to change the subject, so I asked, "How long have you lived in Atlanta?"

He picked up a menu and asked, "Do you mind if we order first? I have to take my medicine with food."

Oy vey. "Sure, I think I'll have the pasta with pesto sauce."

He motioned for the waiter to come over and he ordered for us.

"We'll both have the pasta with pesto sauce and a bottle of Chianti."

I waited for him to start the conversation ball rolling, however, we sat in silence as the waiter poured our wine.

"What kind of work do you do, Will?"

"Computers," he answered as he rubbed his back against the chair.

I tried to ignore his discomfort for fear he would describe his ailment in detail.

"I work in a hair salon."

He closed his eyes and continued to attack the itch on his back with his chair when he stood and said, "I'll be right back."

I assumed he went to the restroom, so I drank my wine. After five minutes, I texted Sophia and told her to expect a fun date report. Ten minutes later, he came back to the table as if nothing had happened.

"Are you okay?" I asked.

"Sure. Why do you ask?"

Was he serious?

I was about to answer when the waiter arrived with our dinner. I took a few bites of my pasta hoping Will would at least ask me a question but was not surprised when he ate in silence.

When I couldn't stand it any longer, I said, "I love pesto when it's made with pine nuts instead of walnuts."

A look of panic spread across his face.

"Nuts? I'm allergic to nuts," he exclaimed.

"Why did you order the pesto?" I asked incredulously.

"Because you did. I was being nice."

"Nice? Oh, my God. Your lips are starting to swell. Do you have one of those pen things with the medicine in it?"

"Yes, but I left it at home."

"Are you kidding me?"

"No. You're going to have to take me to the hospital."

"Let's call 911."

I pulled out my phone and dialed as I watched Will's lips and eyes take over his face. Within a few minutes, I heard the sirens and felt a rush of relief when the paramedics arrived. I moved aside as they gave Will a shot and placed him on a stretcher. I saw him relax a little and he motioned for me to come over to him.

"I have to go to the hospital. Why don't you ride with me and we'll get my car later."

"He's going to be okay, right?" I asked the paramedic.

"He'll be fine. It's routine for us to take him in."

"Listen, Will, I'm going to head home. Good luck to you."

He lifted his head in protest then let it fall as he turned away. They wheeled him out, and I sat at the table and finished my wine. I found my purse and stood up as the waiter approached with the bill. He looked at me apologetically.

"Internet dating is great," I told him. "You should try it."

"Would you like a to-go bag?"

"No, thanks. I think I carbo-loaded enough for one night."

Chapter 38

Fourth of July dawned bright and hot as I got off the
train and joined the thousands of others who were getting
ready for the famous Peachtree Road Race. I instantly forgot about the heat as I made my way through the mass of
people trying to find a familiar face. I was running with a
group of girls from work and their friends. Brightleigh and
Amy were not into running at all, but Bobbie Lee and some
of the others did the Peachtree every year. People were
dressed in red, white and blue and others were wearing
American flag body paint. It was quite the place for people
watching and I loved every minute of it. I was excited when
I finally found Bobbie Lee and the others.

Brittany hugged me and said, "There's a cute guy I
want you to meet."

"The last time you tried this, it didn't work out so
good," I answered.

"It's Bobbie Lee's brother-in-law. His name is
Richmond and he's sweet."

She grabbed me by the arm and stopped in front of a
nice looking guy with blue eyes and brown hair.

"Richmond, this is the girl I was telling you about.
Mona Lisa, this is Richmond."

We shook hands as Brittany walked away.

"What did she tell you about me?" I asked.

"What didn't she tell me?" he replied with a smirk.

I laughed. "I think we may get along just fine. Mind if

I ask you a few questions?"

"Shoot."

"Do you live with your parents?"

"I'm thirty-two years old," he answered.

"Is that a no?"

"Yes, that's a no."

"Any weird allergies, skin conditions or other ailments?"

"Are you serious?"

"As they say in the south, serious as a heart attack."

"None that I know of. Anything else, 'cause you're starting to creep me out a little?" he confessed.

"Nope. I'm good."

"My turn then. Married before?"

"Narrowly escaped it. How about you?"

"I thought it was my turn," he answered.

"Sorry."

"No. Never married. Kids?"

"No kids."

"Last thing, I hear you're from Jersey. What brought you here?" Richmond asked.

"That was how I narrowly escaped marriage."

While we were talking, we moved toward the starting line and in a matter of minutes, we began. Richmond and I kept pace with one another. We talked a little, but mostly enjoyed the crowds and the music. We finished in a little over an hour and I was happy as we crossed the finish line.

"Let's go this way," Richmond said. "We have to get

our shirt. That's the only reason I do this race."

"Seriously?" I asked.

"Yes, ma'am. The shirt is a status symbol around here and I'm not leaving without it."

We picked up our t-shirts and then made our way over to the food stand where I got a peach and a bottle of cold water.

"It sure gets hot here."

"This is nothing. Wait until August when we have days and days of ninety-five-degree weather. I love it. The hotter, the better."

"I'm more of a utopia girl myself. I'd like it to be seventy-five all year round."

"I hate to tell you this, but you're living in the wrong part of the country, Mona Lisa."

"I realize that. Who knows? Maybe I'll grow to like the heat, too."

"I have another question for you if that's alright," Richmond said.

"Go for it," I challenged.

"Would you like to have dinner with me tomorrow night?"

I smiled and said, "I'd love that."

"Great. Give me your number, and I'll call you tomorrow and we can firm up the details."

He stored my number in his phone and I asked, "Can we not do Italian? The last time I had it, it left me very uncomfortable."

Richmond gave me a strange look and said, "Whatever you like. I have the feeling that you have a few dating stories tucked away."

I just shrugged and thought to myself, *And I hope tomorrow doesn't add to my collection.*

Chapter 39

Richmond was a man of his word. He called me the next day and we settled on a Thai restaurant. I even accepted his offer to pick me up. For the first time in a while, I was actually excited about a date. Amy seemed to be able to smell the optimism in my blood and was not one to pass up any opportunity to try and unnerve me. She plopped herself on my bed as I put the finishing touches on my makeup, but she said nothing. I was determined not to speak first, but eventually, I couldn't stand it any longer.

"What?" I asked.

"What?" she asked back.

"I know there's something you're dying to tell me. What is it? Does Richmond have three testicles or something?"

Amy laughed. "You sure are paranoid."

"Don't you think I have a right to be?" I challenged.

I grabbed a pillow off my bed and held it just over her face.

"Spill it. What's wrong with him?" I asked.

Amy burst into a fit of laughter, so I whacked her across the head with the pillow.

"Tell me what you know, or I'll smother you and frame Brightleigh for your murder. I think you forget I'm Italian and from Jersey," I said as I held the pillow lightly against her face.

Amy knocked it out of my hands and said, "I love

messing with you. He's a good guy. Too good for my tastes, but you might like him." She got up off the bed and added, "Word on the street is he only has two testicles. He has three nipples, but only two testicles."

"You're horrible," I said as she sauntered out of my room.

The doorbell rang and Amy yelled, "I'll get it."

"Noooo," I called out as I ran to beat her to the door.

Amy was sitting on the couch, waiting to watch me act like a crazy person.

"I hate you right now," I said as I smoothed my hair and tried to appear normal.

I opened the door, and there was Richmond with a bouquet of peach-colored roses, looking tanned and relaxed. I motioned for him to come in and closed the door. He handed the flowers to me and then gave me a light hug. I might have a true gentleman on my hands.

"Thank you, Richmond. They're beautiful."

"Peach is the state color of Georgia, you know."

"Really?" I asked.

"I made that up. It sounded good, though, didn't it?"

I smiled and then realized that Amy was still there.

"Richmond, I think you know my roommate Amy. She's on leave from the mental hospital so, please ignore anything that comes out of her mouth."

"Hey, Richmond," she said with a small wave. "We've met before at the shop. You two have fun. I'm going back to my padded cell."

Amy walked out of the living room and I grabbed my purse.

"She's funny," Richmond said.

"Yes, she is. She's a great friend, too."

"I heard that," Amy called from her room.

"Good for you. Remember, no operating any heavy machinery until I get home," I answered.

"You're funny, too."

"I prefer to think of it as finely-honed sarcasm. It's a survival skill where I come from."

* * * *

The restaurant was quaint and quiet, and it gave us an opportunity to get to know each other. We made small talk while we looked at the menu and after we placed our order, I sat back in my chair and let out my breath to try and relax.

"Are you nervous?" Richmond asked.

"I think I am."

"Take a sip of your wine and talk to me like you would your roommate. I'm pretty easy going."

"If I talked to you like I do Amy, you might run away. We're from the north and we tell it like it is."

"Tough girl, eh? I think I can take it," he challenged.

"I promise to break you in slowly. How about you tell me more about yourself. What kind of law do you practice?"

"I'm a divorce lawyer. That usually freaks my dates out," he admitted.

"That's nothing. I only freak out when I have to use

EpiPens on my dates."

"You're kidding, right?" he asked.

"Wish I were. I'm thinking of selling my stories to Hollywood so they can make a sitcom out of them."

"One day, you'll have to share them with me."

"I'll wait until we know each other a little better. Tell me about your family. Your brother is married to Bobbie Lee?"

"Yes. They're great together and I love being an uncle. I don't see them that often, but when I do it is fun."

"What about your parents? Do you see them a lot?" I asked wondering what life was like outside the Cicciarelli hemisphere.

"I guess. We have dinner every so often. They're re-tired and live here in town, but they're always going to the club to play golf or something."

"Wow. That's amazing."

"What is?" he asked.

"Dinner every so often. My family has dinner together every Sunday."

"You and your parents?"

"Me, my parents, four sisters, three husbands, one boy-friend, three nephews, one niece, my grandmother and her live-in man friend. He's eighty-one, so I think boyfriend is not an accurate term to use."

"You really do tell it like it is."

"I've always been that way. Lay it all out there and see who has the guts to stick around."

"Just so you know you haven't scared me yet. In fact, I was wondering if you'd like to go to a Braves game with me on Sunday?"

"Baseball, right?"

He laughed. "Yes, baseball. They do have that where you're from, don't they?"

I nodded and thought, *A second date. No nervous tics. No obvious oddities. Things are looking up.*

Chapter 40

I enjoyed getting to know Richmond and the city of Atlanta. We had been on two dates and so far had managed to avoid the hospital and jail, so I felt things were moving in a positive direction. He had gotten me to agree to go to a baseball game, even though I never had one iota of interest in the sport and the temperature was supposed to go up to one hundred degrees. I hadn't ever experienced heat like Atlanta in July and I was not a fan.

I tried to cool off before my baseball date with a shower, but was sweating profusely afterward. I wrapped myself in a towel, snuck into the hallway and turned the air conditioning on full blast. I tiptoed back to my room, turned the ceiling fan on high and laid naked on my bed hoping to stop the waterfall of perspiration. A few minutes passed when I heard a knock on my door.

"What the hell are you doing, trying to turn me into a popsicle?" Amy asked.

I covered up with the towel and got up to open the door.

"This heat is killing me. I needed to cool down before my date, so I turned the air conditioning up. I'm sweating so much, I could hydrate a small town in Africa."

"Oh, my gosh. I have never heard anyone complain about the heat more than you."

"I feel like my mother when she was going through menopause. It didn't matter what was happening. We could be in the middle of dinner and if a hot flash hit, she would stop whatever she was doing, open the freezer and stick her head in."

"So your aversion to heat is hereditary. Is it a Catholic or an Italian thing?" Amy asked.

"Probably Catholic. Our main goal is to avoid the fires of Hell. However, I think right now I may be living in Hell on earth."

"You're a mess. You know it gets hotter in August."

"Yes, I know, and I think it may be a good time for me to go home and visit. There's no way anyone would come down here with this kind of weather."

"You sure are a sensitive bunch. My mother and grandmother are coming tomorrow," Amy boasted.

"Here?" I asked incredulously.

"Yes, here, you idiot."

"Do they know how hot it gets?"

Amy rolled her eyes. "Yes. They come every summer and they live to tell about it. My mom got some of these new fangled pants for women that have the legs cut off. They're called shorts, I think. Plus, when it gets too hot, we can go to the swimming hole," she said dryly.

"As my mother would say, 'No need to be a smart-ass.'"

"You make it too easy, sweaty Betty. Are you going out with Richmond again?"

"Yes. We're going to a Braves game."

"How's it going with you two?"

"It's … nice. So far, there's been nothing weird which is weird, you know? I'm so used to drama with my relationships, it seems unnatural not to have any."

"You need counseling, girlfriend."

"Maybe the heat is frying my brain," I quipped.

"Something is messed up in there. You've got a nice guy who likes you and you can't deal with it because he's normal."

"I sound like a nut when you put it like that."

"As Bubbe says, 'A yenta is a yenta is a yenta'," she said with a smirk.

"What does that mean?" I asked.

"I have no idea, but she says it all the time and it makes me laugh."

"I can't wait to meet her. I will get to meet her, won't I?"I asked.

"Sure. Tomorrow night. They're coming over and cooking all of my favorites. You're welcome to join us, but you are not allowed to use the words heat, hot or sweat. Got it?"

"Got it. Now, if you'll excuse me, I need to put some ice packs in my bra so I can survive my first major league baseball game."

Chapter 41

The baseball game was a lot of fun mostly because of the fans and the beer. I tried to ignore the fact that I might actually be melting and never let on to Richmond how uncomfortable I was. He enjoyed teaching me the rules and telling me fun facts about the players and it helped keep my mind off my impending heatstroke. After the game, we went for dinner and when we were seated at a table, I relaxed as the air conditioning enveloped me. I smiled as I thought about taking my shirt off and fully enjoying the cool air.

"What are you thinking about?" Richmond asked.

"Oh, nothing," I lied.

"Since when does nothing put a smile like that on your face?"

"I got a little hot at the game," I confessed, "and I'm happy to be indoors. That's all. Nothing sinister going on in my head."

"The heat really bothers you that much, huh? It's only July. August is worse."

"Everyone keeps telling me that. I am starting to freak out about next month."

Richmond laughed.

"Stop laughing at me," I admonished. "I don't like extremes in temperature."

"Sounds like you need to be living in California."

"My family would love that. As it is, they think I am

living in another country. California would be equivalent to moving to China. Plus, I'm not a fan of earthquakes."

"What about snow?" he asked.

"I like it to snow once each winter and last for two to three days."

"You have some definite opinions on the weather."

"What can I say? Some people are passionate about religion and politics. I have weather."

"I'll keep that in mind. What about relationships? Ever get passionate about those?" Richmond asked.

Yikes. This was our third date and we only shared a kiss on the last one. It was nice, but passion wasn't a word I would use to describe my feelings for Richmond.

"Sure. I, I …"

"Sorry," he said as he fiddled with his napkin. "I didn't mean to put you on the spot."

"Don't be sorry. The last passionate relationship I had was with my high school sweetheart and his mother, and it resulted in me being left at the altar. In hindsight, it was the best thing that could have happened to me. It forced me to make a big change in my life, and that's how I ended up here in the delightfully toasty south."

Richmond's shoulders relaxed at my explanation and I wondered about myself. *Was I incapable of having a relationship with somebody who was raised in a normal family where boundaries were observed? Did I need to have the drama? No. This is how relationships were supposed to be,* I told myself. *Right?*

I leaned over and kissed him lightly on the lips as if to prove something to myself. Instead of answering my questions, it conjured up more.

* * * *

After Richmond dropped me off, I stripped down to my underwear, turned on the fan full blast and called my sister.

"Soph, it's me. I need some advice."

"Sure. Let me go into the other room. The television is blaring in here. I swear, no one in this family can tolerate quiet except me. Hold on." After a few seconds, she said, "That's better. What's going on?"

"I think there is something seriously wrong with me?"

"Oh, my God. Did you find a lump?" she asked on the verge of tears.

"Jeez, you're as bad as Ma. No, I did not find a lump. I need some relationship advice."

"Mona Lisa, you scared the hell out of me."

"You're the one with the overactive imagination. The phone rings and you automatically assume someone died."

"Something in me snapped once I had kids. At least I come by my neuroses honestly."

"True and speaking of neuroses, I need to talk about mine. I'm dating this guy, and he's nice, and he's a gentleman, but I can't get past it."

"Past what?"

"I seem to have a hard time because he's normal. That's crazy, isn't it?" I asked.

"What do you mean by a hard time?"

"There's not a lot of chemistry."

"That's different than needing him to be a little nutty. How many times have you gone out with him?"

"Three. He's only kissed me twice and it was nice, but nothing to write home about."

"If you wrote home about it, Ma would tell you to buck up and be grateful you had a date."

"Yes, she would and Noni would tell me to skip the kissing and just have sex with him."

Sophia laughed and said, "I miss you so much, Mona Lisa."

"I miss you too. I'm going to come up in a few weeks. You can't believe how hot it is down here."

"I know how hot it is because each Sunday at dinner, Chick reads us the weather report from Atlanta. It's his way of keeping tabs on you."

"He's a head case. I love him, but he needs a hobby."

"His family is his hobby. Now back to you. Do you enjoy spending time with this guy?"

"Yes, I do, but…"

She interrupted me and said, "Stop with the buts and don't overthink this. Have fun with him and see where it leads."

"Ever the voice of reason, you are. So … enough about me. What else is new?"

"The kids are out of school and I'm counting the days until they go back. All I do is drive them places. I swear they need to be entertained all day long and it's exhausting. I use it as an excuse not to cook. We just got back from Giovanni's. I saw your boyfriend there," she teased.

"Joey?" I asked.

"No, Dante. He asked about you. I told him you love Atlanta and he actually looked a little disappointed."

"Was he alone?" I asked, not knowing where this sudden interest was coming from.

"I don't know, Mona Lisa. Why?"

"No reason. Hey, I need to get in the shower before my roommate beats me to it. Thanks for the advice. I love you."

As I hung up the phone, my mind went back to Dante and I felt my heart beat a little faster as I remembered his tender kiss the last time we saw each other. There really was something wrong with me and I hoped a cold shower would clear my head, but I heard the bathroom door slam and the water turn on and knew Amy had beat me to it. I smiled as I thought at least I wouldn't mind if she used all of the hot water.

Chapter 42

The next morning, Amy was up at the crack of dawn. I heard cabinet doors slamming, dishes clanging and managed to remain in a light doze, but when the vacuum cleaner was turned on, I couldn't take it any longer. I got out of bed and went into the living room and watched as Amy moved at a speed I never knew she was capable of. I waved trying to get her attention, but she was in a zone, so I was forced to pull the plug on the vacuum.

"What the hell?" she muttered before seeing me.

"What the hell is right, Amy. Do you know what time it is?" I asked.

Brightleigh shuffled out of her bedroom and looked like she was sleepwalking. Her eyes were half open and her hair seemed to be channeling her inner Don King.

She threw herself on the sofa and asked, "What in the world are ya'll doing? It's my only day to sleep in."

"Don't ask me," I countered. "Ask Mrs. Clean."

"My mother and Bubbe are coming today and this place is gross."

"Does it have to be done right now?" Brightleigh whined.

"I couldn't sleep, so I thought I'd get a head start. Go back to bed and I'll be quieter," Amy promised.

Brightleigh shuffled back to her room, but I stayed.

"I'll help you. I remember how stressed my mom would get when my dad's mother would visit. We joked that it was the only time the refrigerator ever got cleaned out. What can I do?" I asked.

Amy gave me a smirk and said, "How about helping me clean out the refrigerator?"

"That I can do. What time do they get here?" I asked as I opened the fridge door and began removing questionable items.

"Their plane gets in at two this afternoon. I'll take them to their hotel and then we'll come here and cook."

"I guess you'll hit the grocery store first."

"Oh, no. Bubbe will have a suitcase with all the necessary items. According to her, you can't get a decent bagel in this town, let alone a loaf of Challah. I picked up some of the minor ingredients, but she will have everything she needs in her traveling Jewish pantry."

I laughed. "I can't wait to meet them."

"They're both crazy, but I'm excited to see them. And if you tell them I said that, I'll put ex-lax in your kugel."

"Got it. I'm going to talk to Bobbie Lee about taking some time off in a few weeks. I'm ready to ditch this southern sauna for some time with my family, too."

"I hope they have a heat wave up there when you go. It would serve you right for all your grumbling."

"Don't even go there. My parents don't have air conditioning. They have one of those whole house fans that sucks all the bugs onto the screen and just blows the hot air around."

"Maybe you better start praying to the patron saint of

weather."

"Maybe you can clean out these rotten vegetables and moldy cheeses by yourself."

"Point taken. You're good, Mona Lisa. I like it that you can give as good as you get."

"You're a good sparring partner. If only you were a guy."

"Why? Richmond not much into lively banter?" she asked.

"He's pretty literal. Sometimes I say things and I can tell he's not sure what to make of me. So, he just sits there with a smile on his face and says nothing."

"It could be worse. He could be one of those guys who doesn't know when to drop the sarcasm. My grandfather was like that. Always had a smart remark, but never anything nice to say. One day, Bubbe had enough and took her cast iron pan that she fried the *gribbenes* in and told him if he didn't stop with the nasty talk she was going to kill him with the pan in his sleep. He never said another unkind thing to her."

"Wow. What's *gribbenes*?" I asked.

"Fried chicken skin or as I call it, Jewish bacon. I tell you my Bubbe threatened to kill her husband and that's what you ask about?"

"I'm Italian. What can I say? Is it good?"

"What? The *gribbenes*? If you like fried chicken skin, it is. Jeez, remind me not to tell you any more stories."

"What was the point of the story, again?" I asked.

"Hell if I know now," Amy admitted. "Start wiping out that shelf. I'll get enough negative comments about my love life. I don't need them about my housekeeping abilities."

"I think I'm going to enjoy myself tonight," I confessed. "For once, someone else will be the focus of the family dinner."

"Remember, they'll leave in a few days, but I'll be here forever. Payback's a bitch."

Chapter 43

Amy's mother and grandmother arrived carrying two suitcases, which contained enough food to feed a small nation for a month. Amy's mom, Lee, was petite with black curly hair and a warm smile. Bubbe was an older version of Lee with a hint of sassiness. They set the luggage on the dining room table and Amy introduced us.

"This is my mom, Lee, and Bubbe. This is Mona Lisa."

Lee broke into song, "Mona Lisa, Mona Lisa men have named you."

Amy looked at her watch and said, "Well, you managed to embarrass me in record time, Ma."

"Just doing my job, Love Bug."

"Do you have to be so good at it?" Amy asked.

I laughed because I felt like I was transported back home.

"She learned from the master," Bubbe said as she began unpacking an endless supply of groceries.

"Did you take all of this on the plane?" I asked Bubbe.

"Sure. The one suitcase had all of the cold stuff and the other had the food you can't get here."

"Like what?" I asked.

"Oy, you name it. Matzoh, flanken, cabbage."

"Cabbage, Bubbe?" Amy asked.

"Listen, Miss Smarty Pants, one day you'll be making these dishes and you'll understand," Bubbe replied as she took her stash of aprons out of the suitcase and handed one to each of us.

"Me? I don't see myself carrying a suitcase of Jewish delicacies halfway across the country."

"Amy, you need to be proud of your heritage. Plus, your husband will expect you to be able to carry on the traditions," Lee said matter-of-factly.

"Oh, I need to learn to cook for my husband, do I? Maybe, he'll cook for me," Amy challenged.

"I swear, you will never find a man with that kind of attitude," Lee said shaking her head.

"You worry too much about me finding a man, Ma. You did just fine without one."

Lee sighed and said, "Yes, but it was hard and I don't want that for you, Amy."

"Alright, enough with the drama. No need to make a *gantseh megilleh* out of the past. Put your aprons on and let's get to work," Bubbe ordered.

I looked at Amy and she said, "Yiddish for big deal."

"Thank you for the translation," I said.

Bubbe handed me a stalk of celery and ordered, "Chop. No big chunks."

"Yes, ma'am."

"None of this ma'am crap. Bubbe will do just fine."

"You got it, Bubbe."

* * * *

We worked in the kitchen for hours, but I felt like I was with my sisters as I cooked and talked with Amy and her family. I set the table and we sat down to a colorful array of dishes full of meats and vegetables so unlike the sauce-covered pasta creations my family was famous for.

Everyone was seated when Lee stood and said, "I forgot the sours."

"God forbid, you forget those. As if we needed something else to ensure our blood pressure stays in the dangerously high range," Amy remarked.

Lee returned to the table with a dish of olives and other assorted pickled vegetables.

"It's tradition, wiseass. One day, I'll be gone and you'll be wishing I were here to get the sours."

"Unless, of course, you die from high blood pressure," Amy replied.

"You're going right to Hell, you know that," I teased.

"I'm sure I won't be alone," Amy said.

"Let's stop with the idle chitchat and eat," Bubbe interjected. "I'm starved."

Bubbe poured everyone some matzoh ball soup and I was instantly in heaven.

"Oh, my gosh, this is fabulous," I gushed.

"It's just soup," Amy said. "You better pace yourself, because we have a ton of food."

"I'm Italian. We know about eating."

"You're Italian?" Lee asked.

"The name Mona Lisa didn't give it away?" Amy asked.

Lee shot her a look.

"Just ignore her," I said.

Lee laughed and said, "My best friend growing up was Italian. I used to spend every Christmas Eve with Maria and her family. We had smelts, fried dough, and cioppino. Talk about being in heaven. I have dreams about that meal."

"Come to my parents' house on Christmas Eve and we can make that dream a reality. I'm not sure what cioppino is, but we can offer seven different kinds of fish deep-fried for maximum *agita*."

"I'm actually spending Christmas Eve with Maria and her family. We reconnected at our high school reunion a few months ago and it turns out she lives in Jersey. I love that we found each other again. It was the only good thing to come out of that night."

"Why was it so bad?" I asked.

"Oy, just hearing people brag on their jobs and how much money they make. One woman, who was the biggest burnout in high school, is now a forensic accountant. What the hell is that? And how come I never heard about jobs like that when I was in college?" She didn't wait for an answer, and asked, "Ma, why didn't you tell me I could be something other than a teacher or secretary?"

"It's always the mother's fault," Bubbe muttered as she stood to clear the soup bowls from the table. "You want I should have picked your career? You sure as hell didn't listen to me when I told you not to marry that bum. You think you would have listened to me if I told you to get a job at NASA."

I stood to help her, but she waved me back into my seat.

"I know it's not your fault, Ma. Look at Amy. She's a hairdresser in Georgia for God's sake. I didn't do any better by her."

"Well, that's two of us you just insulted," Amy informed her mother.

I smiled. I was enjoying myself immensely.

Amy continued, "For your information, I like what I do. It lets me be creative and I help people feel good about themselves."

"I didn't mean it like that, Amy. I just felt like I could have done something different, but I didn't even know there were options out there."

"Listen, LeeLee, you're a damned good teacher so stop *kvetching* and eat," Bubbe ordered.

I filled my plate with stuffed cabbage, beef and a whole slew of new foods I was dying to enjoy.

"There you have it, Mona Lisa, the Roth family dirty laundry. Have we covered all the skeletons in our closet?" Amy asked.

"Aren't you touchy today, Love Bug?" Lee quickly changed the subject, seeing her daughter squirm. "So Mona Lisa, we heard about the mishap at the altar."

"He should rot in Hell, that one and his mother," Bubbe added.

"And now it's on to your dirty laundry," Amy announced.

165

I smiled. "It's all good, really. It was for the best. I'm happy now."

"Are you dating anyone?" Lee asked.

"Maaaa…" Amy cried.

"What?" Lee asked. "It's a simple question. Yes I am or no I'm not."

"It's none of your business," Amy chided.

"It's fine. I find these questions much less intrusive when they're not coming from my meddling mother," I confessed.

"That is one thing I'll never be. Meddlesome," Lee said.

Amy choked on her cabbage and when she got her breath back she said, "Now, I've heard it all. A non-meddling, Jewish mother. Did the world stop spinning?"

"You think you're so funny, Amy."

"Not think, I know and Ma, you keep giving me plenty of material." Amy stood and kissed her mom. "I love you, you crazy old lady."

Tears welled in my eyes.

"Oh, my gosh, are you crying?" Amy asked with disgust.

"Shut up, Amy," Lee and I ordered in unison.

As I wiped my eyes, I thought of my family who would be having another dinner without me and realized I was missing their opinions and advice about my life. It was definitely time to go home.

Chapter 44

Amy and I cleared the table, as Lee and Bubbe sat on the sofa and watched a game show. Every few minutes, Bubbe yelled at one of the contestants and I laughed each time.

"What's so funny?" Amy asked.

"Bubbe. Noni likes to talk to the people on the TV, too. She especially likes to yell at the Jets and Giants during football season. My sisters won't let the kids be around when she watches football. I think I miss her most of all."

"Stop whining and get on a plane, already," Amy said.

"I know. I'm going to call my parents later and see when a good time would be to visit."

"I've got the rest of the dishes. Go call them now. I'm sick of seeing you cry like a hormonal school girl all the time."

"Thanks, girlfriend. I owe you one."

I poked my head into the room where Bubbe and Lee were engrossed with their show.

"Thank you for a wonderful dinner. I hope I get to see you again before you leave."

"Anytime, sweetheart," Lee called.

"Give us a hug. You're family now," Bubbe added.

I embraced them both and left our guests to their show. I went to my room, plopped myself on the bed and grabbed my cell phone. I saw I had missed two calls from my parents, so I hit their number on speed dial and waited to face the inquisition.

"Hello, Miss I'm too busy to talk to my family. Nice of you to remember the people who gave you life."

"Hi, Chick. It's nice to hear your voice, too. What's new?"

"Getting ready for the family dinner tomorrow which you'll miss again."

"Well, yeah. I live 800 miles away."

"Aren't you just full of sass today? You know what I meant. You miss time with the family. Anyway, here's your mother."

"You gotta stop talking my ear off, Chick," I replied.

My mother answered, "He's a man of few words, Mona Lisa. How are you, honey?"

"I thought I'd come home."

"Oh, my God. That's wonderful. I turned your bedroom into a craft room, but I'm sure I can get your furniture back from Aunt Louise. Did Vinnie give you your job back? I've been saying a Novena since you left so you would come back home."

"Whoa, Ma. I'm just coming home for a visit."

"What? Why didn't you say so? Here I am rambling on like a lunatic. Chick, she's only coming for a visit."

I heard my dad grumble in the background.

"Sorry about that. You took me by surprise and then I was waiting for you to take a breath."

"Oh," she offered meekly.

"Don't sound so disappointed."

"I thought you were moving back," she admitted.

"I'm sorry. I'm excited to see you, though. I miss you a lot."

"I miss you too, Mona Lisa. When are you coming?"

"I have to talk to my boss and arrange for some time off. Do you have any plans in the next few weeks?"

"Who am I? The Queen of England? What could I possibly be doing that would be more important than having my wayward daughter visit?"

"Ma, you kill me. I just wanted to check with you before I made my reservations."

"What do you want to eat when you come home? If it's cooler, we can have soup or gnocchi or shells."

"Ma, I'm coming home to visit. The food doesn't matter."

"Oh, Mona Lisa, of course, the food matters. We're Italian. Or have you forgotten your heritage already?"

"No, Ma. I will eat whatever you make, and I will love it."

"Darn tootin' you will. How long can you stay?" she asked.

"I don't know. At least a couple of days."

"A couple of days? I was hoping for at least a couple of weeks."

"Ma, I don't make any money if I don't work."

"And if you were married, you wouldn't have to worry about things like that."

"So a husband guarantees I make money. Wow, I wish

you had told me that sooner."

"I don't miss your smart mouth. Speaking of husbands, I hear you're dating someone."

"I've been on a few dates, but I don't think it's going anywhere. Don't order the invitations yet."

"Have you ever thought that some men might be put off by your sarcasm?" she asked.

I rolled my eyes and said, "I consider it a gift and if a man can't handle it, then he can't handle me. Listen Ma, I'll call you later in the week when I firm up my plans. I love you," I added and quickly hung up the phone.

I went back out to the kitchen and found Amy still doing the dishes.

"Are you moving in slow motion?" I asked her.

"The longer I stay in here, the less time they have to focus on finding me a husband."

"I just got my weekly dose of 'If you weren't so mouthy, you'd be married by now.' Remind me why I want to go home?" I asked.

Chapter 45

I was nervous about asking Bobbie Lee for time off because I didn't want to discuss Richmond with her. I was feeling guilty for not liking him more, and I wished I had thought more about the ramifications of dating a member of my boss's family.

Seeing Bitsy and Mary on my schedule lightened my mood, though and as always, Mary honed right in on my anxiety and asked, "What's eating you today, Yankee?"

"You scare me, Mary or am I that transparent?" I asked.

"You look like you're about to jump out of your skin," she replied.

"I'm fine. I need some time off."

"And you're afraid to tell Bobbie Lee? If she were any more laid back, she'd be dead."

"No, I'm not scared to ask for time off. I don't want to bother her is all," I lied.

"Don't play poker much, do you? You don't have to tell me the truth. It's none of my business, but if anyone knows Bobbie Lee, it's her G-Mama."

"I know you do. It's Richmond," I admitted.

"The pretty boy brother-in-law?" she asked.

"We've been dating and I'm not sure it's working out. I don't want Bobbie Lee to be mad at me."

"Goodness, child, you are workin' yourself up over nothing. That boy is too white bread for you. You need

171

someone with a little kick to him. And Bobbie Lee won't care. Just let him down easy."

"You think so?"

"Lord have mercy, yes. There is no need to carry on about this any longer. Now, get yourself together before you touch my hair. I do not want to pay the price for your messed up love life. Got it?"

"Yes. Ma'am. And thank you, " I added before I gave her a gentle squeeze.

"No need to get sappy on me, Yankee. Let's get to work. I don't have all day."

* * * *

"Mona Lisa, grab your lunch and join me in my office," Bobbie Lee called out.

"Oooh, you're in trouble," Amy teased.

I discreetly flipped her the bird and grabbed my bag out of my station drawer and walked back to join the boss. Bobbie Lee was at a small table that had been cleared off and was busy spreading out her food. She motioned for me to sit in the empty chair.

"So, what did I do to deserve an audience with you today?" I asked timidly.

"G-Mama was worried about you and I wanted to make sure you were okay," Bobbie Lee replied.

"She's sweet. I love working with her," I said.

"Wow, something must really be wrong because even G-Mama would laugh at someone callin' her sweet. So, what's up?"

I took a drink of my Diet Coke and said, "I need some

time off and I'm afraid you'll be mad at me if I stop dating Richmond."

Bobbie Lee laughed and said, "Is that all? Well, bless your heart, but you have been worryin' for no reason at all. You can take time off whenever you need it. You make your own schedule. I don't say anything unless it gets out of hand. And as far as Richmond goes, I personally don't see you together. You're like a firecracker and he's more like … not. Don't get me wrong, I love him to death, but I see him more with a debutante type."

I let out my breath and relaxed into my chair. "I'm so relieved. I was so worried about talking to you, you have no idea."

"When you have an old lady runnin' interference for you, it must be bad. Have you spoken to Richmond? He deserves that, at least," she said.

"Not yet," I admitted. "I will. We're supposed to go out this weekend and I'll talk to him then. I'd like to do it in person."

"Good. I like a person with integrity. So, where ya headed?"

"I'm going home for a few days. If it gets any hotter down here, I may spontaneously combust."

Bobbie Lee chuckled and said, "You're a lightweight. You'll get used to it in a few years and when winter hits, you'll be wishin' for some of this heat."

I smiled thinking the weather was like my love life— never quite right for my moods.

Chapter 46

I made a date with Richmond for dinner on Friday and was anxious about seeing him. I tried to plan when I would make my announcement about us not being quite right for one another. I wondered if he would even be upset. Nothing seemed to rattle him, which was a nice quality, but he didn't laugh much either and that bothered me a little. Not that I was a stand-up comic, but I had a quick wit and felt that it was one of my better features.

I was putting the final touches on my eye makeup when Brightleigh came in and sat on my bed.

"So, you're going to do it, huh?" she asked.

"What?"

"Break up with Richmond," she whispered.

"Why are you whispering?"

"I feel bad for him," she admitted.

"It's not like we've been seeing each other for that long. I don't think he's going to be that upset."

Brightleigh frowned slightly, which aroused my curiosity.

"Since when do you care so much about Richmond?" I asked.

Brightleigh turned beat red and then it hit me.

"Oh, my gosh, you like Richmond!"

"No, no … Oh, Lord. I do. I'm sorry, Mona Lisa. I think he's beautiful and smart and now you must hate me because I like your boyfriend."

"Wow. How long have you felt this way?" I asked.

"I met him last year at Bobbie Lee's Christmas palooza and I've admired him from afar since then."

"What's Christmas palooza?"

"It's a crazy Christmas party Bobbie Lee throws every year. She has her house decorated with a million lights and even has a snow-making machine so that people can go sledding."

"Man, she must really love Christmas. Do you think she'll invite me this year?"

"I swear, Mona Lisa, I am tryin' to confess to you I harbor feelings for your boyfriend and all you care about is Christmas palooza."

"I've never heard of anything palooza. We don't have that in Jersey. Besides, it makes me feel better to know you like him. I can tell him I have a replacement girlfriend all ready for him."

"Oh, my stars, if you so much as even hint to him I even know he's alive, I will rip your heart out," she threatened.

"Man, okay. I was going to put a good word in for you, but I'll keep my mouth shut."

"Thank you. And I'd rather you not tell Amy about this conversation. She loves nothing more than having something ugly to hold over my head."

"Your secret is safe with me, ma'am," I assured her.

"Promise you don't hate me? I love you to death and it would kill me to know I hurt you."

"Brightleigh, I'm fine. If I had true feelings for Richmond, it would be different. No worries and I love you to death, too." I hugged her.

The doorbell rang.

"Show time," I announced and walked out of my room to greet Richmond.

He looked as sharp as ever. Hair neatly combed, starched oxford with the sleeves rolled up and khaki shorts. This might be more difficult than I thought.

He kissed me on the cheek and asked, "You ready to go?"

"I thought we could talk for a few minutes. Come sit with me."

"This doesn't sound good," he said with a nervous chuckle.

We sat next to each other on the couch.

"I want you to know that I really like you, but I don't think it's going to work out between us."

He had no visible reaction and said, "That's fine. Do you still want to go to dinner?"

I was puzzled. "Do you want me to?"

"Why not? I thought we'd go over to Solids and Stripes and play pool then get some dinner. I asked my brother and Bobbie Lee to join us."

"Sure. Do you mind if I ask my roommate Brightleigh to come along? I don't think she has any plans."

"Not at all."

I walked toward her bedroom and found her hiding in

the hallway, trying to listen to my conversation with Richmond.

"What are you doing?" I whispered before grabbing her arm and pulling her into my bedroom.

"I couldn't help myself, Mona Lisa. I wanted to make sure he wasn't upset," she confessed.

"Hardly. He barely blinked his eyes. I think he may be part mannequin. Anyway, we're meeting Bobbie Lee and Prescott to play pool, and you're coming with us."

"No, Mona Lisa. I look a fright and I would get all tongue-tied around him."

"A fright? You look fine. This is your opportunity to get his attention, so don't blow it. Go put on some lipstick and deodorant and be ready in five minutes."

"You're the best, Mona Lisa."

"Don't forget me when you have a spare boyfriend lying around. I'll be on the hunt when I get back from Jersey."

Chapter 47

The plane ride to Newark was uneventful, but I en-joyed chatting with the passenger in the seat next to mine. She had been in Atlanta for business and was telling me stories about slow southerners and how they irritated her. I told her I felt that same way when I first moved there, but I was getting used to the more relaxed pace and actually en-joyed it. She wasn't swayed by my testimonial, but I didn't care. I was going home.

The walk from the plane to baggage claim seemed in-terminable, but then I saw Sophia and her bright smile. We hugged and squealed like two little kids and ignored the glares from the people around us.

"I'm so happy to see you. I miss you so much, Soph."

"Me too. It's not the same without you," she admitted.

"I'm here now and we're going to have fun. I need some laughs and I'm counting on you to provide them."

"No pressure, though," she chuckled.

We talked about my flight and the weather on the way to her car, but once we got on the road, we gabbed nonstop, catching up on each other's lives.

"I broke up with Richmond," I confessed.

"Don't tell Ma. She rests easier when she knows you have a boyfriend."

"That's abnormal," I replied.

"Since when have you known our family to be normal? So did he take it well?"

"Oh yeah. It was no big deal. Plus I fixed him up with my roommate Brightleigh. They're like Scarlett and Rhett. A much better match than we were."

"Good. Are you happy down there, Mona Lisa?"

"You know, I am. I was able to start over and not have my whole identity tied up with Joey and Alice."

"Speaking of which, they're all getting married next month, and Alice told Vinnie that Joey and his wife are moving in with her so she can watch the babies when they're born. Boy, did you dodge a bullet," Sophia confirmed.

"A bullet? More like a nuclear bomb. Now that I've been away from him for awhile, I can't remember what I ever saw in Joey."

"I think it was the two-for-one-deal that attracted you to him," she said.

"Yeah, marry my son and get me as your new best friend. Let's talk about something else. What's the family scuttlebutt?"

"Ro and Charlie have been secretly dating. She told Nina who told Marilyn who told me. Obviously, Ma and Chick don't know. It's good because Ro was going a little crazy."

"How so?"

"Oh, she was a regular down at Lucky's and let's just say she got lucky pretty often. I was about to get her some pamphlets on STDs when I heard she and Charlie were seeing each other again."

"Get out," I exclaimed. "I go away for a few months and everyone goes nuts. Thank God Chick didn't find out about her wild ways."

"Oh, he did and I think that was a major factor in her getting back with Charlie."

"Why didn't you tell me about this?"

"It was a while back and I didn't want to worry you. Then it worked itself out and there you go."

"Wow. What else has happened?" I asked.

"That's really it. Oh, and I'm pregnant."

"What?"

"Kidding. Noni would have a better chance of getting pregnant than me. My two keep me so busy, I collapse at the end of each night. Exhaustion is wonderful birth control."

We turned into our parents' driveway, but it didn't look like anyone was home.

Sophia put the car in park and said, "I wish I could stay, but I have to pick up Gina and get her to dance class. Even in summer, my taxi is going all the time. I'll see you tomorrow for dinner."

I grabbed my bag out of the back seat and waved before I entered the code on the garage door keypad. I walked into the kitchen and found a note from my mother.

Mona Lisa,

Had to help Mrs. Sebastiani with her grocery shop-
ping. Be back before dinner.

Make yourself at home.

Ma

I went down the hall to my old room and was surprised
to see my bed surrounded by two tables of crafting supplies. Yarn, paper, glue, fabric, and beads were everywhere
and I wondered if Chick had traded my mother for Martha
Stewart. I moved a half-knitted scarf and two canvases off
the bed so I could put my bag down and unpack. However,
when I looked around, there was no place for me to put my
clothes. Make yourself at home, indeed.

Chapter 48

I was trapped without a car and now that I was back home, I wanted nothing more than to go somewhere. I was sad and mad there was no one home and I wanted Noni, but I couldn't get to her, so I settled for a phone call. I picked up the phone and dialed her number.

"Noni, I can't wait to see you."

"Who is this?" she asked.

My heart fell into my stomach.

"It's me, Mona Lisa."

"Who?" she asked again a bit louder.

"Mona Lisa, Noni don't you remember me?"

She let out a hearty laugh and said, "Just messing with you, kiddo. I'm not senile yet."

"I was going to tell you how much I missed you, but now I'm not."

"Jeez, Miss Thin Skin, the south is making you wimpy."

"Sorry, Noni. I was so excited to get here and I'm all alone. Chick's at work and Ma is helping a neighbor. I'd love to come visit you, but I don't have any wheels."

"You want Marshall to come get you?"

"No. That's all right. I feel like a baby. I thought it would be different when I came back."

"Sorry, kiddo, but the world didn't stop when you left. It doesn't mean we don't love you. It's just how it is."

"How did you get to be so smart, Noni?"

"What can I say? You live as long as I have and you pick up a few things along the way. We're coming over for dinner tomorrow, but maybe the warden and his wife will let you borrow a car and you can visit me for a bit tonight."

"Judging from the welcome I got, I don't think they'll care."

"Don't be a martyr, Mona Lisa. Suck it up and get your ass over here and see me tonight."

"Will do," I replied dutifully.

After I hung up with Noni, I heard a car door slam. I peeked out the window and ran to greet my mother. As we hugged, all my resentment faded. I helped her carry in grocery bags and she proceeded to fill me in on her life.

"Mona Lisa, I'm so glad to see you. I've got to clear a few things out of your room. I've been dabbling in arts and crafts. I'm pretty good at it. Who knew? When I was raising you kids, I never had time for things like that, but now I have a whole room to myself. And guess what? I'm taking a knitting and a painting class at the senior center and next month I start Tai Chi."

Who was this woman and what did she do with my mother?

"Tai Chi?" I asked.

"Yes, it does wonders for your balance and reduces stress. If only I could get Chick to go! He is the major cause of my stress."

"That I'd like to see."

"You never know. I'm praying he'll start to calm down

as he ages. I had hoped the grandchildren would mellow him out, but so far no such luck. He's missed you so much, honey."

"I've missed him, especially on Sundays. I've missed you a lot, too, Ma."

"I miss you terribly, but I want you to be happy and if that means you live far away, then so be it. How's your boyfriend?"

I heard another car door and tried to answer my mother before Chick came in, but I blurted out, "We're not together anymore, and I'm fine."

"Who's not together anymore?" Chick asked.

"Hi, Chick," I said as I held out my arms for a hug.

He squeezed me tight and then kissed me on both cheeks like he did when I was little.

"Are you gonna answer my question?" he asked.

"Me and Richmond. No chemistry," I added.

"It's not always about sex, Mona Lisa," Ma chided.

"We barely kissed, Ma. We weren't right for each other."

"Just as well," Chick remarked. "I don't want you marrying some cowboy from Atlanta, so I've arranged for you to meet some real men while you're here visiting. You never know. You may decide to move back. I'm going to shower. What's for dinner?"

As my mother answered, "Manicotti," I rubbed my temples to quiet the pounding in my head.

She kissed my forehead and said, "See how much he

missed you!"

Like the warden misses the prisoners on his day off.

Chapter 49

I made my escape and smiled broadly as I stood on Noni's stoop and waited for her to answer the door. She greeted me with a huge hug before she pulled me into her house.

She stood back and said, "Let me get a good look at you. Not bad," she mused. "You seem relaxed and happy. You must have gotten some recently."

"Geez, Noni, you never change. Tell me again how my mother got to be so straight-laced. It's like living with Mother Teresa. Always helping her neighbor and never, ever talking about sex. I'm surprised she ever did it."

"As your mother would say, 'No need to be uncouth, Mona Lisa.'"

"What can I say? You bring out the best in me, Noni. I missed you so much."

"Come sit in the dining room," Noni said as she led the way.

She had her best coffee cups and plates out, and she even had the matching sugar bowl and creamer filled and ready.

"Wow. I feel like I'm at high tea at Buckingham Palace."

"It's not everyday I get you all to myself. I sent Marshall to the bakery to get us a little something sweet. He's the best. Did I tell you I'm going to convert for him?"

"Get out? Have you told Father Flanagan? Holy crap,

have you told Ma?" I asked.

Noni burst out laughing.

"You should see your face, Mona Lisa. Absolutely priceless."

"You are a mean old lady," I reprimanded as she fanned herself to cool down from her fit of hysteria.

"That was a good one. I'm running out of Yiddish phrases to bug your mother with so I thought I'd drop that little gem at Sunday dinner. Somebody's got to keep things lively. Chick and your mother are so serious. I like to lighten the mood."

"You kill me, Noni."

"I try, kiddo."

The back door opened and Marshall walked in carrying four pastry boxes.

"Mona Lisa, I'm so happy you're here. Nice of Chick and Ange to let you come over on your first night home. They're the best."

Marshall put the parcels down on the table and kissed my cheek and then Noni's.

"I'll get the coffee," he announced.

"And he's really nice, too," I whispered. "Does he care that you like to harass Ma and Chick?"

She shrugged. "He loves me for who I am, smart mouth and all."

Marshall returned, filled three cups and asked, "Do you two want some time alone?"

"You're sweet, Marshall. Please join us."

He sat, and I fixed my coffee as Marshall opened up the boxes.

"I wasn't sure what you like so I got a little bit of everything."

"It's been so long since I had anything like this. Thank you," I said reaching for a powdered sugar doughnut filled with vanilla custard. "I have dreams about these."

"Tell us about your life in Atlanta," Marshall asked.

I wiped the sugar off my mouth and said, "It's good. I love my job and my roommates. It was very hard at first. It seemed like everyone and everything was in slow motion, but now I'm starting to like the slower pace. The people are nice and there's a lot to do."

"Have you met anyone special?" he asked.

"My dating life has been another story. I just broke up with a guy I'd been seeing for a short time. I'm still waiting for my prince charming to show up. You have any single male relatives, Marshall?"

"Yes, but they're older than I am," he admitted.

"Wouldn't that shut Chick and Ma up? We could double with you and Marshall. Hit the movie matinee and early bird buffet. Although, I'm not sure I'm ready to make small talk about my lack of good bowel movements. Don't make any calls yet, Marshall because Chick informed me he has a whole line up of Jersey's finest bachelors ready for my inspection. I guess he didn't learn his lesson when he tried to fix me up with Dante Colletti."

"You could do worse, Mona Lisa," Noni replied. "I

188

saw him at Mass last week with his mother and he is one good-looking boy."

"I'm sure he's a nice guy, but the timing was all wrong. I also don't want to give Chick the satisfaction. He's barely tolerable now. Imagine if he managed to fix me up with someone I actually liked or married. There would be no living with him. I'd have to name all of my kids Chick. What's new with you two?" I asked.

"Life is great, Mona Lisa. How could it be anything less with this one here?" Marshall said as he squeezed Noni's hand. "She's the cream cheese to my bagel and it doesn't get any better than that. I hope you don't mind, but it's been a long day and I need to relax for a few minutes before bed. I'll see you at Sunday dinner, Mona Lisa."

He kissed us both again and I watched as Noni's expression exuded contentment. She was in love and enjoying every minute of it.

"I envy you two," I admitted.

"Your time will come, Mona Lisa. Hopefully not when you're my age."

"I'm patient, but not that patient." I looked at my watch and said, "I'd better get going. I hear the warden starts checking cells at ten."

"I'll bring you a cake with a file in it tomorrow so you can escape."

"No need. The girls are coming to break me out at lunchtime."

Chapter 50

The next morning, I found my mother sitting at the kitchen table doing the Jumble. *Now I'm home*, I thought to myself. I squeezed my mother from behind and she jumped.

"Mona Lisa! What are you trying to do? Give me a heart attack?"

I laughed.

"It won't be so funny when you're picking my outfit for the casket," she chided. "I thought you were going to sleep forever. Chick wanted to take you to the diner, but he couldn't wait any longer."

"It's eight o'clock."

"You know Chick. Patience is not his middle name."

"I don't think it's in his vocabulary either."

"Don't be sassy, Mona Lisa."

"I can't help it. It's my middle name."

My mother tried to suppress her smile.

"I saw that. Why don't you and I go out for breakfast?"

"Why? We have so much food in the house. Let me make you some eggs or pancakes."

"Coffee first, then maybe I'll have something later. Sit and talk with me. The girls will be here in a few hours so let's take advantage of the quiet."

"Are they coming for lunch? Nobody told me."

"We're going out to lunch."

"I guess I'm going to have to come to Atlanta if I want

to see you," she said, sounding hurt.

"I'm here now. Have some coffee with me and I can tell you all about my new and glamorous life."

She poured us both a cup of coffee and said, "Maybe you need to focus less on glamour and more on finding a husband. I saw this show where they talked about how after a certain age women's eggs start to shrivel up. I hate to say it, but you're approaching that age."

I groaned. "Ma, give me a break. I'm not going to get married just so I have better eggs. I'm not a chicken, you know. I haven't found the right guy yet."

My mother started to clean off the counters, and I realized we needed a new topic of conversation and not one that focused on me.

"Show me what you've been working on in your craft room. Maybe I'll get inspired and take some classes myself. I hear that's a great way to meet men."

Her face lit up. "Sure. It's a mess, though. I need to organize everything."

"Why don't I help you with that," I suggested.

"Really? That would be great."

We grabbed our coffee and walked back to what used to be my bedroom. My mother pulled two boxes from under my bed.

She opened the first and said, "This is my yarn, but I overdid the buying part. I hide it in this box, so Chick doesn't see."

There had to be over fifty skeins of yarn.

"I guess I know what you'll be giving everyone for Christmas. You better get to knitting, Ma."

"I know, but then I started taking this painting class and I love that, too."

She opened the second box and it was filled with paints and brushes.

"Wow, you really go all in, don't you?" I laughed.

"Don't laugh. If Chick ever found out how much I spent on this stuff, he'd shit a brick."

"I've never seen this side of you, Ma, and I have to say I love it. Stop worrying about what Chick thinks. This is something that's just for you. He has nothing to do with it."

"My generation isn't used to that way of thinking," she admitted.

"I know, but you worked your butt off taking care of Chick and us girls. You deserve this and I want you to promise me you'll keep it up."

She smiled at me and then was back to old Ma.

"Help me get this stuff put away, so I know what I have. How long until your sisters get here?" she asked.

"About three hours. We have plenty of time."

"Good. I want to be finished well before they arrive."

"When will Chick be home?" I asked.

"He'll be at that diner for at least another hour or two. It's his new Saturday routine. He goes and hangs out with his cronies and then comes home and takes a nap. See why I needed a hobby?"

"Yes, I do," I agreed as I began to sort the yarn into

piles. "You should come to lunch with me and the girls. It will be fun."

"I'm your mother Mona Lisa, not your friend."

One step forward and two steps back.

"Can't you be both?" I asked.

"That's sweet, but no. I don't need to hear about your sex lives. It's upsetting to even think about it."

"Ma, you act as if all we talk about is sex. A wise woman once told me there's more to life than just sex."

"Very funny. You go to lunch and discuss all the sordid details of your lives and I'll stay here with my nice pure art supplies."

"I'll be sure and take notes," I offered.

She smiled and said, "You can give me a report at dinner."

Chapter 51

My sisters arrived with a flurry of excitement and squeals as we greeted one another. The constant chatter continued for the ten-minute car ride to the restaurant.

I sat in the front with Sophia and said, "I miss this so much."

"What? The noise level?"

"No. All of us being together. I'm jealous. You get to do this all the time," I admitted.

"You think we do this all the time?" she laughed. "We haven't done this since you left. Sure we see each other at Sunday dinner, but we're all so busy these days. I'm doing good just to text one of the girls during the week."

"I know it's immature, but I'm so happy you told me that."

Sophia parked the car and said, "You're turning into a head case. I think you need to move home again so you toughen up!"

We walked into the restaurant and sat at a table near a window so we would not be disturbed. As the waitress approached, Marilyn put her hand up.

"No need for menus. We'll have two pizzas—one meat, one veggie and a pitcher of beer with five glasses."

"Nice to see she hasn't changed," I whispered to Nina. She giggled and Marilyn raised her eyebrow at me.

"Causing trouble already, Mona Lisa?" she asked.

"No, ma'am."

"Ma'am?" Ro asked. "Is that something you picked up down south? Next thing you know she'll be saying ya'll."

"Very funny, Ro. Let's cut to the chase. I hear you and Charlie are dating again," I blurted out.

She gasped. "Who told you?"

The other three looked down.

"Does it matter?" I asked. "We all know. I want the details."

"Yes, we're dating, but I want to keep it quiet. It's going well and I don't want to jinx it."

"Why don't you want to tell Chick and Ma?" Nina asked.

"Because if it doesn't work out, they'll have a stroke. I don't want to get their hopes up."

"Is it weird dating your husband?" Marilyn asked.

"It was at first," Ro admitted. "We were both nervous, but now we have fun together. We forgot how to do that. We go into the city and walk around. We went hiking in the mountains. I enjoy being with him again."

"So, have you done it?" I couldn't help asking.

"Geez, Mona Lisa. You're as bad as Noni," Marilyn admonished.

"What can I say? She taught me well. So, yes or no?" I asked again.

"Yes, you moron. Many times. Satisfied?" Ro asked.

I smiled and said, "Very. It's good to know someone in this family is doing well in that department."

"What about you?" Nina asked.

"I've had a few dates and none of them memorable, except if you count the guy who had to be taken from our date in an ambulance. That was probably the most exciting one. Seems he had a nut allergy and thought pesto would be a good entrée choice. At least I didn't have to do mouth-to-mouth on him."

We traded stories for the next hour or so when out of the corner of my eye, I saw Dante Colletti being seated. He was alone and I felt the sudden urge to say hello to him. I excused myself from my sisters and walked by him, pretending not to see him.

"Mona Lisa?"

I smiled before turning around.

"Dante? Sorry, I walked right past you. How are you?"

"I'm well," he replied. "What about you? Have you moved back or are you here for a visit?"

"Just a visit. I missed everyone and came up for a few days."

"I saw your sister not too long ago."

"She told me. The girls are around the corner. We're having a reunion lunch and catching up."

"I didn't mean to keep you," he said.

"That's fine. I'm glad I ran into you. I felt bad about our last … I'm not even sure what to call it, but it was an awful time for me, and I apologize for being so rude. It had nothing to do with you."

"I understand."

I stood there a moment, butterflies in my stomach,

wanting to talk more but not knowing what to say.

I hugged him and said, "It was really nice to see you again, Dante."

"You too."

I turned to head to the restroom when he tapped my arm.

"How long are you in town for?" he asked.

"Five days," I replied.

"Would you like to have coffee or a drink now that the timing is better?" he asked with a grin.

"I'd like that. How about tomorrow?"

"Great. I can pick you up," he offered.

"Oh, no. Chick would have a field day with this. Give me your number and I'll figure out a way for us to meet up."

He wrote his number on a napkin and pressed it into my palm with a lingering squeeze that sent a tingle up my spine.

Suddenly, it was great to be home.

Chapter 52

I needed an accomplice if I was going to meet Dante without Chick or Ma finding out so I sat through the rest of lunch deciding which sister would be the best for the job. In the end, it was an easy choice. Nina was someone I could always count on, and I knew she wouldn't make a big deal out of my date, so I waited until we got home, followed her into the hall and pulled her into my old room.

I put my finger to my lips and said, "I need your help."

Her eyes widened.

"Relax. I need you to cover for me. Remember, Dante Colletti?"

"The guy Chick tried to fix you up with?" she questioned.

"Yes. I saw him today at lunch and he asked me out, but I need you to pretend I'm doing something with you."

"Okay. Why do you need to hide it?"

I stared at her in response until a knowing look crossed her face.

"All I need is for Chick to find out and I would never hear the end of it. He had us married and living next door before I had the chance to meet the guy. Imagine if he knew we were seeing each other. Besides, I'm curious and it's just coffee."

Nina smiled.

"What?" I asked.

"I hope you fall in love with him and move back."

198

"You're a hopeless romantic, Nina. Please don't tell anyone about this. Like I said, it's no big deal and I want to keep it that way."

"It would definitely be a big deal to Chick. So what time are we getting together tomorrow?" she asked.

"Let's say ten and then Dante and I can have breakfast, and it won't interfere with Sunday dinner. Coffee doesn't give you enough to do. I think it will be less awkward with a meal. Don't you think?"

"Definitely. I'll pick you up at 9:30 and drop you off with Dante. Call me when you're done. No one will suspect a thing."

"Aren't you the sly one?" I asked.

A loud knock on the door caused us both to jump.

"Chick's looking for you two," Marilyn called through the door.

I shook my head. "Some things never change."

We made our way into the living room where Chick was holding court with my mother and sisters.

"Nice of you to join us, girls," Chick admonished.

"I didn't know you called a family meeting," I replied.

"Sorry," Nina answered.

"This isn't a meeting, Mona Lisa. Thanks to you and your new life, I never have all my girls together at the same time, and I thought I'd enjoy it while my memory is still intact," Chick said.

"What's wrong with your memory?" Marilyn asked. "Are you keeping something from us?" She turned to my mother and asked, "Is he sick?"

"Oh, for crying out loud, nothing is wrong with him. He's being dramatic," my mother replied before slapping the top of Chick's head. "You need to stop overreacting, Marilyn," she continued. "I swear. I don't know where you get it from."

The rest of us covered our mouths or put our heads down so she wouldn't see our smirks.

"I see you smiling, girls," she said. "One day, I'm not going to be here anymore and you'll be sorry you made fun of me."

"Who's being a drama queen now?" Chick asked.

My mother responded with another whack. "You better quit while you're ahead, Chick," she warned.

"What time is dinner tomorrow?" I asked trying to change the subject.

My parents looked at me as if I had shaved my head and joined the Hare Krishna's.

"Are you kidding me?" Chick asked in disgust.

"Mona Lisa, I realize you no longer live here, but I find it hard to believe that two months in Georgia has erased a lifetime of family dinners. We eat at one like we always have."

"You are so disrespectful," Chick chimed in before he and my mother retreated to the kitchen.

"Jeez, I was trying to change the subject. I think I'll stop by the church and make my confession. Bless me Father for I have sinned. I forgot what time Sunday dinner was."

My mother called from the kitchen, "I heard that. You can talk to Father Flanagan after Mass in the morning. I'm sure he'd love to hear your laundry list of sins."

Great. I can start with the fact that I'm skipping Mass and lying about who I'll be with. Dante better be worth risking my salvation for.

Chapter 53

I was able to appease my parents and my conscience by getting up early and attending Mass. It was the speedy Mass—no music or singing, and I was out of there in thirty-five minutes thanks to a short sermon by Father Flanagan. I said a quick hello to him and made my escape in case my crazy mother had actually called to tell on me.

The church was only three blocks from home and I enjoyed the walk back thinking about my breakfast date. I had almost an hour to get ready. I wanted to look good but didn't want to arouse suspicion. I was hoping Ma and Chick would still be asleep but knew I was kidding myself. When I opened the door, they were up, dressed and having coffee.

Chick was still holding a grudge and didn't acknowledge my presence. I took a deep breath and realized that I'd never understand my dad. He whines because I don't live here anymore and then when I'm here, he gets mad and ignores me. There was no pleasing him

"How was Mass?" my mother asked.

I wanted to say enlightening, but I held my tongue and said, "Fine" to avoid getting in more trouble with my parents. "Father Flanagan says hello," I added hoping to score a few points.

"Good."

I stood there for a minute and then poured a cup of coffee for myself. I added my cream and sugar, and when I couldn't take the silence anymore, I said, "I'm going to change for breakfast with Nina."

"I don't know why you have to waste money on food when there is plenty to eat here."

There was no winning this one.

"I know, Ma. I want to spend some time alone with Nina. I miss her."

My mother's face softened into a smile.

"And she misses you. You're a good sister, Mona Lisa. Have fun."

I felt a huge pang of guilt, and for a nanosecond, I thought about coming clean with my mother, but quickly came to my senses and said, "I will."

                              * * * *

I couldn't handle any more lies, so I kept an eye out for Nina and ran out to her before she had a chance to get out of the car. I opened the door and shut it as if I had robbed a bank.

"Let's go," I ordered. "You can see them later. The guilt is going to give me a heart attack," I said.

"We'll corroborate our stories on the way home. I had pancakes. You had an omelet. No one will suspect a thing unless you come home with a hickey on your neck," Nina replied.

I laughed. "You're starting to sound like me."

"I learned from the master."

"I'll take that as a compliment. Ma and Chick might not agree, but I do."

"They still think I'm that shy five-year-old who was afraid to go to kindergarten. They treat me like an infant."

"Oh, Nina. Get used to it. They're not going to change. We'll always be little girls to them."

"Sometimes it makes me crazy. The other night Ma called to tell me I was tired and needed to go to bed. When I answered the phone, she said, 'Why are you still up?'. When I said it was because I had to answer the phone, she told me not to be fresh. I feel like I can't win."

"And you never will. That's why you're driving me to my date. Some things are better kept from them. It's easier that way."

"I hope I don't act like that when I have kids."

"I do, too but let's face it, it's going to happen. Thirty years from now, my daughter may be sneaking out to meet a guy her father tried to fix her up with."

We both laughed as Nina pulled into the parking lot of the coffee house. Dante was there and I caught him checking his watch.

"Wish me luck," I told Nina.

"Have fun. I'm gonna call Ma and give her my report."

"Don't you dare and don't go too far in case I need to make a hasty exit."

"Call me and I'll come running."

I got out of the car and walked over to the entrance of the restaurant where Dante was waiting. I was about to give him grief about checking his watch when he leaned in and brushed his lips against mine with a light kiss. It took my breath away and I realized that heaven was over-rated.

Chapter 54

Dante and I were led to a booth where we sat opposite from one another. We both ordered coffee and when the waitress left us alone, he sat back, crossed his arms and a look of unbridled satisfaction crossed his face.

"What are you so smug about?" I asked.

"I'm in shock, really that you're here. I think the last time we saw each other you threatened to cut my tongue out if I so much as said hello to you ever again."

"I think I said I'd cut your eyes out if you ever looked at me again. Seriously, was I that bad?" I asked.

"Close, but you were going through a rough time so I forgive you. Anyway, I'm glad you're here."

"Me, too," I admitted.

We each glanced over the menu and when the waitress brought our coffee, we ordered.

When she left us, Dante asked, "So where do your parents think you are right now?"

"Here, but with my sister, Nina."

"Is she the one who dropped you off?"

"Yes, and aren't you the observant one? It was a very stealthy operation. Lots of planning and lying, which is hard to do right after attending Mass."

"Yet, you pulled it off. Maybe you missed your calling as a C.I.A. agent," he said as he raised his coffee cup to cheer my efforts.

I clinked my mug to his and said, "I'm fine in my current profession. This was a little stressful, but unless you'd like Chick to start planning our wedding, I think it's best to keep him in the dark."

"For right now anyway. Eventually, we'll have to tell him and your mother," Dante quipped.

"I think we should see how breakfast goes before we start making out the guest list."

"I see the south hasn't changed you."

"You know what they say about taking the Jersey out of the girl, but honestly it's been good for me. I'm still as sarcastic as always."

"Tell me about your life these days. I fly into Atlanta sometimes and think it's a great city. The people seem friendly."

"I know, aren't they? At first, I was a little distrustful of everyone, but now I really like it. Not that I don't love Jersey, but it's a different attitude down there and it was what I needed."

"Are you working?"

"Yes. Vinnie, who owns the salon I worked at up here has a cousin down there who gave me a job. She's great, and my two roommates both work there, so it's all good. What about you? Flying much?"

"I've hardly been home. Sometimes I wonder why I have an apartment here. My mother has been pushing for me to give it up and move back in with her, but there's no way."

"That's a relief, because after Joey, I only date men

who live away from home."

"Glad I qualify."

The waitress brought our meals and after the brief interruption, Dante asked, "Are you seeing anyone special in Georgia?"

"Let me think ... special? No. Interesting? Most definitely. I'm thinking of turning my dating experiences into a sitcom, but I'm not sure people will believe my stories."

"It can't be that bad," Dante countered.

"Really? One day, I'll tell you all the gory details, but for now, let's say it hasn't been dull. And yourself? How's the dating world treating you?" I asked, not sure if I wanted to know the answer.

"Like an outsider. I haven't had the time. Since my grandmother passed away, I've spent every free minute with my mom trying to settle her estate. There's so much paperwork. It's really involved when you die."

"As hard as it is for you, I'm sure it was worse for your grandmother."

Dante laughed, "I guess you're right. I'm surprised I didn't get struck by lightning just now. My grandmother was some sort of Italian fortune teller. She was always having feelings about people and loved to go to psychics. It drove my mother crazy."

"My grandmother loves to push my mom's buttons, too. I'm sure you noticed her love of the Yiddish language. I think it's hilarious."

"Of course you do," Dante remarked. "That's what I like most about you."

"What? The fact that I like to see my grandmother goof on my mother?"

"No, your sense of humor. You have a unique way of looking at things and you make me laugh. That's important."

Wow.

"This might be a first. I think you're at a loss for words," he remarked.

"I guess so. I've always thought my quick wit was an asset, but the guys I've dated never seemed to agree. Even my ex-fiancé didn't think I was funny. I would crack a joke and he'd look at me straight-faced and say, 'I'm laughing on the inside, Mona Lisa.' Good thing I didn't marry him, huh?"

"I'm glad you didn't," he answered as he reached across the table to grasp my hand.

The warmth of his touch brought a chill to my spine and a smile to my lips. We continued to talk and relaxed into a fun and easy conversation. I lost track of time and panicked when Nina appeared at our table.

"Mona Lisa, I've called you ten times." She turned to Dante and said, "Hi. I'm Nina and we have to go."

"What's the rush?" I asked getting the answer from my watch. "Shit. We're going to be late for dinner. I'm in enough trouble with Chick already." I began to scramble, looking for my purse and feeling like a teenager who had missed curfew. Nina walked away to give us a moment to say goodbye.

"Dante, it was wonderful. Call me?" I asked.

He answered with a long, hard kiss that almost brought me to my knees. I caught my breath, stared into his eyes and pulled him in for another kiss. I was already late. What difference would another minute or two make?

Chapter 55

As soon as Nina and I got in the car, I began to concoct our story.

"We can say we got to talking and forgot about the time."

"Why don't you tell them the truth?"

"That would be the worst possible thing we could do," I said, though I doubted Nina's ability to pull off the lie. "They will go crazy if they find out I was with Dante."

"It doesn't matter what we say. They're gonna be pissed that we're so late," Nina admitted.

"I'll think of something. Let me do the talking and hopefully, they won't go ballistic." As we approached the back door, I said, "We can do this."

As I turned the knob, all eyes turned to us.

"I'm sorry. It was totally my fault. I made Nina take me shopping and I lost track of time. They don't have any good stores in Atlanta," I lied.

Marilyn walked by me and whispered, "Yeah, right. Did you leave the bags in the car?"

I glared at her and she quickly lost the smirk on her face.

Chick said, "Mona Lisa, I expect this kind of behavior out of you, but must you corrupt your little sister?"

"Jeez, Chick, you act like I committed murder. Ma, I'm sorry I wasn't here to help get dinner ready. I'll do all of the dishes."

My mother ignored me as she handed plates to my sisters. They avoided my eyes as they brought the food to the table.

I put down my purse and walked to the stove to carry the pasta to the table, but my mother said, "Go sit. You're a guest."

Ouch! I started to protest, but felt my eyes welling and went into the dining room as I was told. Noni and Marshall were seated with my brothers-in-law and I slid onto the seat next to hers.

"You better watch it. The warden's gonna put you in solitary," Noni said quietly.

"That would be better than having to sit through this dinner. He's pissed."

"Were you two at breakfast this whole time?" she asked.

"I was, but not with Nina. I was with Dante Colletti and if you say a word, I will put you in a home. And not a nice one, either."

Noni chuckled, "You are full of surprises, Mona Lisa."

"And I'm also in deep shit, so you better keep your mouth closed."

The girls and my mother joined us, and we waited for Chick to sit. I was relieved he did not mention my multiple acts of disrespect while giving the blessing, however as soon as we finished the sign of the cross, he started in on me.

"Mona Lisa, can you explain to all of us why you felt it

necessary to put shopping above being with your family for dinner?"

Suddenly, I felt like I was going to burst into tears. Why did I allow my father to turn me back into a child? I tried to come up with an answer that would satisfy him when Nina spoke.

"Chick, it was my fault. I made Mona Lisa go with me to the city. I wanted to get some tickets as a surprise for Nick and it took longer than I thought it would. I'm really sorry."

The look on Chick's face softened because he never got mad at Nina. He still referred to her as the baby and she could do no wrong in his eyes.

"And then I stopped in a few shops and we ended up getting back late," I added.

"No harm done," Chick admitted. "We're all together now, and Mona Lisa is home, so let's eat."

I guess that was his way of apologizing for practically setting me up before the firing squad. I was thankful I picked Nina to be my co-conspirator because she saved me from excommunication from the family. I was relieved, but also annoyed. Everything was okay now because the baby lost track of time and it wasn't Mona Lisa being selfish.

We ate in silence for a few moments when my brother-in-law Dom asked, "What's it like in Atlanta, Mona Lisa?"

"It's great. Really hot now, though. I had to get out of there for a few days."

"So that's the reason you came for a visit?" my mother

asked.

"No. I missed all of you," I answered sensing my mother's sadness, but feeling like the family outcast.

"Isn't that nice," my mother commented.

"Yes, it is, Ange," Noni replied. "I'm thrilled Mona Lisa came to visit and you should be too."

"Of course I'm happy she's here," my mother said to Noni, "but she has to understand the world does not revolve around her. She's always been your favorite, Ma. You will defend her to the death."

"I'm in the room, you know," I interrupted. "Can we talk about something else? How's your new job, Mike?"

How did I always manage to cause such disruption to the family? I was going to have to toe the line for the rest of my visit. That meant I wasn't going to be able to have another date with Dante. Then I thought of our kiss, and I knew I would have to figure out a way to see him again before I left. Selfish Mona Lisa would do it, but the question, was would she get caught?

Chapter 56

Somehow I made it through dinner, but in the back of my mind, I was trying to figure out how I could see Dante again. I had less than forty-eight hours until I went back to Georgia and I was going to have to be very careful so that I didn't cause another international incident. I planned to spend Sunday evening with my parents, but had to speak with Dante and hatch a plan.

When everyone left and the dishes were done, I said, "Hey, Ma. I have to call my roommate and make sure she's clear on the time to pick me up at the airport. What's going on tomorrow?" I asked casually.

"Some of us have to work," Chick remarked dryly without taking his eyes off of the television.

"I have a painting class tomorrow at the Center, but I can skip it if you like," she answered.

Perfect! "No need. What time is it? I thought I'd visit Noni again before heading back."

"Eleven. I can drop you off on my way."

Damn! "Let me talk to her. She mentioned something about sending Marshall for me."

"Whatever Noni and you want. The rest of us are just here to serve you," she replied.

I was going to let that remark slide. I went to my room and shut the door. I grabbed my phone, but all of a sudden I was nervous. What if he didn't want to see me? I took a deep breath and dialed. He answered after one ring.

"Hi, Mona Lisa. I'm glad you called."

"Really?" I asked.

He laughed. "Yes, really. I had a nice time with you. Can I see you again?"

"I had a small window of time open up tomorrow. Are you available around eleven in the morning? I'm sorry it's such short notice, but both of my parents will be busy then and I think it's best to keep this under wraps."

"For now," Dante added.

"Yes, for now," I conceded. "Does eleven work for you?"

"Sure. How long do you have?"

"Probably two hours and I cannot be late. I'm still paying for today's lapse in time management."

"Seriously?"

"Come on, you met my parents. Guilt is our family pastime."

He laughed. "You're not alone. My mother told me yesterday that grandchildren increase life expectancy. How do you answer that?"

"Take a deep breath and bite your tongue. It's how I've survived my trip," I admitted.

"Great strategy, unless of course, you like to eat or talk. Hard to do with a bruised tongue."

"Don't I know it. I'd love to talk more, but they're going to send the troops out looking for me if I don't surface soon. Want to pick me up at my house? The coast should be clear by then."

"Great. I'm looking forward to seeing you again."

"Me, too," I said before I hung up.

I immediately dialed Noni's number. Unlike Dante, she took forever to answer and when she did, I was out of patience.

"I need your help," I said not allowing her to even say hello.

"You got it, kiddo. What do you need?' she asked.

"I have another date with Dante and I need you to cover for me. I'm going to tell Ma I'm having lunch with you and Marshall, okay?"

"Sure. You must like him a lot, huh?"

I thought about it for a second and said, "I guess I do. I've dated so many lunatics in the past few months, I never thought I'd find someone normal. And Dante's normal and nice."

"Wow, wait until Chick finds out about this. There's gonna be no living with him. You know you're going to have to name one of your kids Chick. Or Carmine," she added.

"I forget he has a real first name and there's no way I'm naming anything Chick. Not even a dog."

"Carmine it is," Noni concluded.

"Listen up, Noni. It's only a date. I'll let you know when you can put the announcement in the paper. Thanks for helping me out, though," I said.

"Anything for you, Mona Lisa, you know that."

"Back at ya, Noni. If you ever need anything …."

"Don't get all sappy on me. We gotta stay sharp if we're going to survive in this family."

"No kidding. I need you to be especially sharp about tomorrow. You're sending Marshall to get me at eleven o'clock and we're having lunch at your place, got it?"

"Hey, I have the easy part. You need to set an alarm so you're not late again."

"I will and thanks."

"Anytime and tell Dante I'll babysit little Chick whenever you two want."

Chapter 57

I was incredibly nervous about my second date with
Dante and had no one to talk to about it, so I tried to keep
busy by doing little chores around the house. I only succeeded in irritating my mother.

"Mona Lisa, what are you doing to that toaster oven?"

"I'm cleaning it. I thought I'd do a few things to help
you out."

"So, what? I don't know how to clean my own house?
You move away and suddenly you're Heloise?"

"No, Ma. I'm cleaning out the crumbs, that's all. I
thought this would be appreciated."

"Oh, my gosh. What is that smell?"

"I'm cleaning the coffee maker with vinegar."

"For crying out loud, what has gotten into you?"

"Nothing. I wanted to do something nice."

"You're nice to people by insulting the cleanliness of
their home. I thought the south would improve your manners, but it seems to have made you more uppity."

More uppity? She thought I was uppity before? "I'm
sorry, Ma. I was trying to be helpful."

"Go take a shower and get dressed. You'll be late for
lunch with Noni. She may think it's fine when you run late,
but Marshall is a nice man and doesn't deserve to be kept
waiting."

I wanted to say Noni was nice and she didn't deserve
bad behavior, but I said, "Sorry," instead, as it seemed to be

the theme of my trip—The Mona Lisa Apology Tour.

* * * *

When I finished dressing, I opened the door from my bedroom in the hopes that everyone would be gone for the day, but my mother was standing right outside.

"I need to get my art supplies out of your room. You took forever in there. I hope I'm not late. Maybe I should stay home and go to Noni's with you."

I started to sweat and said, "No!" a bit too loudly.

My mother looked hurt and said, "I wouldn't want to intrude on your time with my mother."

"I didn't mean it that way, Ma. You always put Chick and us girls first, and now you need to do things for yourself. I would feel bad if I was the reason you missed your class."

She smiled and seemed appeased by my answer. Score one for me.

"I do want to go, so help me carry my things to the car."

She handed me a canvas along with a bag of brushes and paints and said, "Take this for me."

I carried her supplies to the garage and placed them gently on the passenger's seat as my mother got into the driver's side and started the engine.

"Have fun," I said before closing the door and heading back to the kitchen.

I sat at the table and took a deep breath hoping to slow my pulse down. I heard the doorbell and immediately my heart started to race again. I walked to the door but first checked my teeth and my armpits for any last minute hygiene issues. I opened the door and was relieved to see Dante's confident smile.

"Pretty bold move getting out of the car. I can hear old lady Spagetini now. 'Angie, I saw that Colletti boy at your house when you and Chick were out. I certainly hope Mona Lisa knows how damaging that can be to her reputation,' I said closing the door behind me not giving Dante the chance to come in.

"Wow. You have some imagination," he said as he opened the car door for me.

"Imagination, nothing. That old bag used to love to get me in trouble."

"Should we wave to her as we leave?"

"No need. Ma says she has really bad cataracts. The good thing is she can still drive. Isn't that comforting?"

"If I didn't know any better, I'd swear you make these stories up," Dante admitted.

"They're too crazy to be made up. It's just my life, Dante. Have I scared you off yet?"

"It will take more than that, Mona Lisa. Do you want to know where we're going?"

"Sure. Remember I have a curfew."

"We're not going far. There's a great spot for a picnic along this trail where I like to hike. It's out of the way and no nosy neighbors will see us."

"Sounds great." We sat in silence for a moment then I

asked, "So when do you work?"

"I was supposed to work today, but I got someone to cover my flight. I was optimistic about the possibility of seeing you again. I fly to Orlando tomorrow."

"I was hoping you might be going to Atlanta."

"I can't do anything about tomorrow's flight, but I'll work on getting a flight there sometime soon," he said as he parked the car. "If you want me to," he added.

I answered him by leaning in and kissing him with every ounce of my being. Dante looked shocked then came back for some more.

After a minute, he said, "I think we better get out of the car."

I nodded, and we gathered up the picnic basket and blanket and walked a few yards into the woods. We stopped at a spot next to a stream and I spread out the blanket and sat.

"It's beautiful here. I can't believe I never knew about this spot before."

"I love to get up early and come here for a run and watch the sunrise. We'll have to do that next time you visit."

Dante opened the basket and had three different kinds of cheese, crackers, sandwiches and fruit. It was an incredible feast.

"So did you pick out all this stuff yourself?" I asked suspiciously.

He rubbed his chin as he contemplated his answer.

"Sorry to say that I had help. There's a specialty market down on Somerset and the sales woman there put it together for me. I have some wine, too," he said pulling a bottle out of the basket.

"I think I'll pass. Based on that kiss in the car, I need to keep my wits about me. Plus, I need to keep an eye on the clock," I replied.

"I feel like I'm out with a married woman."

"I understand. I feel like I'm cheating on my parents. I hate that I have to keep this from them, but they always take things too far. If I say I had a date, they want to know if it's serious. As far as they're concerned, my whole life is a series of steps which have to lead to the altar and then the maternity ward. It's tough to live up to their expectations."

"I get it, but I've been wondering where we go from here. We live 800 miles apart. That doesn't make for an easy relationship."

"No ... but can't we just see what happens? Do we have to know how things will be a year or even a month from now?" I asked.

This time he pulled me into him and answered with a kiss.

Chapter 58

At ten minutes before one, Dante and I were back in his car and I was on my way home. I was sad at the prospect of not seeing him for a while.

As if he could read my mind, he said, "I know it will be tough not being together, but we can still talk. Do you ever video chat?"

"We tried a few times during the Sunday dinner, but its gets so awkward when there are ten conversations going on in the background. It's easier for them to pass the phone around and I talk to whoever is in the mood that day. We can try it, though. I guess that means I'm going to have to put on makeup before hand."

"Don't do it on my account. I like the natural look."

"Aren't you the perfect man?" I teased. "It's too bad I wasn't in the right frame of mind when we first met." *Why was I so anxious? Maybe because I was starting a relationship with someone who lived in another state. And not just another state, but five or six states away depending on how you went. Do two dates make a relationship?*

"Don't overthink things, Mona Lisa. If it's meant to be, it will work out and then your father will take all of the credit."

"You said it. I'll try to relax. I was thinking I'd like for you to drop me at my grandmother's. Then I won't be a total liar."

"Sure. Just tell me where to go."

"Turn left up here on Essex and then take the third right."

Dante followed my instructions and within minutes we were in Noni's driveway.

I turned to him and said, "Thank you for a fun weekend. Why don't you call me tomorrow night once you get settled in Orlando?"

He touched my cheek and said, "I will and Mona Lisa, I have a good feeling about us."

He kissed me gently.

I dragged my weakened legs out of his car and onto Noni's porch. I turned and waved before I rang the doorbell.

Noni opened the door and said, "You've got it bad, kiddo."

"Am I that transparent?" I asked following her into the house.

She sat on the couch and said, "Yes."

I sat beside her and said, "My head is spinning and I needed to come by for a bit before I go back to my last night in the loony bin."

"Marshall and I are coming for dinner, not that I'm not happy to spend extra time with you."

"I can't talk about Dante in front of them. Chick will go crazy."

"What's going on?"

"I don't know. We had two dates and he's pretty amazing, and now I'm going back to Georgia and who knows when I'll see him again."

"Anything else?" Noni laughed.

"Well, yes because I could have gone out with him when Chick set us up and I might not have moved to Georgia and things would be so much easier."

"Easy is just a word, Mona Lisa. Life is complicated and fun and sad and happy, and I suggest you get over yourself and stop thinking about what could have been. Take some time to get to know each other. Stop worrying and live a little."

"I know you're right. Why can't I figure these things out on my own?"

"Because that's my job. I like to think of myself as your guardian angel—a guardian angel with attitude."

"I think that sums you up. So, Noni, you better protect me at the last supper tonight. I need to leave on a good note."

"I've got your back, kiddo. I only ask for one thing. I want to be there when you tell your parents about Dante because that will be one show worth watching."

Chapter 59

As I sat at the table for my last family dinner before heading back to Atlanta, I had a difficult time paying attention to the conversation. I wanted to hole up in my bedroom and talk with Dante. Not that I was love-struck and couldn't be without him, but it was more my control freak need to know what was going to happen next. Plus, I was developing a major crush on him and wanted to know what he was thinking, so yes, my thoughts were obsessively revolving around Dante Colletti and my wandering mind surely did not go unnoticed.

"Earth to Mona Lisa," Chick announced.

I looked up and said, "Sorry, Chick, what did you say?"

"Since you're leaving tomorrow, it would be nice if your mind was here with your body."

I opened my mouth to defend myself but slumped back in my chair knowing I was already defeated. Noni knowingly patted my leg.

"I was asking everyone to raise their glass to Rosie and Charlie, who have come to their senses and realized that marriage vows are not disposable. *Salute!*"

The cheers were followed by a huge gulp of Chianti on my part.

"And," Chick continued, "here's to Mona Lisa's visit, though short and not enough time spent with her parents. *Salute!*"

This time, I finished my glass. If he brought up my lack of a husband prospect, I was going to have to open another bottle. Thankfully, the spotlight was removed when Charlie stood to address the family.

"Chick and Ma, I love you both. The past few months have been tough and I missed you two almost as much as I missed Ro."

What a suck-up Charlie had turned into, I thought as I caught Sophia rolling her eyes in my direction. We both suppressed our smiles.

"I am so grateful to be back with my beautiful wife and even more so to be back with the family."

I looked at Soph again who made a gagging gesture. I had to put my hand over my mouth to cover my grin. This time Noni gave me an elbow to the ribs, so I pulled it together.

Charlie continued, "And if getting back together wasn't enough ...."

"I'm pregnant," Ro called out stealing Charlie's thunder.

He looked like he was about to cry, but got a grip when squeals of joy erupted from my mother. We all stood taking turns hugging and patting Ro's belly and asking questions. The sisters huddled around her.

"When did you find out?" I asked.

"Why didn't you tell me?" Marilyn asked with a hint of hurt.

"I found out a couple of weeks ago. Charlie and I still

had to work out a few things between us. We were moving in the right direction but were hardly rock solid. I was scared."

"Are you good now?" Nina asked.

"Yeah, we're pretty good and we still have some time to focus on our relationship before the baby gets here."

Chick broke into our little circle and hugged Ro. "Thank you for giving your mother and me another grandchild. My mind and heart are at ease now." Then he fixed his gaze on Nina and me.

Here it comes.

"Now, as for you two," he said cornering us. "Nina, it's time you and Nick made it official. If you want, I'll talk to him."

Nina's eyes bugged out of her head.

"Chick, please don't," she pleaded. We are talking about it, okay?"

"I don't want to butt in. I'm here if you need me."

I almost choked at his words. He didn't want to butt in? He never butted out.

"Mona Lisa, I hope you don't mind, I invited someone over to meet you."

I had a fleeting thought it might be Dante, but that dream was quickly squashed when he said, "His name is Primo Manganella, but he goes by Bucky."

"Geez, Chick, where did you find this guy, Ellis Island?" I asked in horror. "He sounds like he's a hundred."

"He's a little older than you, but I think his stability

will be good for you."

"How much older?" I asked.

Chick paused and said, "I'm not sure, but he should be here any minute."

As if on cue, the doorbell rang and Chick announced, "I invited a friend to come by and meet Mona Lisa. Everyone be on your best behavior."

As he went to greet his friend, I held my breath. I was sad, then mad when he returned with a man who looked like he would be closer in age to Noni. He looked to be about sixty, with a mustache dyed to match the jet-black hair on his head. He was able to walk on his own which was a plus, but he was also a good forty pounds overweight. I could feel all eyes watching as Chick escorted Bucky to me.

"Mona Lisa, this is my friend Bucky. Bucky, my beautiful daughter Mona Lisa."

He grabbed my hand and kissed it. I had sunk to an all-time low.

"You two sit," Chick ordered as he pointed to the sofa. "I'll help your mother with the dishes."

In all my years, I'm not sure Chick ever helped my mother with the dishes, I thought as we did as we were told. I looked for help and gave Sophia the "save-me" eyes. She started to make her way over when Chick grabbed her arm and shook his head.

I decided to play along and try to have some fun.

"Tell me about yourself, Bucky."

"I'm a simple man, Mona Lisa. My wife and I moved here from Sicily twenty years ago, and we had a good life until she passed last year."

And, so you're looking for a replacement? "Do you have any children?" I asked.

"Sadly, no, but I am hoping to remarry and start a family."

I can't even go there. "Good for you. I guess my father told you I live in Atlanta. I'm very happy there."

"I think I might like it there as well. The warm weather would be good for my arthritis."

What? Great. He wants a wife and a nurse. "I'm sure you're a great guy, Bucky, but I'm not available." I scrambled to think of something and blurted out, "My parents don't know this, but I'm thinking of becoming a nun."

He made the sign of the cross and said, "God forgive me. I had no idea."

"No, don't give it another thought. Nobody knows and I'd appreciate it if you didn't say anything to Chick just yet. It's still in the early stages."

"Of course," he said, "but what do I say to your father about us?"

I thought for a moment and replied, "Tell him it would be too difficult with me in Atlanta." *And you can add you don't want to marry someone who will be spending eternity in hell for lying and impersonating a nun.*

Chapter 60

I didn't sleep well on my last night and was groggy on the drive to the airport the next day. My parents insisted on taking me, even though I would have loved some time to talk alone with Sophia. I told her bits and pieces, but I wanted to have a long chat with her about Dante. We planned to talk that night, and I was grateful to spend a little more time with Ma and Chick, even if it was a thirty-minute car ride.

"I'm sorry I didn't hit it off with your friend, Chick," I lied.

"He's like an old man. Afraid of a relationship because of a little distance."

Like an old man. He is an old man.

"You'll find someone, honey," my mom reassured me.

"I know, Ma, but I'm really happy. I don't need a husband."

I heard her suck in her breath.

Chick replied, "That attitude will turn you into a cat lady, Mona Lisa."

"Maybe that's my destiny, Chick. Except for the fact that I'm allergic to cats. Maybe I'll start a new trend. Turtles? Fish? I don't know. It will have to be something without fur. I'll keep you posted."

"Mona Lisa, men don't appreciate sarcasm in women," my mother advised. "It makes you seem hard."

I chose not to answer and instead, opted to change the

subject. "When can you two come down and visit? There are a lot of great restaurants. We can go see a Falcons game if you want."

"You know I only watch the Jets or the Giants," Chick reminded me.

"I know that Chick, but maybe you can step out of your box a little. Hell, I can get tickets for when the Falcons play the Jets or the Giants."

"We'll see."

"Ma, you and Noni can take a girls trip and come down. That would be so much fun."

"Mona Lisa, I'm married."

"So, you can't get away for a few days by yourself?"

"Hey, just because you're not married, don't go meddling in other people's marriage," Chick admonished.

"Sorry. It was only an idea. I'd love for you both to come visit and see where I live and work. I miss you guys."

"I'll check our calendar and see what we can do," my mom offered.

Thankfully there was no reprimand for moving away.

"That would be great. Fall in Atlanta is supposed to be fabulous," I said.

We approached the exit for the airport and my heart hurt a little at the thought of leaving. "Terminal B, Chick," I said.

"Got it."

He pulled up to the departure area and put the car in park.

"Don't get out," I said before leaning into the front seat and giving my father a kiss. "I love you, Chick."

"You, too and don't forget to have your tires rotated."

My mother got out of the car and opened my door. I stood and she hugged me tightly. I could not stop my tears.

"I love you, Ma. I miss you already."

"I love you, too and I promise, we'll see you soon," she said wiping the tears from my face.

She got back in the car and we all waved. I opened my purse to look for a tissue when I felt a hand on my shoulder. I turned and Dante greeted me with a long, hard kiss. When he released me, I looked back to see my mother staring open-mouthed as they drove off.

Chapter 61

"What the hell was that?" I blurted out.

"I thought you'd be happy to see me," Dante replied.

"My mother! She saw you. My parents are going to kill me."

"Don't you think you're being a little paranoid, Mona Lisa?" he asked.

"Are you kidding me? I spent this entire trip lying to them and making up stories so they wouldn't find out about us. I am so screwed."

"Is it that horrible if they know we've been out a few times?" he asked.

"Yes … no …. I don't know. They get so wrapped up in my life and my lack of a husband. Whenever I go out with someone, Chick starts calling the VFW hall to check for available dates."

Dante laughed.

"You think I'm exaggerating? Chick has the priest on retainer. You forget I made it all the way to the church. It killed my parents' peace of mind when I was left at the altar. An unmarried daughter is number three on my parents' list of stressors."

"They have an actual list?"

"Yes. One and two are fear of cancer and purgatory. In that order," I added.

"Wow. I thought you were making that up," Dante admitted.

"Cicciarellis do not kid about such things. One day, if you're lucky, I'll tell you what's on the rest of the list."

"I can't wait. Why don't we go in and you can call your parents," he suggested.

"No way. Not until I get safely back to Atlanta and have a few drinks in me."

"Mona Lisa, you're a mess."

"Yes I am, but it's part of my charm."

Dante kissed me lightly and said, "Yes it is."

"Want to come to Atlanta with me?" I asked with a grin.

"I wish, but I have to check in and get to work on the other side of the airport. I've been hanging out here waiting for you and I'm going to be late if I don't get going now."

He kissed me on the forehead and when I looked at him questioningly, he said, "I didn't know if any more of your relatives might be lurking around. Text me when you land so I know you got back okay."

I watched him disappear into the crowd and rolled my bag into the airport. I walked to the security area. There was no line, so I breezed through and was at my gate with time to spare. In fact, I had two hours to spare so I found a seat away from the other passengers and called Sophia.

"Hey," she answered. "You still in town?"

"I'm at the airport. I'm still on Cicciarelli time, so I'm here four hours before my flight."

"Seriously?" Sophia asked.

"No, you moron. I have two hours. Who gets to the

236

airport that early?" I asked.

"Ma and Chick," she replied. "What's up? Any last minute crises?"

"Of course there are. Dante was waiting for me at the airport. He surprised me with a kiss, and Ma saw us."

"Oh, my gosh. That's funny. You spent the whole time hiding him from them and they see you together at the airport."

"It's not funny. They're going to be even more pissed at me. As if that were even possible. It seemed like every word that came out of my mouth caused a fight. What am I going to do?" I whined.

"Get over it, Mona Lisa. If they get mad, they'll recover quickly. Chick will call Father Flanagan and set a date for the wedding, and all will be forgiven."

"That's what I'm afraid of. We've only been on a few dates and live so far apart. I don't want to get my hopes up, let alone theirs. I feel like I can't date anyone without them obsessing over whether or not it will lead to marriage."

"You know how much they worry about you being alone," she said.

"Yes, it's number three."

"I forgot about the list. Mona Lisa, you remember the craziest things."

"How can I forget? Chick loves to remind me about the dangers of too much stress. God forbid he ever has heart trouble. Forget that he thinks eating peppers and onions with his sausage makes it health food. My lack of a husband will be blamed."

"Wow, you're wound up today, aren't you?" Sophia challenged.

"They know how to get under my skin and I dread calling them when I get home."

"You'll survive. Call me after you talk to them and if I hear anything, I'll give you a heads-up. Do you feel any better?"

"Yes. Thanks for talking me down off the ledge, Soph. It was great to see you. I miss you."

"I miss you, too. Call me later."

I took a deep breath and closed my eyes. My shoulders began to relax and then it happened. My cell phone rang and the caller ID read Ma and Chick.

Chapter 62

I took a deep breath and answered the phone, "Hello?"

"Mona Lisa?" Ma asked in a soft voice.

"Who else would it be? You called my cell phone."

"You've got me all confused. I'm sure you know why I'm calling," she murmured.

"Ma, why are you whispering?"

"Because I don't want your father to hear. Hold on. Chick, I'll be in my art room if you need me. Mona Lisa, are you still there?"

"Yes, Ma."

"As I was saying, I want to talk to you. Since your father didn't see you make a public spectacle of yourself, I thought it best not to bother him."

I wasn't about to volunteer any information, but she wasn't going to ask, so we waited in silence for about thirty seconds until she caved.

"Are you going to tell me who that was mauling you at the airport?"

I laughed and then tried to cover it up with a cough. "This may seem funny to you, young lady, but it's embarrassing to watch your daughter practically have sex in public. Especially when she's never mentioned she's dating anyone unless of course you're in the habit of kissing total strangers."

"Wow. Okay, Ma. We were not having sex. It was just a kiss and it was not a stranger. It was Dante Colletti," I mumbled.

"Did you say Dante Colletti?" she asked in disbelief.

"Yes, but please don't go crazy and don't tell Chick," I begged. "I'm sorry."

"Sorry for what? Not having the decency to tell your parents you're dating someone? Sorry for sneaking around and lying? I assume you saw him while you were up here."

"Yes."

"I guess we have Dante to thank for your visit. Why else would you come home?" she asked, sounding hurt.

"Ma, that's not fair. I had no idea I would see Dante when I came home. I ran into him when the girls and I had lunch. We had two dates and that's it. I didn't want to tell you and Chick because I was afraid you would get all excited. We barely know each other and we live in different states, so it's going to be challenging at best."

"That was a pretty heavy kiss for someone you've only been out with twice."

There was no good response to that remark, so I said, "I like him a lot, but you have to promise me you and Chick won't be obsessing over this. I disappoint you both every time my relationships don't work out. I hate that and don't want to do it anymore."

"Mona Lisa, you don't disappoint us. We just don't want you to be alone. We want to know you will have someone to take care of you."

"I know. You worry."

"Number three," we both said in unison and then

laughed.

"Your father tends to get carried away when it comes to his girls. He does it because he loves you, but maybe I'll keep this tidbit of information to myself for right now. Would that be okay?" she asked.

"That would be great, Ma. I love you so much."

"I love you, too, Mona Lisa."

"He's a nice guy, Ma. I don't know when we'll see each other again, but we're taking it slow and I'll let you know when the baby is due."

"Mona Lisa, are you trying to kill me?"

I laughed, "Sorry, Ma. I couldn't resist. But seriously, forget about it for awhile and if things progress, I promise to let you know."

"Alright, but please don't let your father find out from someone else. He may seem like a tough guy to you, but he has feelings too."

"Point taken, Ma. And have I told you lately how much I appreciate you?" I asked.

"No, but if you're smart, you won't forget it. I better go now, I need to call Dante's mother and invite her over for dinner so we can discuss the wedding details."

My heart stopped beating for a second, but then I said, "Tell her hello. I've got to buy a home pregnancy test. Bye."

Chapter 63

As I slid the key into the lock of my apartment door, I suddenly felt exhausted. My trip had been physically and emotionally tiring, and I was looking forward to collapsing in my bed. The kitchen and living room were empty, so I walked into my room and collapsed on my bed. Amy appeared out of nowhere and plopped down next to me.

"Welcome back," she announced.

I nearly jumped off the bed.

"Geez, you scared the shit out of me."

"A couple of days in Jersey and your potty mouth comes right back, huh?"

"Listen, bitch, keep sneaking up on me like that and I'll show you Jersey. They renewed my badass card when I was up there."

"In your dreams, sister. You've been southernized. I'm surprised they let you back in the state."

"Let me back in? They named a street after me."

"You win," Amy conceded. "How was your trip?"

"Complicated."

"Great. I want all the details."

"Where to start," I contemplated aloud. "I ran into a guy my dad tried to fix me up with right after the 'Joey mess' and needless to say, I wasn't interested then. However, this time when our paths crossed something clicked. I snuck away for a few dates with him. Then my mother saw us kissing at the airport. At first, she was pissed I was sneaking around, but she's good with it and I guess I'm now in a long-distance relationship."

"Nice," Amy remarked as her face broke into a wide grin. "That all?"

"You idiot. Yes, that's all. What's new with you?"

"I don't know if you heard the news because my mother had it broadcast up and down the east coast, but I had a date with a Jewish doctor. So cliché of me, huh? And believe me, they are not easy to find."

I sat up. My interest was piqued. "How did you meet him?"

"It was fate. He had an appointment with Brightleigh for a haircut and she was running behind. He was in a hurry and I was free. The rest is what Yiddish fairy tales are made of."

"I guess the date was a good one."

"Oh, yeah. We've been out three nights in a row and as much as I hate to admit it, I like him a lot. He thinks I'm funny, which is amazing."

"You are funny and interesting. Any guy would be lucky to be dating you. Plus, you live in the same state. That's always a good thing."

"What's the status with you and this guy? Does he have a name?" Amy asked.

"His name is Dante and don't you dare make fun of him."

"I'd never dream of it. I wouldn't want the Don to come after me."

"You suck and what also sucks is that I don't know how this is supposed to work. Are we dating other people? Are we keeping it casual? He's calling me later, but it's the not knowing that is killing me. Take my mind off of it. What are you doing tonight?" I asked.

"I'm going on a date. A fancy one. I have to wear a dress."

"I've never seen you in one," I replied.

"It's a rarity, but I'm willing to make the sacrifice. He seems like a keeper and whatever you do, don't repeat that to anyone, especially my mother. She's already taken a trip to the diamond district."

"Our parents are cut from the same cloth. And speaking of parents, I told mine I'd call when I got back." I reached into my purse and found my phone.

Amy stood and said, "I'm going to take a nap."

I dialed and my father answered.

"Hi, Chick. I'm back."

"Good. Hold on a minute, I need to go into the next room."

I heard a door close and then he said, "Do you mind telling me who that was kissing you at the airport today? Thank goodness your mother didn't see."

My stomach immediately knotted up. "It was someone I had a few dates with while I was home. I didn't want you to worry about it, so I didn't tell you guys."

"So you went sneaking around? That's really mature, Mona Lisa. What if something happened to you? You have to start thinking about how your actions affect others."

I fell back on my bed defeated. "I hope he's Italian at least. Oh, dear God. He's not a Protestant, is he? Bucky had it all, Mona Lisa. This guy better toe the line, whoever he is."

"Chick, I can tell you who …."

"Don't bother," he said cutting me off. "I won't tell your mother about this, but from now on, no more secrets. I'll let her know you got back safely."

I heard a click on the other end letting me know our conversation had ended. I let out a cry of frustration and pulled a pillow over my head. I was eight hundred miles away and thirty-one years of age, yet I was reduced to a thirteen-year-old in a matter of seconds. Dante Colletti better be worth it.

Chapter 64

I was anxious about my conversation with Dante because I was unsure of so many things. I texted him that I arrived safely and he replied he would call me around eight that night. At 7:30 I popped open a beer and answered emails until my phone rang precisely at 8 o'clock.

"Prompt, aren't you?" I asked.

"Hello to you, too. How was your trip?" Dante asked.

"Uneventful, however, my conversations with my parents were another story."

"Are you going to tell me or make me guess?"

I took a gulp of my beer and said, "My mother called me while I was still at the airport because as a Cicciarelli I have to be there two days before my flight leaves, so I had some time to kill. Anyway, she basically accused us of having sex right there at the curbside drop-off. In an attempt to calm her down, I assured her it was just a kiss and it was okay because I was kissing Dante Colletti. Once she came to and got her wits about her, she immediately called the *Star-Ledger* and put our engagement announcement in the paper."

"You are a nut," he laughed. "Tell me what really happened."

"It's all true, except for the newspaper part and there's still time for that to actually happen so you never know. She did agree not to tell my father, though, until there is something to tell."

"Great. It sounds like you made some progress with your mother."

"Not so fast, buddy. When I called my parents to tell them I was safely back in Georgia, Chick informed me he saw us kissing, and he was going to spare my mother the humiliation. I tried to tell him it was you, but he cut me off and told me to act my age."

Dante laughed again and said, "You can't make this stuff up. You sure keep things interesting, Mona Lisa."

"Don't I know it. I wish my life was a little more boring," I admitted.

"Don't say that. I like interesting."

"Good thing. So, how was your day?" I asked.

"Great. I fly to New York City in two days, then Boston, D.C., Pittsburgh, Orlando again and home in two weeks. I'm working on getting Atlanta added to my route."

"I'd love to see you again. Phone dating is nice, but it doesn't compare to the real deal."

"I know, but for right now, it's all we've got," he stated.

"You're right, Mr. Reality Check. I can dream though, can't I?"

"Of course, you can. Tell me, what are you doing right now?"

"I'm having a beer. Would you like to join me? I hate to drink alone."

"Sure, since I'm not flying tomorrow. Let me check the minibar."

I heard him rummage around and he said, "Got one. You better be worth it because this beer is going to set me back at least ten bucks."

"You sure know how to flatter a girl."

"You haven't seen anything yet. Maybe on one of these dates, I'll order room service."

"Wow, I can hardly wait. I'll stock up on frozen dinners so I can microwave something scrumptious for myself."

"Excellent. We have to keep our senses of humor if this is going to go anywhere."

"That's my strong suit–keeping it light."

"Good girl. Do you work tomorrow?" he asked.

"Sure do, and I'm ready to get back into my routine. I miss my customers and my coworkers."

"I'm glad you like your job so much."

"Me, too. I'd better get going, though, because I have a bunch of stuff to do to get caught up," I said.

"No worries," Dante said. "Maybe we can have a dinner date next time. Check your schedule and let me know when would be a good time."

"I will. Good night and thanks for the beer."

I hung up the phone, and it immediately started ringing. I thought Dante forgot to tell me something, but I saw it was my parents. I felt guilty when I didn't answer their calls, but I didn't have the energy for another conversation with them. Whenever I didn't answer, I assumed they were calling to inform me of a tragedy so I listened to the voice mail as soon as the alert sounded.

"Mona Lisa, it's Ma. I bet you're talking to you know who," she whispered. "Call me if there's anything to report. Love you."

A sense of humor might not be enough.

Chapter 65

I was very ready to be back at work and happy to see Bobbie Lee's mother and grandmother were on my schedule. I was a bit homesick after getting back to Georgia, and a no-nonsense dose of Mary Willbanks would straighten me out. I quickly found out Bobbie Lee's grandmother was the southern version of Noni and she didn't let me get away with anything remotely self-pitying. When they walked in the door, my spirits lifted immediately.

"Hey, Yankee. I see you came back. The north's not all it's cracked up to be?" Mary asked.

I smiled. "What can I say? I'm turning into a glorified southerner thanks to you."

"Not so fast. It takes years to become a member of that club and you're going to need a sponsor. If you're lucky, I'll take you on."

"Mama, I swear you're incorrigible," Bitsy admonished. "Mona Lisa, forgive her. Maybe you can wash away some of that sassiness with shampoo."

"I'll see what I can do," I said winking at Mary. "Who's first?"

"Bitsy, of course," Mary answered. "I need to see what kind of work you're doing today before I let you touch my head. I know you were visiting back home and I want to make sure you're not going to give me big Jersey hair today."

"Mama, I swear you say things just to get me all riled

up."

Her mom returned my wink and said, "Bitsy, I'm having a little fun with the Yankee here. I'm going to act all proper now and sit and read my *Southern Living* magazine."

I motioned for the shampoo girl to take Bitsy over to the sink and I carried Mary's bag to the sofa in the waiting area.

I sat next to her and said, "I do believe I missed you, Mary."

"I'm not surprised. I'm shocked you came back, though. We must be growing on you."

"You are. It was nice to be home, but I like it here. I'm staying for awhile anyway."

"Just awhile?" she asked.

"When I was home, I started seeing someone. He lives in Jersey. I live here. It's complicated."

"That's the motto for your generation. You know why it's complicated? Because you make it that way. How many dates did you go on?" she asked.

"Three."

"Oh, three. Now I know why you're so confused."

I laughed. "When you say it like that, it sounds silly."

"It is silly. If I've learned anything in this long life of mine, it's that we have control over very little. Don't invent problems."

"You're very wise, Mary."

"Yes, I am. Now I'd appreciate it if you start working

on my daughter's hair. I haven't got all day."

"Yes, ma'am."

I walked over to my station, and Bitsy was washed and ready for me.

"I love your mom," I confessed.

"She's a hot mess and that mouth of hers about puts me over the edge."

"I appreciate her candor. She reminds me of my grandmother."

"She's available for weekends if you like. No charge."

"I'd take her anytime," I offered.

"You know, I'm only kidding, Mona Lisa. I love her to death, but some days she could test the patience of Jesus himself."

"I think you and my mother would get along very well. My Noni is a lot like Mary. I think that's why I like her so much."

"Don't tell her that. She can smell weakness and she'll use it to her advantage. Enough about her. How was your trip?"

"It was great. I was happy to be there and now I'm glad to be back."

"Brightleigh tells me you've got a new beau. Oh, my word. I hope it was okay that she told me."

"It's fine. I'm not sure what will happen with him, but I'm trying not to worry about it. Dr. Mary Willbanks gave me that advice."

"Lord, have mercy. I'm not sure my eighty-year-old

mama is who you should be goin' to for dating advice, darlin'."

"It was more like life advice and it was helpful."

"I'm glad. So when will you see this young man of yours?"

"That is the million dollar question. However, I am not going to obsess about it."

"Good girl."

I combed her hair and grabbed my scissors, but put them in my pocket and said, "Excuse me for one quick minute." I ducked into the restroom and pulled out my phone. No texts or emails from Dante, so I texted him and asked, "When can we have another date night?"

I caught my reflection in the mirror and shrugged. Obsession wasn't a problem if you admitted it, right?

Chapter 66

I had to wait three days for a "date" with Dante and by the time it arrived, I was in a bit of a funk. Amy was quick to pick up on my mood.

"What's with you?" she asked in her usual caring tone before she plopped herself on the couch next to me.

"I have a video date tonight and all of a sudden I'm not looking forward to it."

"Why not? Sitting at a computer screen trying to make conversation isn't appealing to you?"

"It's awkward at first. It takes some getting used to."

"Yes it does," she stated.

"Thank you for your assessment, Captain Optimistic," I chided.

"Hey, when have you known me to sugarcoat any-thing? Being direct is part of my DNA. Kind of like eye color, but more fun."

"You're a lunatic," I said.

"Yes I am, however, this lunatic is going to dinner and a movie and you, my friend, are having a cyber date. My life is looking pretty good now, isn't?" she asked.

"I hate you."

"No you don't," Amy said. She stood and kissed me loudly on the top of my head. "You're mad because I'm right."

I plunged an invisible knife into my heart and said, "You sure know how to kill a girl. At least I don't have to get all dressed up for a video date. Hell, I don't even have to shower or brush my teeth. I only have to look good from the neck up."

"You're delusional, Mona Lisa," she called as she walked down the hallway to her room.

I sat on the couch for a minute, then followed her and curled up on her bed with a stuffed rag doll.

"I am, aren't I?" I asked Amy as she put mascara on her lashes.

"Pathetic?"

"That too. I'm not cut out for long-distance romances."

"A computer kind of takes the romance out of any relationship."

"You're right. I'll see how it goes tonight."

"Good luck, Cyber Sally."

* * * *

I sat at my computer with a plate of pasta, a glass of Chianti and felt like an idiot. That is until I answered the video chat and saw Dante's face and bright smile.

"Cheers," I said holding up my glass.

"Cheers," he replied clicking his water bottle against the screen.

"Where are you?" I asked.

"I'm in D.C., but I have an early flight out tomorrow. Headed to sunny Orlando."

"Atlanta is also sunny," I quipped.

"Yes it is, but I seem to be having some difficulty getting a trip there."

"That's disappointing."

"I know, but something will come up. Eating pasta I see?" he asked.

"Yes, but it's not natural to eat while talking to you on the computer. I'll save it for later," I said moving my dish to the side.

"I'm still waiting for room service to bring up my sandwich."

There were a few seconds of awkward silence and then Dante asked, "How has your week been?"

"It's nice to be back in my groove. I love my job and I love Atlanta, though right now the heat is a bit much."

"You know there's this state called New Jersey and it doesn't get as hot there. You should give it another try."

"You're a funny guy, Dante Colletti. If I lived in Jersey now, you'd be in D.C. so we'd still be computer dating," I replied.

"Point taken. I'm home next week for a day. Want to meet me?" he asked.

"I'd love to, but I have this pesky thing called a job."

"Can't hurt to ask."

"True. So tell me what you do when you're not flying."

"Mostly I sleep and get ready for my trip the next day. It's not as glamorous as it seems. If I have time, I go to local restaurants and hang out. I love to people-watch."

"Me, too. I make up stories about the people I see. Their job. How they met their spouse. What kind of work they do."

Once the initial discomfort passed, we talked for over two hours. We made plans for at least our next twenty dates and laughed the entire time. It ended up being an incredible night … until we had to say goodbye. Dante had better get to Atlanta soon because kissing the computer screen good night was going to get old quickly.

Chapter 67

Work had become my focus as it kept me busy and my
mind off of Dante. We talked every few days, and we had
another computer date, but we had no concrete plans for an
in-person visit. I needed to vent, but not to Amy because
she was totally unsympathetic and Brightleigh was overly
caring. I needed someone who would listen, but who would
also kick my ass if needed.

On my way to work, I called Sophia.

"Hey, what's going on?" I asked.

"Let's see. I had a root canal two days ago and haven't
been able to eat anything besides applesauce. The only silver lining is I lost three pounds. Anthony had the stomach
bug yesterday and you would think a twelve-year-old boy
would be able to make it to the bathroom, but no, so I had
the carpet cleaners come yesterday afternoon. Then in the
middle of the night, Gina comes into my bedroom and
throws up on my bed. Then Dom says 'Well, at least she
didn't puke on the carpet.' Gina responded by getting sick
all over my bedroom rug and leaving a trail into the bathroom. Now I'm waiting once again for the carpet cleaners.
How are you?"

"I'm great," I lied. "Just wanted to say hello, but I
think I'll hang up because I feel a little nauseous."

"Welcome to my world, Mona Lisa. I'll call you when
things settle down. Love you."

I finished my drive to work trying to think of anything

besides Sophia and the kids and eventually my stomach stopped churning. I pulled into the parking lot, and Bobbie Lee followed right behind. I slowly gathered my things and waited for her.

"Hey, girl," she called out.

"Hey, yourself. Do you have time for a cup of coffee before we open?" I asked.

"I think I can manage that. Somethin' on your mind?"

"Just need some advice from an unbiased third party. You up for the task?" I asked.

"Sure am. They don't call me the Dear Abby of the hair industry for nothing."

She unlocked the door, and I put my bag in my cabinet and put the coffee on to brew.

"Come in my office when you're ready."

I checked my station and made sure I had everything ready for my first client. I poured two cups of coffee and joined Bobbie Lee on the sofa in her office.

"What is it? Man trouble?" she asked as I handed her the mug.

"What else? I've sort of been seeing this guy from New Jersey that my father tried to fix me up with days after I was left at the altar. Needless to say, we didn't click at the time, but we reconnected on my trip home. We had a few dates when I was up there, and I thought we had potential, but he hasn't come to visit me yet, and this long-distance dating is for the birds."

"Hmmm."

I waited for her to say something else, but she didn't. I looked at her expectantly and asked, "Is that all you have to say?"

"No. I'm just thinkin' and processin'."

I waited another few uncomfortable seconds until she finally asked, "How long has it been since you've seen him?"

"Three weeks. He keeps saying he'll get a flight here, but he hasn't yet. And he's a pilot, so it's not a stretch for him to spontaneously get on an airplane."

"Hmmm," she repeated.

If this was all she was going to contribute, Dear Abby's job was safe.

"My Aunt Netty had a saying. No one likes a hungry gator."

"And that means…?" I asked.

"Men are turned off by women who are needy. Take a step back and maybe go on a date with someone else. If and when he comes to visit, then you can talk about your expectations. But for now, go out and do things and don't wait by the phone. I guarantee he'll come a runnin'."

"Alright, then. I'll give it a go. For how long, though?"

"As long as it takes," she said.

Patience was not my strong suit, but I was willing to try and I was soon put to the test. After work, I had a voicemail on my phone from one of my new clients who was a doctor.

"Hi, Mona Lisa. It's Harrison Alexander. I hope you

don't mind, but Bobbie Lee gave me your cell phone number. She said you wouldn't mind because I'd like to know if you would have dinner with me on Friday. Call me back."

Chapter 68

As much as I hated doing it, I called Harrison back and accepted his date. For the next three days, Bobbie Lee acted as if she were the queen bee of matchmaking. I had to admit I was looking forward to my night out. I hadn't heard from Dante since I talked to Bobbie Lee and was feeling good about my decision to see Harrison. I agreed to let him pick me up at my apartment and heard the doorbell ring as I finished putting on my lipstick.

I opened the door and he greeted me with a light hug.

"It's great to see you outside of the salon, Mona Lisa."

"You too. Let me get my bag and we can head out," I said.

I grabbed my bag and my cell phone rang.

"Sorry about that. Let me put it on silent," I said while looking at the caller ID.

It was Dante, of course, as I was the poster child for poor timing. I turned the ringer off, careful not to answer the phone because that would also be par for my course. I dropped it back into my bag and said, "Let's go."

We made small talk in the car and pulled up to the valet at a very fancy French restaurant. He escorted me inside.

The maitre d' greeted him, "Hello, Dr. Alexander. It's nice to see you again."

We were seated and I couldn't resist saying, "It seems as though you're a regular here. Is this where you take all of your dates?"

He blushed and replied, "I work at the hospital across the street and I took care of the owner's wife, so they're very nice to me. I'm sure it will wear off soon, but I used my pull to get us a table tonight."

"Did you save her life?" I asked.

"Hardly. I gave her a boob job and her husband is incredibly grateful."

"Get out. Why didn't I know you were a plastic surgeon?"

"I don't like to tell people what kind of doctor I am because then they want me to analyze all of their body parts. There's no good answer to 'So, do you think I should have liposuction?'"

I laughed and said, "Well, I guess I won't ask about my nose then."

"Thank you, and I won't ask you if I'm losing my hair."

"Excellent. What else don't I know about you?" I challenged.

"I'm from Florida, but came up here to go to medical school and stayed. I've been in practice for five years and it's been great. What about you?"

"I've only been here a few months, but I really feel at home. Although my mother would take a stroke if she heard me say that."

"Take a stroke?"

"Sorry, that's one of my mom's phrases. We call them Angie-isms. In our family, we don't have strokes or heart attacks. We take them like other people take vacations."

He laughed which was a good sign. Not that he had to think I was good enough for stand-up, but he seemed to appreciate my sense of humor.

"What do you do for fun, Harrison, besides alter the anatomy of the Atlanta metro area?"

"Hey, that has a nice ring to it. I may use that in one of my brochures. I like to go bike riding and hiking. Have you ever been to Stone Mountain?"

"No, I haven't."

"We should go," he suggested. "We can hike up the mountain and then stay for the laser show."

"Laser show?" I asked.

"It's an Atlanta institution. Makes you relive the Civil War in neon lights."

"Sounds interesting," I feigned.

"It's fun. You have to have an open mind."

Have an open mind. Be patient. I had a lot of directives coming at me, but at the end of the night, I felt it was worth it. Harrison was fun and his good night kiss was nice. No fireworks, but it was more than I got from Dante in a long time. I listened to his voicemail after Harrison dropped me off.

"Hi, Mona Lisa. It's me. I guess you're out. Hope you're having fun. Let's talk soon."

"Thanks for that scintillating message, Dante," I said aloud staring at the phone. "I am having fun and now I don't feel so guilty about reliving the Civil War with Harrison next weekend."

Chapter 69

I waited until the next night after work before calling Dante back. I felt like I was back in high school. *Don't call him. You don't want to appear too anxious.* That's what all the romance magazines preached.

I dialed his number but was disappointed that he didn't answer. After the beep, I said, "Hi, Dante. It's me, Mona Lisa. Sorry I missed your call. Bye."

That was as underwhelming as his message was for me. My mood needed a lift, so I called Noni.

"Hey, kiddo," she answered. "What's the word?"

"Frustration," I quipped.

"Over what? Or should I ask over whom? Does his name start with Dante Colletti?"

"You think you're so smart, Noni," I answered.

"What can I say? I'm right, though, aren't I?"

"Well, yes. I've been waiting for weeks for him to visit and it doesn't seem like it's that important to him."

"Don't wait around, kiddo. Men like the chase. That's how I snagged Marshall, you know."

"You made him chase you? That I would have liked to have seen," I said dryly.

"You know what I mean, wiseass. He didn't like it when Stanley Stasnisky started sitting next to me at bingo. It didn't hurt that I laughed at all of Stanley's jokes. And believe me, that was no easy feat. That man's jokes are older than dirt."

"If Dante and I could ever be in the same city, I would take him to bingo and give that a try, but we're not so I can't."

"A little testy today. Is it your lady time?"

"Jeez, Noni. Thanks a lot."

"Just trying to chill you out, Mona Lisa. So, is it?" she asked.

"Yes, you crazy old lady. It is. Remind me again why I called you?" I asked.

"Because you know I'll tell you like it is. Go out with friends. Have some fun, relax a little and stop thinking about it."

"I miss you, Noni."

"Marshall and I were talking about taking a trip down there in a few weeks. What do you think?"

"I think that would be great. I can't wait for everyone to meet you. You're going to love my roommates. You can stay in my room."

"I think we'll make a reservation. Marshall's been pretty frisky lately, so we'll need our privacy."

"Thanks for the visual, Noni."

"Grow up, Mona Lisa. We're old. Not dead."

"I know that, Noni. It's kind of pathetic my grandmother is getting more action than I am."

"It's how it is right now, kiddo. Your time is coming, but you can't sit around and wait. Get on with your life and if it's meant to be, it's meant to be."

"You're right."

"Yes, I am and now I have to go because Marshall and I are hitting Atlantic City. Noni needs a new pair of shoes."

"Call me if you win big."

I hung up and contemplated my next move. I nervously dialed Harrison's number and took a deep breath to calm myself.

"Hi, Mona Lisa," he answered.

"How did you know it was me?" I asked.

"I have this thing caller ID. I'm glad you called."

"Why is that?" I asked.

"I thought maybe we could see a movie tomorrow night."

"I'd love that. I get done with work at seven."

"I'll pick you up at eight."

"Great, Harrison. I'm glad I called."

"Me too," he replied.

I hung up and felt pretty pleased with myself. Then the phone rang and it was Dante. It took every ounce of willpower not to answer the phone, but I let it go to voicemail. I waited anxiously to see if he would leave me a message and jumped when the alert sounded.

"Hi, Mona Lisa. I was hoping to catch you. This phone tag is getting lame. I miss you," he said and then paused. "Call me," he added before hanging up.

"Yes it is lame, Dante Colletti," I replied to my phone. "But, I think I'm getting your attention."

Chapter 70

The next day I was in a great mood at work, even though I felt a bit guilty about Harrison and wondered if I was using him to make Dante jealous. I worked hard to put that out of my mind and focused on enjoying my clients.

When I got home, I showered and dressed and was looking forward to our night out. When I checked myself one last time in the mirror, my phone rang. It was Dante and this time I had no willpower, so I answered.

"Hey, stranger. Where are you these days?" I asked.

"I'm in Chicago. It's rainy and nasty, and I want to see you."

I couldn't help but grin. "Sounds like someone is having a bad day," I sing-songed.

"Sorry. It's been a tough one. We had a drunk man on the plane who thought it would be a great idea to tell his wife he was in love with the nanny halfway through the flight. Then she told him she was sleeping with their son's math tutor and it went downhill from there."

"You sure do have a glamorous job, Dante."

"It used to be, but I think people are getting crazier by the minute. Sorry I'm such a downer."

"No worries. I, on the other hand, had a great day. And Noni and Marshall are coming to visit."

"That's terrific. You're lucky to have her."

"I am. She's always been there for me."

"I want to be there for you," he offered pathetically.

"You know where I live."

"I know. I'm trying."

The doorbell rang, and I knew it was Harrison.

"Dante, I'm really sorry, but I have to go. Can I call you later?"

"I heard the doorbell. Are you expecting someone?" he asked, sounding hurt.

"A friend from work is coming over," I said feeling the sting of my white lie.

He was silent for a second. "Have a good night," he muttered.

I hung up and felt immensely guilty, but went to greet Harrison.

When I opened the door, he stepped in and presented me with a beautiful bouquet of lilies. I took them and breathed in the fragrance.

"Harrison, these are gorgeous and they smell incredible. Thank you."

"I wish I could take credit for them. I let the lady at the florist shop have free reign."

I kissed him on the cheek and said, "I love them. Let me put them in some water. Have a seat."

I went to the kitchen and put the flowers in a vase and added some water. I returned to the sofa and set the flowers on the coffee table before sitting next to Harrison.

"What movie are we going to see?" I asked.

"Would you mind seeing the new James Bond film? I figure it's got something for the both of us. Action for me and a hot guy for you."

"That sounds perfect."

"We've got a little time before it starts. Would you like to go for a drink?"

"I've got a nice bottle of Pinot Noir if you want to hang out here."

"That's fine."

"Relax, and I'll get the wine and some glasses."

I returned and handed him the bottle and the corkscrew.

"I'm not very adept at opening wine bottles. I'm a whiz with a beer bottle, though."

"Everyone's got their strong suits. Between the two of us, we won't go thirsty."

I laughed. "Priorities. Gotta have 'em."

"Food is my other weakness," Harrison admitted.

"Now you're speaking my language. For Italians, food is more important than oxygen."

Harrison smiled at me dubiously.

"You think I'm kidding? Every family get-together, Sunday dinner, weddings, funerals, baptisms, birthdays. It all revolves around what we're going to eat."

"That sounds good to me. Can I convert?" he asked.

"Sorry, but it's a society you have to be born into. Even the ones that marry in are never truly accepted. You'll have to take my word for it."

"I guess I'll have to live vicariously through you. But so you know, Italian food is my favorite."

"I think you're saying that to get on my good side."

"Is it working?" he asked.

"Maybe. I'll keep you posted."

"All this talk of food is making me hungry. I'm ready for popcorn."

"Fair warning, when it comes to popcorn, I don't share. I need my own and soda too."

"I'll make a note of that. Anything else?" he asked.

"No, that's it. I like to think I'm pretty low maintenance."

"Uh-oh. You know what's worse than a woman who's high maintenance? The ones who think they aren't."

I grabbed a pillow and hit him in the chest. He retaliated by kissing me. It was a sweet kiss. Not totally without merit, but nothing that caused my heart to palpitate.

* * * *

That came later when I listened to yet another voice mail from Dante.

"Mona Lisa, I'm coming this weekend. I'll be there late Friday and can stay until Sunday."

Let the chase begin.

Chapter 71

My head was swimming after I heard Dante's message. I was excited, nervous and unsure as to what to do about Harrison. I took a deep breath and channeled my inner No-ni. I was going to take it day by day and see how the weekend went before I made any snap decisions. I breathed deeply again, but it wasn't working. I was freaking out and needed someone to talk to, so I walked to Amy's room in the hopes that she was home. I opened her door and waited while I tried to determine if she was asleep.

"What?" she shouted. "Someone better be dead or missing a limb."

"Good. You're awake," I said flipping on her light switch.

"What the hell…?" she barked. "In case you didn't notice, I was sleeping."

I quickly turned the light back off.

"Sorry. I need advice and Brightleigh is sweet, bless her heart, but I need someone who is not so nice."

"Thanks for waking me up to receive that compliment," she said before rolling over.

I sat next to her. "You know what I mean. You always tell me the truth even when it's not easy to hear and I appreciate that."

She sighed and sat up. "What's the problem?"

"I've been playing hard to get with Dante trying to get him to come visit because I have no idea if this relationship is going anywhere since we haven't spent any more time together since I went to Jersey. So, I've been on a few dates with Harrison, the plastic surgeon, and it's been nice. He doesn't give me butterflies in my stomach, but we have a good time and he thinks I'm amusing which always helps. Anyway, I've been busy the past few times that Dante has called and it finally worked because he'll be here Friday."

"That was a delightful monologue, Mona Lisa. Can I go back to sleep now?"

"No. I need you to tell me what to do."

"About what?" she asked.

"Haven't you been listening to me?"

"It's hard not to," Amy said dryly. "Tell Harrison you have plans this weekend because a friend from home is coming to visit. See how it goes with Dante and then you can decide which of them you want to keep around. Problem solved. I swear, do you need me to start picking out your clothes each morning too?"

I laughed. "I sound ridiculous when you say it like that. My head goes crazy, and all these thoughts start swirling around and the next thing you know, I can't think straight."

"No kidding. If you start hearing voices, you're going to need to find another place to live. As it is, I'm going to have to lock my bedroom door and sleep with a baseball bat."

"I'm not crazy," I countered. "Maybe just a little obsessive."

"A little?" she challenged.

"Okay. More than a little. Thank you for listening."

"Did I have a choice?" Amy queried.

"Not really. Any time you have irrational thoughts, feel free to wake me up," I said.

"Wow. Thanks for the offer, Dr. Phil. Right now, I'm good except for the fact that my roommate won't let me sleep."

"I'm wide awake. Want to get up and have some ice cream with me? I'll make you a banana split just the way you like it. No strawberries and extra hot fudge."

She hesitated a moment then acquiesced. "Extra whipped cream too. When you realize you're going to have to decide whether or not to sleep with Dante, I'm going to need the extra sugar."

"Shit. I didn't even think of that. Forget the ice cream. I need a drink."

Chapter 72

It was the longest week of my life that culminated in the longest day. Thank goodness I had work that day to keep my busy brain occupied because once I got home, I was a nervous wreck. Dante insisted on taking a cab to my place and I never asked if he was planning on staying with me. I changed the sheets just in case and vacuumed my room. I cleaned the bathroom as best as I could before showering and shaving every area twice. As I covered my entire body in perfumed body lotion, I panicked about the possibility of Dante seeing me naked. *Why didn't I go to the gym more?* I chastised myself. *Why did I eat that banana split and polish it off with two beers? Why didn't I lose those last five pounds?*

Pounding on the door propelled me back to reality.

"Hey, you're not the only one who might be having sex tonight so hurry up in there," Amy demanded.

I wrapped myself in a towel and opened the door to find her waiting with arms crossed.

"Will you stop reminding me about the sex part?" I asked. "I am freaking out."

"What else is new? You're acting like Glenn Close in *Fatal Attraction*. Keep this up and you won't have to worry about sleeping with your Italian stallion. He'll run for his life."

"You're adding to my stress," I exclaimed in exasperation.

"It's fun," she admitted.

"You act like a five-year-old."

"Got to do what I do best."

I groaned and walked to my bedroom. I tried to shut my door, but Amy followed me.

"I'm sorry I'm busting your chops," she said.

"Can I get that in writing? I didn't think you ever admitted remorse," I challenged.

"I don't, but if you want some help, I'm available. When will he be here?" she asked.

"An hour. He got an earlier flight and he's going to text me when he lands."

"What are your plans? Open the door and lead him straight to the bedroom?" she asked with a grin.

"Nah. I think we'll go ahead and do it right in the doorway and get it over with, you moron. We're going to dinner at that tapas place down the street."

"Is he staying here?"

"I don't know," I confessed.

"How can you not know?"

"I never asked. I didn't want to seem overly anxious."

"Part of the chase?" she asked making quotation marks with her fingers.

"Shut up."

"I can tell you're not in the mood for jokes, so let's find an outfit. First, put on your nicest lingerie just to be prepared. Then let's get something sexy. How about this?" she asked pulling a halter dress I recently purchased out of my closet.

"You don't think it's too much?"

"Are you trying to get laid or get invited to the Junior League?"

"Get laid," I mumbled.

"Good and put a little perfume in your cleavage. It drives men crazy."

"Thanks for the advice. I didn't know you were a sex therapist, too."

"You know what they say about desperate times and desperate measures."

"No kidding. Seriously, Amy. Thanks."

"You tell anybody I'm actually nice and you'll pay, sister."

"Your secret's safe with me."

My phone chimed letting me know I had a text message from Dante.

Just landed. Will drop my bags at the hotel and be there soon.

I read the text to Amy and said, "I guess I've been worrying for nothing."

Chapter 73

My anxiety melted away when I opened my door and
saw Dante's boyish grin and the pastry box from Uncle Luciano's Italian Bakery.

"I don't know what I'm more excited about–you, or
what's inside of that beautiful white box."

Dante reached for my waist with his free hand and
guided me to him. He hesitated briefly before kissing me
slowly and longingly. I felt a chill on the back of my neck
and let out a soft moan. He pulled away slightly and
smiled.

"Okay, you win," I admitted.

"You bet I do. Can I come in?" he asked.

I grabbed his hand and led him to the sofa. He put the
box on the coffee table and sat next to me.

"I'm so happy you're here," I said before kissing him
lightly on the lips.

"Me, too. I'm sorry it took so long, but I hope now that
I'm here it will have been worth the wait."

"Judging from your arrival, I think we're off to a
wonderful start," I confessed. "Would you like a drink or
are you ready to go to dinner?"

"You know what I'd really like?" he asked with a
glimmer in his eyes. My heart began to beat rapidly and my
palms began to sweat. "A cannoli. I know I bought them
for you, but it was torture carrying this box. I'll have you
know some guy on the plane offered me fifty bucks for it."

"You're my kind of man, Dante Colletti. Dessert first is surely the way to my heart."

"I've learned a few things over the years."

I grabbed the box and motioned for him to join me in the kitchen. He sat at the island, and I put out plates and napkins. I opened the box and gasped at the assortment of Italian pastries.

"Uncle Luciano's makes the best *sfogliatelle*s. How did you know his bakery is my all-time favorite?" I asked, gingerly putting one on my plate.

"I had a little help from a certain grandmother of yours."

"Noni? I miss her and I've missed Uncle Luciano too."

I took a bite and couldn't help but let out a squeal.

"Sorry. I have a problem when it comes to these," I said before licking my fingers.

"I like a girl who enjoys her food."

"Then you're gonna love me," I blurted out. I felt my face flush, embarrassed at using the L word.

Dante laughed and took a bite of his cannoli, but didn't respond.

"I think I can wait a while for dinner now. How about you?" I asked.

"Sure. All I want is to spend time with you."

"Why don't we sit and catch up?"

"That sounds great."

We made our way back to the sofa and Dante draped his arm gently around as I snuggled closer.

"I really do hate that I couldn't get here sooner," he said.

"I know. I got frustrated, but let's not dwell on it."

He kissed me. This time deeper and longer.

Who needs dinner?

After a minute, we came up for air.

"I think we should go eat now. I'm not sure I can control myself," Dante said.

"I'm not complaining."

"I know, but let's take it slow."

How slow? We only had two nights, and I wasn't getting any younger or thinner.

* * * *

In the end, we had a wonderfully romantic dinner, and when I pulled up to the entrance of his hotel, Dante asked, "Will you come up to my room?"

My heart began to beat wildly in anticipation. It had been a long time for me and I was nervous, but I was ready. "Yes." I put the car in park.

The valet opened my door and helped me out. Dante reached for my hand as he guided me through the lobby to the elevator. We were silent on the ride to the fourteenth floor, but he never let go of my hand until we arrived at the door to his room.

Once inside, I spotted a bottle of wine and two glasses on the nightstand. "Pretty sure of yourself, huh?" I asked teasingly.

"I prefer the term optimistic." He sat on the bed and

motioned for me to join him. "Are you nervous?" he asked.

"Just a lot," I answered truthfully.

He leaned in and kissed me lightly at first, then with a greater urgency as we gently eased onto our backs. He reached for the top button of my blouse but then hesitated.

"You sure?" he asked.

"Oh, yeah," I replied with a grin.

This was going to be way better than the Junior League.

Chapter 74

Our weekend flew by and as we lie in bed on Sunday afternoon, a wave of melancholy washed over me and I couldn't help but tear up. I was having very real feelings for Dante, but I wasn't ready to share them, so I went to the bathroom to splash some cold water on my face. I wished I could call Noni or Amy—someone who would calm me down, but then a knock came on the door.

"You all right, Mona Lisa?" Dante asked.

"Fine. Be out in a second," I called to him. I wrapped myself in the hotel bathrobe and crawled back into bed.

He pulled me into his arms and asked, "Did I turn the air down too low?"

"It's fine. I get cold easily."

"Anything else going on?"

I paused and answered, "Yes. No. I don't know."

He sat up and moved the pillows so I could sit up as well.

"Which one is it? Yes, no or maybe?"

I opened my mouth to speak and burst into tears.

"I'm so sorry. I don't know why I'm crying, but I can't seem to stop," I said trying unsuccessfully to choke back my tears.

Dante smiled and kissed my forehead.

"Oh, great. Now you feel sorry for me because I'm mentally unstable."

He laughed. "A little emotional maybe, but I don't

283

think you're crazy."

"You're probably just saying that to throw me off while you figure out how fast you can get to the airport," I said.

"I think you've been watching too many made-for-TV movies."

"I know how these things go. The guy says 'I'll call you' and then he changes his name, has plastic surgery and you never hear from him again."

"Now, I'm a little scared," Dante quipped.

"You can leave. I won't cause a scene."

"Mona Lisa, please stop. I'm not going anywhere."

"Really?" I asked.

"Really. I'm sad that our weekend is almost over, too, but I'm a guy. I have an inherent lack of sentimentality that bites me in the ass sometimes. But I'm glad you show emotion. I always know what you're feeling and I like that."

"Can you repeat that so I can record it for evidence?" I asked.

"Sure and you can record this too. I want to see you again very soon."

"Next week?"

"Probably not that soon. I have flights scheduled already, but I should make it back here in two, three weeks tops. I like being with you and if you're up for a challenge, I have a proposition for you."

"Hmmm. You certainly know how to pique my interest," I admitted. "Bring it on."

"I don't want you … us to see other people."

He must have sensed I was seeing someone. I thought for a split second about Harrison but had no problem agreeing to Dante's request.

"Okay."

"Okay to us seeing only each other?" he asked, somewhat disbelievingly.

"Yes. It's what I want too. I was afraid to bring it up before this weekend."

He kissed me and pulled me under the covers, but I held back and said, "I don't want any secrets between us. I've been on a few dates with a guy."

Dante looked wounded.

"Nothing happened, but I plan to tell him in person about us and I wanted you to know what I was going to do. I'm too old for games, Dante, and I want us to have a clean slate. *Capish*?"

He pouted and mumbled something incomprehensible.

"Look who's the emotional one now. Was that a yes?" I asked.

"Yes, but I want you to tell him soon. *Capish*?" he asked with a grin.

"You got it. And speaking of telling, did you let anyone back home besides Noni know you were coming for a visit?"

"Just Chick and your mother."

I paused to make sure he was kidding. "Thanks for that. First you make me cry, and then you give me a heart attack. Way to leave a lasting impression, Colletti."

"I think I've got a better way to do that," he said before pulling me under the covers.

Chapter 75

The next day, I called Harrison the first opportunity I had, but he didn't give me much chance to talk.

"Mona Lisa, I missed you. I hope you had fun with your friend. Please say you'll have dinner with me tonight. I already have a place in mind. Just name the time."

"Harrison," I began. "I was hoping we could talk."

"Sure. Let's do it over dinner. What time should I pick you up?" he asked.

"Can I meet you there? I have a few errands to run."

"Of course. How about Tuscan Grill at seven-thirty?"

"I'll be there," I replied, happy to have an exit strategy as the night was not going to end well for poor Harrison.

* * * *

I practiced my speech in the car on the ride over but forgot everything when I walked in and spotted Harrison sitting at a table with a bottle of wine and flowers. Waves of dread and guilt came over me as I slowly made my way to him.

I felt someone grab my arm and a strange woman pulled me to her and whispered, "He's a keeper, that one."

I looked at her and asked, "Do I know you?"

I heard, *tisk-tisk*, the sound of her disapproval as she turned to her friend and said, "These girls today don't ap-preciate a gentleman."

I opened my mouth to argue with her but needed to save my energy for Harrison. This was going to be more difficult than I thought.

He stood and greeted me with a light kiss.

"I'm so happy to see you. It was a long weekend without you." He motioned for the waiter to come to the table who opened the wine and served us.

"You can bring the appetizers now," Harrison told the waiter. "I hope you don't mind, but I took the liberty of ordering a special meal for us. I think I know what you like so you should be pleasantly surprised."

Did I just enter the twilight zone or was I on Candid Camera *because that seemed to be the only explanation for the altered reality I was in.*

"Harrison, I need to talk to you. This weekend changed some things for me."

"Me, too. I realized how much I like you and I want to take our relationship to the next level."

"Wow," was all I could muster.

"Is that all you have to say?" he asked looking and sounding hurt.

"I'm sorry, but …."

"Great. I go to all this trouble and you're dumping me. That's what this is, isn't it?"

This was not how I hoped it would go. "Well, I didn't want to tell you this way. It has nothing to do with you."

"Oh, that's original," he said sarcastically. "It's not you. It's me."

"Harrison, you're not making this easy for me," I protested.

"I'm sorry," he mocked. "Go ahead. I'll try not to interrupt."

He had a severe storm of sarcasm brewing.

"I didn't mean to hurt you, but an old friend has turned into something more and it came to light this weekend. You and I have only been out a few times, so I thought …."

"You thought wrong," he said before standing up and throwing his napkin on the table. He started to walk away, but then came back to leave me with one final jab. "And don't come running to me when you decide to get that nose fixed."

Ouch!

Just then the waiter delivered a large antipasto and asked, "Shall I wait until the gentleman returns?"

"He won't be coming back. He had an emergency," I lied.

Out of the corner of my eye, I saw the "He's a keeper" lady point at me and whisper something to her friend.

"Do me a favor," I said to the waiter. "Take this to that table over there and tell them that I sent a snack to go along with the show."

Dante Colletti, I'm all yours. You better be worth it.

Chapter 76

I had hoped Harrison would find another place to get his haircut, however, I was not that lucky. I saw him walk in from the corner of my mirror while I was working on a client. I thought about totally ignoring him, but I wanted to be the bigger person, so I excused myself for a moment and walked toward Harrison. I caught his eye and smiled, but he held his hand up for me to stop. His facial expression bordered on contempt with a hint of disgust. He succeeded in stopping me in my tracks and causing my hand to reflexively cover my nose. I had never even thought of changing any part of my face, but Harrison's comments made me self-conscious.

I didn't let the incident bother me for long as Dante and I were growing closer despite the physical distance between us. It had been two weeks since I saw Dante, but we talked every night no matter how late and I looked forward to our phone dates. Noni and Marshall were finally coming to visit, so that helped quiet my longing for Dante. I was frantically cleaning up the apartment before their arrival when Amy decided it would be a good time to harass me.

"Doing the family clean?" she asked as she sat on the sofa.

"Yes. I guess you forget what a nut you were when your mom and grandmother came to visit. I think you woke up at six am to defrost the freezer."

"That's the first place they look. I hope you already did

it because it takes a lot of time. They also like to check out your medicine cabinet and nightstand. Better hide that stash of condoms," she warned.

"This is my grandmother we're talking about. She'd be mad if I didn't have any. My mother is the one I need to hide them from, but I think my wedding is the only reason they would ever set foot in the state of Georgia," I admitted.

"Now that you pissed away your chance with Harrison, you may never get hitched. Did you see the look he gave you when he came in for a haircut yesterday? I couldn't tell if he was sad or if he was plotting his revenge."

"Oh, he wasn't sad," I countered. "He was probably thinking about ways to botch up my face with a nose job gone horribly wrong, so I would have to live out the rest of my life in hiding."

"Wouldn't that be something?" she asked. "The locals would tell stories about you and how you got that way and on Halloween, the neighborhood kids would dare each other to trick or treat at your house. You could be famous."

"I'm glad you find happiness at my expense," I replied.

"It does bring me joy. I can't wait for your pilot man to come back and visit. That will be a lot of fun."

"You will not be allowed within fifty feet of Dante. I'm taking out a restraining order on his behalf. As much as I'm enjoying our little banter session here, I need to keep cleaning. How about making yourself useful and clean the bathroom?" I asked.

"What's in it for me?" she asked.

"A sanitary toilet and my undying gratitude. Please?" I begged. "I've got to pick them up in an hour."

"Okay, but that's not nearly as fun as getting under your skin," she said before heading toward the bathroom.

"Love you," I called after her.

"Yeah. Just remember this when I'm old and I need someone to change my diapers."

"I hope we're not still living together by then," I shot back.

I finished cleaning and arrived at the airport in plenty of time and even made a sign with their names on it from the Cicciarelli limousine service. It took awhile to get their baggage and maneuver our way to the parking because while their brains were sharp as tacks, their bodies sometimes moved at a snail's pace.

Once inside the car, I thought they might collapse, but Noni surprised me and asked, "What have you got planned for us today, kiddo?"

"I'm going to drop you at your hotel and give you some time to freshen up and then we're going downtown for dinner and a show at the Fox Theater. You're going to get the full tour tonight and then tomorrow, it's up to you. There are some outlet malls nearby, a winery about an hour away, and a casino about three hours from here."

"Hot damn," Noni squealed. "I've been feeling the itch to go to Atlantic City. I'm not sure my sciatica can take all that time in a car, though."

"We don't have to decide right now, my little *bubba-la*," Marshall said as he patted her hand.

"You're right," she agreed. "Let's wait and see how we feel."

She rested her head on Marshall's shoulder and I felt a pang of loneliness. It would be so much fun if Dante were here, but I was thrilled to have Noni and Marshall with me and was going to enjoy every moment of their visit.

After we pulled up to the hotel, I helped them out of the car and hugged them both fiercely.

"Thanks for coming you two. Get some rest because we're gonna have fun tonight. My roommate Amy is going to be my date and our driver, so look out Atlanta."

Chapter 77

I took a short nap after I dropped off Noni and Marshall, because despite the fact that they were older than me, I sometimes had a hard time keeping up. I wanted them to have a great visit, so I followed my rest with a shower and an energy drink. I was dressed with plenty of time to spare, so I thought I'd bug Amy while she got ready.

I plopped down on her bed and said, "You need to get moving, sister. We're going out with old people. If you're on time, they think you're late. They like to get everywhere fifteen minutes early."

"I'm doing the best I can. Perfection should never be rushed," she countered.

Her phone buzzed signaling a text and she sent a quick reply.

"I think I'm going to pass tonight. I just got a better offer," she announced.

"What? I bought four tickets for the Fox and you were supposed to be the DD. Come on. You're kidding, right?"

The doorbell rang and she asked, "Will you get that? I'm not ready."

"Seriously. You're ditching me at the last minute and you want me to entertain your date while you finish dressing? You suck," I mumbled before heading to let Amy's boyfriend in.

When I opened the door, a scream escaped because there was Dante. I grabbed him and planted the biggest kiss ever on his lips.

When we came up for air, I asked, "What are you doing here? Did Amy help you plan this? Oh, no. I owe her an apology."

"You got that right," she said with a smug look on her face. "Your pilot man got my number last time he was in town and let's just say we've been working on this for awhile."

I hugged Amy and whispered, "I'm so sorry."

"Don't get all sappy on me. I have a reputation to uphold. Go have fun and hey Red Baron, no drinking tonight. You're taking my place as the designated sober person."

He saluted Amy and said, "Will do. Are we picking up your grandmother and Marshall?"

"Yes. I can't believe you're here. Wait until Noni sees you. Oh? Was she in on it too?" I asked.

"No. Just Amy." He turned to her and said, "You had every detail down pat. I never met someone so organized."

"I'm good. What can I say?" Amy asked not expecting an answer.

"I appreciate you," I admitted.

"Ahh. I love it when you're indebted to me. If you'll excuse me, I've got a hot date with a man of my own," she said before heading back to her room.

A moment of panic went through me as I realized I had not done the big pre-date prep. Surely we would be spending the night together. Damn Amy for not preparing me. What underwear did I have on?

"Mona Lisa? You there? You disappeared for a minute. What's up?" Dante asked.

"Nothing. It's just if I knew you were coming, I would have dressed a little nicer," I said.

"You look beautiful. It's dinner and a show right?" he asked.

I didn't want to blurt out that I was afraid I was wearing a bra from Target and not Victoria's Secret.

"You're fine, but if you want to change, I'll wait."

"No. I'm sure Noni and Marshall are already pacing the lobby."

"We can come back here later and you can pick up a few things on our way to my hotel," Dante said casually.

"What makes you so sure I'll be staying with you?" I asked.

"Playing hard to get?"

"I thought about it, but you've already got me," I admitted.

He touched my cheek and said, "I'm glad."

I responded by wrapping my arms around his neck and kissing him so deep and long that it sent a shiver up my spine.

"Are you sure we can't be a little late?" Dante asked.

"For dinner? Have you met my Italian family? If it's one thing that trumps all others, it's food."

"Maybe later I can help straighten out your priorities," he said.

"Once we dump those two back at their hotel, have at

it."

Chapter 78

Noni and Marshall were surprised and excited to see Dante. As we waited for the elevator to take us up to the restaurant, Noni whispered to me, "This must be getting serious between you two, huh?"

"It's got potential, but keep that to yourself. You know how Ma and Chick get their hopes up. If and when there's something to tell, I'll fill them in. For right now, I want to enjoy this time without them constantly asking, 'So, do you think this is the one?'"

"I understand, kiddo," Noni replied. "Your mother still asks me when Marshall is going to make an honest woman of me. I swear it's like she's the parent and I'm the child."

"Welcome to my world, Noni."

We exited the elevator and were seated near a window that gave us an extraordinary view of the Atlanta skyline. The restaurant was at the top of a hotel and it slowly rotated so that you could get a panoramic view of the city. It was an Atlanta landmark, however, Noni wasn't quite sure that she was going to have a good time.

"I'm afraid to get up to use the bathroom. I might break a hip trying to get off this ride. The toilets don't move, too, do they?" she asked.

"I'm sure they don't, Noni. I've never been here before, but the view is incredible," I answered.

"It certainly is Mona Lisa," Marshall concurred. "Thank you for bringing us here."

"I wanted to take you somewhere special on your first night. And also because you're my first official guests," I added.

"What was I?" Dante asked with a pout.

"You're in a separate category," I said patting his hand. "These two are the first family members to break free from the New Jersey chokehold and actually vacation somewhere other than the tri-state area. The only reason my sisters came with me on my first trip to Georgia was so Chick could ensure my safe return from the underworld of the south."

Our waitress approached and handed us menus and took our drink order. When she returned, we toasted to our night together and compared notes about what we wanted. I ordered the salmon, but the rest of my crew ordered the steak, which was a specialty of the house. Once we handed our menus back to our server, Noni set out on a fact-finding mission.

"So, Dante, when will you two see each other again?" she asked.

"I'm hoping to get back here one more time and then Mona Lisa will come to Jersey for Thanksgiving and Christmas," he answered.

"When will you go public with Chick and Angie?"

"Noni," I admonished, "I said we want to keep it quiet for awhile."

"I'm not going to tell anyone. I want to make sure I'm around when they find out. I love to have a front row seat for these types of family events," she admitted.

"You're so bad, Noni. You enjoy torturing my parents, don't you?" I asked.

"Only when it comes to family matters. I get great enjoyment out of watching those two try and control every aspect of all of our lives. I've learned a few things in my day and the most important is that we have control of very little."

"You got that right," Marshall chimed in.

"Promise me I'll be the first to know when the news breaks?" Noni requested.

"Of course," Dante replied. "Mona Lisa, you're in charge of keeping Noni informed. Do you mind if I call you Noni?"

"Not at all. I hope I can call you grandson in the near future," she quipped.

I groaned and said, "Marshall, would you mind refilling my wine glass. Let's change the subject. Noni, how long do you and Marshall intend to go on living in sin?"

"*Touché*," she said. "I've missed you, kiddo. Nobody goes head-to-head with me like you do."

"I've missed you too. Here's to us," I said raising my glass.

We all took a drink, and I started to ask Marshall about his kids when I heard Noni whisper to Dante, "I'm not going to be around forever. Another grandson would be nice."

Chapter 79

As I stood at the airport saying goodbye to Noni, Marshall and Dante, I wanted to cry. I knew the old adage about enjoying the moment instead of weeping because it was over, but I couldn't do it. I wasn't that way and today was no different.

Noni sensed my mood right away and said, "Thanksgiving is in six weeks, Mona Lisa. Get a grip."

Dante laughed, but Marshall gave my shoulder a gentle squeeze.

"At least Marshall is a little sympathetic. Thank you," I said to him. "Don't let Noni turn your heart to ice like hers," I added.

Marshall took Noni's hand and kissed it. "Not my beautiful *shiksa*. She has the heart of an angel," he said gazing at her.

"Noni, you've got him fooled."

"Don't I know it," she agreed. "I hate to break up this love fest, but I hear Atlanta security can take forever."

I hugged Marshall and said, "Thanks for coming. I'm so glad you and Noni have each other."

"She's a gem and so are you," he said. "I can't wait to come back."

Despite her earlier admonition, tears welled in my eyes as I reached for Noni and pulled her into a long embrace.

"Please don't cry, Mona Lisa. I had a wonderful visit and haven't laughed this much in a long time. The next six weeks will fly by," Noni added.

"I know. I'm so happy we got to spend this time to-gether."

"Me too. I'll call when we get home." She turned to Dante and gave him a peck on the cheek and said, "You hurt her and I'll kill you."

Dante nodded and said, "Understood."

"Marshall, let's get going and give these two lovebirds time alone."

The tears returned as I watched them disappear around the corner. Dante wiped them away and pulled me to him. His sweet gesture only succeeded in bringing the water-works on full force.

"You're a little emotional today, huh?" he asked.

"It's a double whammy," I admitted. "Two of my fa-vorite people are leaving me."

"Wow, you must really like me," he said with a grin.

I smiled and said, "I guess so."

"Am I number one or number two?"

"That's for me to know and you to try and get the number one position."

"Is that a challenge?" he asked, "because I'm very competitive."

"Let the games begin," I said.

Dante gently placed his hands on my cheeks, leaned in and kissed me with such intensity, such passion, I think I stopped breathing.

I pulled back ever so slightly, inhaled and said, "I believe you just took first place."

Chapter 80

I tried to keep myself busy and bide my time until Thanksgiving. The weeks seemed to drag by and thankfully I had my job to keep me going. I was booked solid each day with clients getting ready for the holidays as well and most evenings I collapsed into bed exhausted. Dante and I spoke nightly. We had agreed to spend the holiday with our respective families. His mother knew we were dating, but it was not an issue as she did not suffer from marital obsession the way my parents did. His sister was coming in from upstate New York with her two sons and her husband, and we talked about my meeting all of them.

"You can come for dinner on Friday," Dante suggested.

I was sorting clothes and trying to pack for my trip and was half paying attention as he spoke, and when I didn't answer, he busted me.

"Or I can come to your house and tell Chick you're pregnant and I'm not sure the baby is mine," he remarked.

"Maybe ... Wait. What?" I asked as I suddenly realized what he said.

"Do I have your attention now?" he asked.

"Sorry. I'm trying to coordinate my outfits and talk at the same time. Obviously, I'm not a good multitasker. I'll sit and you talk." I sat on the edge of my bed.

"I'd like you to meet my mom and sister if we can work it out. We have a whole week together in the same town. Surely we can find an hour for you to see my family," he said.

"I'll make it happen. I want to meet them. I have to plan what to tell Chick and Ma," I admitted.

"Mona Lisa, how long are you going to do this?" he asked.

"Do what?"

"Play this game with your parents. Why not tell them about us?" he inquired.

"Because every time I talk to them, they will ask how it's going with us and do I think we'll get married because you know, you're not getting any younger, Mona Lisa, and your ovaries shrink by twenty-five percent each time you get dumped by a guy."

Dante couldn't help but laugh and said, "Alright. I won't push it this time, but I think we should tell them soon."

"My mother is picking me up from the airport. Let me chat with her a bit and get a read on her Mona Lisa Marriage Barometer. I'll let you know if any storms are brewing or if it's smooth sailing."

* * * *

When I stepped outside the baggage claim doors, my mother was in her car waiting. I put my suitcase in the back and quickly took my place in the front passenger's seat.

"Hi, Ma," I said excitedly as I leaned over to give her a kiss and hug.

She gave me a quick squeeze and said, "Buckle up.

That cop has been giving me the stink eye since I got here."

I did as I was told and my mother floored the gas pedal thrusting me back against my seat.

"Since when did you join NASCAR?" I asked.

"Very funny, Mona Lisa. I see living in the genteel south hasn't dulled that sharp tongue of yours."

"I'm afraid it's self-sharpening. I missed you, Ma."

"I missed you too. I'm glad you're going to be here for a while. So tell me, how are things with Dante? I purposely drove to the airport without Chick so we could talk," she said.

I looked at my watch and replied, "I think you set a new record. It only took twenty-seven seconds for you to ask me about my love life."

"So hilarious, you are. Again, how are things with Dante?"

"We don't get to see each other much and we're taking it very slowly, but things are good."

As she often does when she gets excited, my mother broke into song. "Love is a many splendid thing." And as always, she never knows more than the opening line, so she substitutes "la la la" for the words until she tires out or one of us loses our minds.

"Ma, knock it down a notch. I'm not ready to tell people we're dating so try and be cool."

"That's my middle name, Mona Lisa," she said.

"No, I think crazy is your middle name, but I still love you," I said. "Dante is up here for Thanksgiving and we're going to try and see each other when we can."

"I'll cover for you with Chick. I'm your wingman, Mona Lisa."

"What are we, in Top Gun?" I asked. Then I thought for a moment and said, "Thanks, Ma. I'll take you up on your offer. It's good to be home."

Chapter 81

The entire family gathered for dinner at my parents' house on my first night back in New Jersey and it was like old times. There was a lot of laughter, tons of food and I couldn't have asked for a better homecoming. I missed everyone, especially my sisters. After the dishes were done, the five of us sat in the formal living room to talk. No one ever used it, so it was the perfect place to get away from the rest of the crowd and talk. I decided to tell Marilyn and Ro about Dante. Sometimes, they felt left out because Nina, Sophia, and I were so close and I wanted to prevent any unnecessary hurt.

We settled in on the sectional sofa, and when the squeaking of the plastic covers subsided, I said, "I want all of you to know something."

"Tell me you're not pregnant, too," Ro muttered.

"Geez, you're as bad as Ma. No, I'm not pregnant, you goof. I'm dating someone. Dante Colletti to be exact."

A chorus of happy squeals erupted, but I quickly shushed them. "Listen, it's all still very new and I want to keep it that way for now. Chick knows and Ma knows, but they don't know the other one knows."

"What?" Ro asked.

"It's complicated but please don't talk about it and I'll tell you when it's safe to discuss in public."

"Maybe you'll marry him and move back home," Nina said.

"Don't even say the M word. Let's talk about something else. What's new with you, Marilyn?" I asked.

"Let's see. I basically live in my car which smells and looks like a locker room. I feel like I exist in testosterone-ville. I want another girl in the house," she admitted.

"Why don't you have another baby?" Sophia asked.

"Mike and I talked about it, but I'd probably have a third boy. Plus my guys are pretty self-sufficient now and I don't think I can go back to the baby stage."

"I always thought I'd have five girls just like us and now that I have two kids, I can't imagine having three let alone five," Sophia confessed.

"I sure hope I like having kids," Ro chimed in as she patted her growing belly.

Nina gasped. "How could you not like kids?" she asked.

"I'm pretty happy with my life right now. Charlie and I are good, and I'm hoping this little one doesn't rock the boat."

"I want six kids," Nina said. "Three boys and three girls—just like the *Brady Bunch*."

"Talk to me after you have the first one," Marilyn quipped.

We laughed and looked up to find that Chick had joined us.

"Hey, girls. I need to talk to Mona Lisa for a minute," he said.

They stood and made a mass exit without question.

What did I do now? I wondered.

"What's wrong, Chick?" I asked as he sat beside me.

"Nothing. I wanted to talk about Dante," he whispered.

"It's all good," I replied. "We're taking it slow and still keeping it under wraps. He's up here for Thanksgiving, so we're going to spend a little time together if I can get away without too much trouble."

"You make the plans and I'll handle your mother. She'll be upset that you're going out, but I'll smooth it over for you. You can use my car, too. I have a good feeling about this. I know you resisted my interference in the beginning, but I have a gift for this sort of thing."

"Yes you do," I lied, "but let's not get carried away. I'll let you know if it gets serious, okay?"

"Of course. You know me. I'm Mr. Even Keel. I know how to keep things in perspective."

"Thanks, Chick. You're a great wingman," I said trying not to smile.

"I am, aren't I?" he boasted. "And when you become Mrs. Dante Colletti your happiness will be thanks enough."

Chapter 82

It was remarkably easy for me to get out of the house the next night and the night after that. I felt like a kid who was suddenly told they no longer had a bedtime. It was exciting and liberating and the teeniest bit disconcerting. Being a Cicciarelli meant that I was always waiting for the other shoe to drop. My newfound freedom would surely come with a price. I wasn't sure if it was an Italian thing or a Catholic thing, but in my family whenever fate smiled upon us, we never fully enjoyed it. In the back of our minds, we knew we would somehow pay for our good fortune and after a classic fog-up-the-windows make-out session in Dante's car, my fun times came to an end.

It was a little past midnight when Dante dropped me off at my parents' house, and as I turned the knob on the front door, I went flying across the threshold and was suddenly face to face with my father.

"What's wrong, Chick? Did somebody die? Is Noni alright?" I asked, my heart pounding.

"She's fine. It's your mother you have to worry about," he replied.

"What's wrong with Ma? Does she need an ambulance?"

"She's in the kitchen."

I ran into the kitchen to find my mother sitting in the dark. I flipped on the light and asked, "Ma, what's wrong? Are you sick?"

"Sick to my stomach, Mona Lisa," she responded. "Chick and I are on to your little game. What exactly did you hope to accomplish by having me lie to your father? How do you think that made me feel? After forty-two years of marriage, you cause me to be unfaithful to my husband."

"Unfaithful?" I challenged. "I ...."

"You know what I mean, Miss Smarty Pants," she interjected. "You forced Chick and me to lie to each other so that you could go gallivanting around with Dante Colletti. Lord only knows what the neighbors think, running around like a teenager with no morals or common sense."

"Isn't that a little harsh?" I asked.

"I'll tell you what's harsh," Chick answered. "Harsh is carrying on a torrid affair under your parents' roof and thinking of no one but yourself."

"Wow. Okay. Let's talk about this rationally," I began. "I apologize for asking you both to keep my secret, but in my defense ...."

I was interrupted by snickering from both of my parents.

"In my defense," I continued, "you each found out at separate times, and I left town before we could all be together and talk. Then it got harder to figure out a way to broach the subject without you both going crazy. Plus you guys seemed to enjoy sharing this with just me and I liked having this bond with you," I took a breath to assess their take on my explanation.

Ma looked like she was starting to soften, but Chick

was stone-faced. I needed to come up with something, so I kept babbling.

"I also didn't want to disappoint you in case Dante and I didn't work out. I know how badly you want me to be married, especially to a Catholic Italian, but you both go overboard with questions and plans. Chick, I've only been home a few days and you've mentioned marriage to me like ten times."

His shoulders relaxed a little, but I wasn't home free yet.

"I was going to tell you both tomorrow," I lied, "because I invited Dante to come for dessert. He's having Thanksgiving with his mom and sister but can join us later. I hope that's alright." *I'm going straight to Hell. And I was taking Dante hostage because I made plans for him without asking.*

They both gave me challenging stares, but I had the balls to ask, "So can I tell him he's welcome to have dessert with us or what?"

"Of course he can come, Mona Lisa. What do you take us for? Our welcome mat is always out," my mother proclaimed.

My parents were like Ellis Island. Give us your hungry, your eligible bachelors ....

"Thank you. I'll be up early to help you with dinner," I offered.

"Get a good night's sleep," Chick ordered. "You don't want to be worn out by the time Dante gets here. Maybe

Nina can do your makeup, so you don't look so …"

"Let's quit while I'm still sane. I'm going to bed." I said.

I kissed them both and went to my room and quickly texted Dante.

The jig is up. Please, please, please come for dessert tomorrow or I'll be in Cicciarelli prison and won't be eligible for parole until I'm a senior citizen.

His reply came within seconds. *I'm here for you, Mona Lisa. Will bring a cake with a file in it. You're gonna owe me big time and I can't wait for you to pay up.*

I typed back. *Name your price, sir.*

Again, he responded quickly. *Dinner with my family on Friday. I love you and I want everyone to know it.*

I stared at my phone. Holy shit. He just said he loves me. In a text? Not exactly romantic, but as my Great Aunt Julia used to say, "Eh, what are you going to do?" I contemplated what to write back. I love you too? I did love him. I was afraid to admit it until now, but I was falling in love with Dante Colletti. I was startled by the ringing of my phone.

It was Dante and I answered, "So you love me, huh?"

"Yes and please don't tell our grandchildren the first time I professed my feelings for you was in a text. It just came out."

"So you didn't mean it?"

"Oh, no. I meant it, but I was hoping to say it in person the first time," he admitted.

"I'll let you have a do-over. If you can say it and mean it after dessert tomorrow, the story of your text will go away forever. Get some rest. You're going to need it."

Chapter 83

Thanksgiving dinner was lively and fun with lots of talking and laughing. The kids went outside to play while the adults finished the meal. Everyone was in a good mood, even Chick and Ma. Chick usually tired of my brother-in-law Mike's jokes, which tended to get more off color with each cocktail he consumed. And Ma always got frustrated because the meal took six hours to prepare and was eaten in less than thirty minutes. Today, however, they were both positively euphoric. And that was not a word that ever came to mind when describing my parents. My mother didn't even flinch when Noni patted her belly and proclaimed the dinner to be *geshmak*. I looked at Noni as if to say, *what gives*? She replied by shrugging her shoulders.

Then the blitz began. Ma stood up and said, "Girls, let's get this table cleaned off. Mona Lisa, when that's done, take this dirty tablecloth off and put the white one from the closet on. The good one that my cousin Adeline brought me back from Italy. Marilyn, you put on the coffee and Nina, you make the espresso. Ro and Sophia, help me get the desserts ready."

We all sat there for a second trying to absorb the multitude of commands when Chick hollered, "You heard your mother. Get moving. Dante will be here in thirty minutes."

And there it was. The source of Cicciarelli contentment and the impetus behind putting on a dessert display worthy of the Vatican. Dante Colletti. I glanced at Noni and shook

my head before I started gathering plates. The five of us
worked like the KP Division of the army washing, drying
and finally setting out a table full of treats that were enough
to feed an impoverished nation for days. My sisters and I
joined the others in listening to Mike tell about how he de-
livers packages to a guy who answers the door completely
naked. My mind began to wander to Dante as I had heard
that story many times before. I looked over at Chick and
saw him tap the face of his watch while frowning at my
mother. That was Cicciarelli code for he's late and you
know how I feel about people being late. I turned my attention back to my brothers-in-law who were trying to outdo
one another with outrageous stories. They got progressively
louder as they talked over each other, but when the doorbell
rang, there was immediate silence. Chick's face broke into
a huge grin as he once again tapped his watch, but smiled at
my mother as if to say, how about this guy. Right on time.

My father stood to answer the door, but I said, "Chick,
I'll get it if that's okay."

He opened his mouth to no doubt tell me it was his
house and he should answer the door, but my mother
grabbed his arm and silenced him with one word, "Chick."

He sat back down and I made my way to the front
door. I opened it and threw myself into Dante's arms which
were occupied with flowers and a bottle of anisette.

"Can I come in?" he asked.

I motioned for him to enter and shut the door. "Are either of those for me?" I asked.

"Sorry. I need to score some points with your parents," he replied handing me his tokens of appreciation and bribery while he removed his coat and hung it on the rack. He then looked to make sure the coast was clear before giving me a quick kiss.

I handed him back his ammunition and asked, "Did you get enough sleep? Have you had anything to drink because you are officially getting ready to board the crazy train? Your conductor is Chick and he will be assisted by Angie. You should be aware that the rest of the passengers are escapees from the local mental institution and anything they say or do should be ignored or forgotten."

"And what is your position on the crazy train?" he asked.

"Crowd control," I quipped. "Take a deep breath 'cause once you board, there's no going back to the station."

I grabbed his hand and led him to the dining room. A chorus of hellos ensued as everyone rose to greet Dante. Chick beamed when Dante gave him the bottle and my mother literally blushed when taking the flowers. He shook hands with all of the guys and kissed the women on their cheeks. Noni gave him a soft pat on the rear—her signature move indicating she liked you. We were all used to her grabbing our backsides, but Dante's eyes grew huge and I had to laugh.

My mother flitted around nervously.

"Everyone sit," she ordered. "Nina, please bring out

the coffee. Marilyn, pass the cookie tray around."

Chick motioned for Dante to sit next to him as he got out the shot glasses and began to pour the anisette. I sat on the other side of Dante and when we were all assembled, Chick stood and held up his glass.

"Oh, no," I muttered to Dante. "I guess it's not enough that you've been fondled by my grandmother. Now you're going to be the subject of my father's toast."

Chick waited for me to finish and said, "To my wonderful family, I am thankful for all of you. And Dante, it's nice to have you join us again. I knew in my heart this day would come and that you two would realize what a good match you make. I have a talent for bringing people together and I'm glad you both came to your senses. *Salute*."

"*Oy, vey*," I said to Noni who was seated on the other side of me.

"I couldn't agree more, Mr. Cicciarelli," Dante said raising his glass in support.

"What's with the formality? You're practically part of the family. Call me Chick."

"Sure thing, Chick," Dante replied before taking a sip of his drink.

I swallowed mine in one gulp, which was of course seen by my mother who gave me the "act like a lady" glare.

Luckily everyone stopped gawking at Dante and regular conversation resumed, however, Chick had Dante's ear and wouldn't let go.

"I knew you'd be back at this table one day. Mona Lisa was too proud to see that, but thankfully she realized she doesn't always know what's best for her," Chick said proudly.

"Well, Chick, I think the timing was very bad. Mona Lisa knew she didn't want to jump into another relationship until she fully healed from what that jerk did to her. Luckily, we found each other again and so far, so good."

My hero. For once Chick was at a loss for words, so he turned and said something to my mother trying to hide the fact that he was just put in his place. That was great until my nephew, Anthony wandered over from the child's table said, "Aunt Mo, Grandpa Chick said you better marry this guy because you've got some years on you."

"Well, Dante," I said, "the crazy train never disappoints."

Chapter 84

My dinner with Dante's family seemed about as un-Cicciarelli as you could get. His mom greeted us with a warm smile and was soft-spoken and reserved. Those were two words that weren't even in my family's vocabulary. She led us into the living room, and there was an array of fancy cheeses and meats that looked like it was prepared by a television chef. Dante poured us each a glass of an expensive French wine and I waited to give my nervousness a chance to subside. Not to be outdone, I pulled a wrapped gift out of my bag and handed it to his mother.

"Mrs. Colletti, Dante told me you're a big fan of the *Barefoot Contessa*. This is her most recent book. I put the gift receipt inside the jacket if you'd like to exchange it for something else."

"It's perfect, Mona Lisa. That was so thoughtful of you. And please call me Margaret. "

"Thank you, Margaret. Will your daughter and her family be joining us for dinner?" I asked.

"Yes. I sent them on a little errand so we could get to know each other for a few minutes first. The four of them bring a lot of commotion, and I thought it would be nice to chat in peace and quiet for a bit."

Wow. His mother exuded calm. "I'm one of five girls, so I'm used to chaos," I admitted. "Our family dinners are like a big free-for-all. Poor Dante. I'm sure he was a little shell-shocked after being at my house last night."

"I think I held my own," he replied.

"I don't know your parents well," Margaret admitted, "but your grandmother is a riot. I love to sit next to her at bingo."

"That she is. She's sharp as a tack and keeps the rest of us on our toes," I replied.

"Dante tells me you live in Atlanta. You must miss your family a lot."

"I do, but the move has been good for me."

A look of recollection came over Margaret's face as she remembered why I moved away. It's a very small town and everyone knew about my incident with Joey. She nodded in reply.

"I like it there. My job is great and I've met a lot of wonderful people."

"But you don't get to see my handsome son very often being that far away," she said.

"Ma …." Dante chimed in.

"What? I'm making conversation," Margaret responded.

"More like an inquisition," Dante challenged.

"You're not getting any younger and I'd like a few more grandchildren before I die," she said giving me a wink.

Yes! I knew there was a meddlesome, Italian mother in there somewhere.

I winked back, but our moment was interrupted by the arrival of Dante's sister and her family. They came in with four pastry boxes and took a minute to get settled.

Then Dante made the introductions. "This is my sister, Lucia, her husband Declan and their boys Seamus and Nico."

I greeted each boy with a handshake and said, "Cool names."

Lucia spoke up. "We have a mixed marriage. Italian-Irish. We each named a kid. I guess you can figure out who named who."

Margaret looped her arm in mine and said, "Mona Lisa, come keep Lucia and me company while we finish preparing dinner."

Dante started to protest, but I waved him off. We sat at the kitchen table and Margaret squeezed my hand and said, "I'm glad you're here."

"This must be serious because Dante hasn't brought a girl home since …." Lucia tried to recall. "Let's just say it's been a while. So tell me, Mona Lisa, what are your intentions with my brother?" She was stone-faced.

I opened my mouth to answer, but she broke into a huge smile and said, "I'm totally kidding. Dante said you have a great sense of humor, so I was just messing with you."

"Lucia," her mother admonished. "You'll scare her off and then Dante will live with me forever."

I laughed and thought these could be my people.

Chapter 85

The weeks between Thanksgiving and Christmas
seemed to fly by because I was extremely busy at work, but
they also seemed to drag because Dante and I had no time
together. I took two weeks off from work during the
holidays and I planned to get my fill of family, but more
importantly Dante. He had to fly on Christmas Eve, but the
next morning he arrived at my parents' house to have
breakfast with me. It was quite calm as it was only the four
of us. My sisters were with their families and in-laws, and
the entire clan was going to gather again for dinner as we
had the night before.

My mother and I made a frittata and fruit salad, and the
four of us enjoyed a conversation free of talk about marriage, children and the age of my ovaries.

When we finished eating, my mother said, "Chick, you
and I can do the dishes. Mona Lisa, you and Dante can enjoy some quiet time together."

"It's a Christmas miracle," I blurted out.

"Listen here, you better be glad it's the birthday of our
Lord, or I'd smack you for being such a wisenheimer."

"Well, Merry Christmas to me," I replied. "Thanks,
guys."

"Yes, thank you for breakfast and especially for some
time alone with my girl," Dante added.

"Of course," Chick replied as if he came up with the
idea himself.

Dante and I went into the family room and sat by the Christmas tree.

"Real or fake?" he asked.

"I beg your pardon?"

"Do you like real or fake trees for Christmas?" he asked with a grin.

"I like real, but we had one once and my mother had a fit with all of the needles dropping everywhere. She was convinced the house was going to burn down from it, but I love how it smells. My turn, Midnight Mass—yes or no?" I asked.

"No. It's too long and crowded," he answered. "Ravioli or turkey on Christmas?"

"Ravioli. Seven fishes on Christmas Eve?"

"We've narrowed it down to smelts and seafood, but we still don't eat meat," he replied.

"I can work with that," I remarked.

"Do you want kids?"

"Whoa. I wasn't expecting that one," I admitted. "Sure, I want kids. I'd like to reserve the right to decide how many after I have one, though. My sister Nina wants six kids and she's not even married. Me, I'll deal with it when and if the time comes. Why all the questions?"

"I just want to know you better."

"Don't you want to know more important things like how many family members are currently being treated for mental illness?" I asked with a smile.

"I love you, Mona Lisa. I know the important things,

now I just want to know the fun stuff."

"Sure you don't want to say that again in a text?" I asked with a laugh.

"You promised never to speak of that again," Dante admonished. "Now I'm not going to give you your Christmas present."

"That's a little drastic, don't you think? Listen, I will never use the words text and love in the same sentence again. Can I have my present now?" I begged.

He handed me a small gift bag. I reached inside and took out a beautiful silver bracelet with one charm in the shape of a train.

"The crazy train?" I asked. He nodded and I smiled. "Open this."

He unwrapped the gift I handed to him. It was a train key chain that I had engraved, "Welcome Aboard."

We both laughed and I said, "I won't even mention the obvious."

"Same train of thought?" he asked shaking his head. "Let's move on. Open this one," he said.

It was a paper scroll and on the inside was an invitation to join Dante on New Year's Eve for dinner and fireworks.

"Fireworks, huh? Pretty proud of your skills in the bedroom, aren't you?" I teased.

"You have a dirty mind, young lady. I'd tell Chick, but then I'm afraid he won't let you go with me. You will go, won't you?" he asked.

I reached over to the table and grabbed my phone and

texted him.

Yes, I'd love to be your date on New Year's Eve.
BTW... I love you too. Now we're even.

Chapter 86

I splurged on a new outfit for my date with Dante and was almost giddy with excitement. Sophia came over to help me get dressed.

"I feel like I'm getting ready for the prom."

"I'm living vicariously through you," Sophia admitted. "My night will consist of pigs-in-a-blanket and trying to stay up until midnight."

"Get this. Ma basically gave me permission to have sex."

"What did she say?"

"'Mona Lisa, I'm not as naïve as you girls like to think. I understand if you don't come home tonight. I don't like it, but I get it.' How about that?" I asked

"You're kidding?" she challenged.

I heard the doorbell ring as I put the finishing touches on my lipstick. I took a step back and smiled as I not only looked sexy, but I felt that way.

"Mona Lisa, you look beautiful," Sophia said before giving me a light squeeze. "It's been so nice having you back home. I miss you."

"Me, too. Thanks for your help. Let me get out of here before Ma and Chick rethink the whole curfew thing."

* * * *

We ate at a quaint restaurant that specialized in decadent multi-course dinners. It was lit totally by candlelight and we were seated at a table next to a large stone fireplace.

328

It was warm and romantic, and dinner was the best meal I had ever eaten. Dante and I talked and laughed and by the time dessert arrived, we had been at the restaurant for over two hours.

"I feel bad that we've taken up the table for so long," I said.

"Don't worry. I'll make sure the waiter gets an excellent tip. I'm not letting anyone rush us tonight. I love being with you, Mona Lisa."

"I do too. I hate the thought of going back to Atlanta," I admitted.

"Then don't," he said casually.

"Don't what?"

"Don't go back. I was going to wait until midnight, but ...." He reached into his pocket and got down on one knee.

My heart began to pound wildly and I felt like I couldn't catch my breath. He was about to propose and I had no idea it was coming.

"Mona Lisa Annette Cicciarelli, I love you with all of my heart. You make me laugh and you make me incredibly happy. Will you marry me?"

I couldn't focus and felt as though I might pass out. Dante took the ring and placed it on my finger. The other patrons in the restaurant broke into applause as I sat there frozen. Dante kissed me and sat back in his seat.

"Wow. I mean ... wow. I am shocked. I don't know what to say."

"How about yes?" he asked.

"Wow. I wasn't expecting this. Wow."

"Will you stop saying wow," Dante chided, his feelings obviously hurt.

"I need some time to think about it." I stood and said, "I love you. I really do."

I started to remove the ring, but he said, "Don't take it off. Once you do there's no going back."

"I think I want to go back to my parents' house and clear my head."

"They're supposed to meet us at the hotel," he replied.

"What?" I screeched. "They know about this?"

"Yes, they know. I asked your father for his permission. I have a champagne breakfast reserved for us."

My phone rang. Reflexively I checked it. My parents. I let it ring. When it stopped, I saw they had called four times and left four messages. No doubt to pick a date for my nuptials. Then a text came in from Marilyn.

Noni was taken to the hospital. Call me ASAP.

"Noni's in the hospital," I told Dante. I listened to my voice mail. Each one was more urgent than the previous. I needed to get to Kennedy Hospital.

Chapter 87

Dante held my hand as I cried and prayed silently on the ride to the hospital. When we arrived, we went to the emergency room waiting area to join my parents and sisters.

I hugged my mother tightly as we both let our tears out. She reached into her purse and handed me a tissue.

"I'm sorry we ruined your big night," she said sadly.

I kept my left hand out of sight and said, "She's going to be fine Ma. She's tougher than the two of us combined. Is Marshall with her?"

She nodded. My sisters and I sat around my mother as if protecting her from any bad news. I looked over to see Chick talking to Dante, no doubt asking if he popped the question yet. Dante shook his head and looked over at me.

We waited quietly and finally, Marshall came out with a huge smile on his face.

"She's going to be fine. No heart attack. She had a bad case of indigestion. It seems as though she overdid it with the fried foods at lunch and then we had pizza with everything on it for dinner, and it was too much for her. Ange, you want to go in?" he asked my mother.

My mother leaped up, and I motioned for Marshall to sit in her spot next to me.

"I don't know what I'd do without her, Mona Lisa," he confessed. "She makes me laugh every day."

I squeezed his hand and said, "I know. I need her too."

"Life is too damn short, Mona Lisa. Don't waste any of it."

I nodded wondering if I killed my chances for happiness with Dante.

A few minutes later, my mother came out and said to me, "Noni wants to talk to you."

I walked into her room and burst into tears at the sight of her in the bed with all of the machines and tubes. I hugged her tightly and then said, "You scared the shit out of me, Noni. You have the eating habits of a teenage boy, you know that?"

"I know. It was stupid, but oh that fried appetizer plate sure was good."

"Promise me you'll take better care of yourself. I need you, you crazy old broad."

"Looks to me like you're doing fine without me. Let me take a look at the ring."

I held out my hand and asked, "Did you know too?"

"Yes," she admitted. "Dante and I talked on Christmas. Shouldn't you be more excited? I realize it probably took a back seat to my imminent death, but now that you know I'm gonna make it …."

"I didn't say yes."

"You said no?" she asked in disbelief.

"I didn't answer him. He slipped the ring on my finger before I had a chance to say anything. Then he told me once I take it off, that was it."

"Sit down and listen to me, Mona Lisa. That boy loves

you, quirks and all. And believe me, this family is enough to send anyone running for the hills and yet, he seems to find us endearing. Do you love him?" she asked.

"Yes."

"I will say my piece once and then it's up to you, but here is a man with a job who is smart, funny and kind. He loves his mother and sister, and he survived two holidays with your mother and Chick. Do I need to slap you or can you see for yourself how lucky you are to have found each other?"

I waited for a second and smiled. "You would really slap me, wouldn't you?" I asked.

"If you turn that boy down, you bet your ass I'll slap you."

I hugged her fiercely and said, "I love you so much, Noni."

"I love you more, kiddo. Get out of here and take care of business."

I walked back to the waiting room and sat next to Dante who was resting his head against the wall.

"How is she?" he asked.

I responded with a long, deep kiss. I pointed to the ring and he looked dejected until I asked, "Can I have a do-over?"

Epilogue

As I sat in the bride's room of St. Luke's church, I marveled at the twists and turns my life had taken since I'd been there last. I thought my life was over then, but now I was grateful that it turned out as it had. Dante and I were good, no—great together and I loved him more than anything. Our engagement endured a few bumps, the biggest being where we would call home after our marriage. There was something I loved about the South—the slower pace, the friendliness of the people, but Atlanta was too far from home. Noni's health scare was a wake-up call, and I knew I wanted to spend more time with my family and to do that I would have to live closer. We settled on a small town in Southern New Jersey that was a two-hour drive from my parents, but only thirty minutes to the airport. I would be starting over at a new salon, but coming home to Dante would make it all worth it.

My mother came in and brought me back to reality. "It's time to put your dress on, Mona Lisa."

As I slipped into my gown, I pushed the thoughts of déjà vu out of my head. No one had mentioned my previous try at marriage thankfully, though I'm sure if anyone would bring it up, it would be Amy who was one of my bridesmaids. I locked eyes with her and she gave me a smirk. I smiled back knowing that she and I would be friends no matter where we lived.

I put on my veil, and after my sisters made their fuss, I

said, "You know I'm not the mushy type …."

"You can say that again," Amy muttered. "I'm sad I'm not going to see you every day now. I'll have to save up all my catty remarks for when we visit."

I looked at her and said, "And I expect nothing less. As I was saying, I love all of you and I'm glad that you're with me today."

We had a group hug and there was a soft knock on the door. Chick poked his head in and said, "Ange, they're ready for you."

I hugged her and said, "I love you, Ma. Thank you for everything."

"I love you back, Mona Lisa. Let's get this wedding underway, so I can be that much closer to more grandchildren."

I could only smile. I checked myself one last time in the mirror and took Chick's arm as we made our way to the vestibule of the church. The wedding coordinator lined the bridesmaids up, but I had to stop for a minute.

"Wait," I blurted out.

"What's wrong?" Chick asked. "You better not be getting cold feet."

"No, there's one thing I have to do before I can go through with this," I replied.

I handed Chick my bouquet, walked to the door of the church and peeked in. As if he had been expecting it, Dante smiled and gave me a covert thumbs up.

"Now I'm ready," I said to Chick with a grin. And I

was.

Acknowledgments

Thank you to Barbara Terry and Waldorf Publishing for this wonderful opportunity. It has been such a joy to work with you.

And to Valerie Clark for your guidance and help in writing *Mona Lisa.* Thank you for always laughing at the funny parts and for stopping me from using the word "just" so much.

While the Cicciarelli's may think they have cornered the market on family, I like to think that I did too. My parents, who are NOT Chick and Angie, (maybe a little) have always been immensely supportive of their kids and for that I am extremely grateful. I am also thankful for all of the traditions you have passed on to me. Thank you to Vera, Tricia and Joe for reading, editing, advising and for always making me laugh. Alex, Nick and Gina - you are the most caring, funny, hard-working and all around best kids a mom could ask for. And Mark, what an amazing journey our life has been. Looking forward to sharing what lies ahead.

Author Bio

An avid reader, Robyn Sheridan had always dreamed of becoming a writer. Though she pursued a degree in chiropractic and has a successful practice, she still felt the call to write a novel. Though it would take a few years for it to come to fruition, *Facing Forward* was published in 2009 and it was nominated for a 2010 EPIC award and the 46th annual Georgia Author of the Year Award. Her current book, *Mona Lisa* is a light-hearted book that allows Robyn to use her sarcasm and wit for good, not evil.

A native of New Jersey, she moved to Atlanta for school and though she vowed to return North before the ink on her diploma was dry, she never left. Robyn currently lives with her husband and together they have three children who are grateful she has found an outlet for her energy so that she will have less time to focus on them.